Riders of
Buck River

Center Point
Large Print

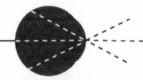

**This Large Print Book carries the
Seal of Approval of N.A.V.H.**

Riders of
Buck River

William
MacLeod
Raine

CENTER POINT LARGE PRINT
THORNDIKE, MAINE

This Center Point Large Print edition is published
in the year 2014 by arrangement with
Golden West Literary Agency.

This novel appeared serially under the title
Riders of the Rim Rocks.

The text of this Large Print edition is unabridged.
In other aspects, this book may vary
from the original edition.
Printed in the United States of America
on permanent paper.
Set in 16-point Times New Roman type.

ISBN: 978-1-61173-993-0

Library of Congress Cataloging-in-Publication Data

Raine, William MacLeod, 1871–1954.
  Riders of Buck River / William MacLeod Raine. —
  Center Point Large Print edition.
    pages ; cm.
  ISBN 978-1-61173-993-0 (library binding : alk. paper)
  1. Large type books. I. Title.
PS3535.A385R53 2014
813'.52—dc23
                                                2013036167

Riders of
Buck River

I

Calhoun Terry drew up at the edge of French Mesa and looked down on Round Top, a sprawling cluster of houses that nestled in the saucer formed by the body of the mountain and the spur which thrust itself out into the desert. It was an ugly little place, bleak and sun-dried, but ever since he could remember, it had been his town. Here he had come with his father in a buckboard, a very small boy, and exchanged his nickel for striped stick candy from a jar on the counter of Clint Evans's store. And here he had come later to see the elephant, knee to knee with other lads in whose company he had ridden the range and listened to windies from oldtimers at countless campfires.

They had been good days, those carefree ones before he had been bitten by the urge to make of himself something more than a thirty-dollar-a-month cowpuncher. It had been a gay world. Money had burnt a hole in his pocket, and he had counted friends by the score. Half a dozen years had made a change. He had developed from a hired hand on horseback, one of a hundred who rode the Buck River country, to a man of weight in the community. A seasoned man, hard and steely, he followed with no lack of assurance the path he had picked out for himself. If his popularity had vanished and his friends had dropped away, that was the price he paid for success.

He rode down along a rocky watershed now hot and dry, a bed plowed out for itself by a turbid stream in the rainy season. It brought him to a draw that debouched into the straggling outskirts of the town. Parallel to the dusty road ran the railroad tracks. From the loading pens in the yards came the bellow of beef cattle awaiting shipment. A freight train snorted past, the smoke of the engine rising into the untempered air of the high plains in long, black billows.

A young man in shiny leather chaps met and passed him without a flicker of recognition in the blue eyes, grown suddenly hard and cold. He was Bill Herriott, joint owner with his father of a small ranch near the Diamond Reverse B. Terry had known him ever since they had ridden their first roundup. A dozen times they had stood together, a pair of gangling boys, in the stag line of country dances.

The road ran into the courthouse square. Terry swung from the saddle and hitched at a rack in front of Clint Evans's store. His gaze drifted along a row of false fronts and took in a scene as familiar as the palm of his hand. He had seen it, just as he did now, basking in a hazy amber light of afternoon, so often that he could not count the times. Jerry Spindler's Crystal Palace, the post-office, Pegleg Jim's pool room, the Evans store, the Home Range Restaurant, Black's drugstore: they would have fitted themselves automatically into place in his memory if fifty years had intervened without his seeing them again.

He strolled through the dust, a deceptive indolence in the drag of his step. His spurs jingled on the board sidewalk when he moved along it.

Two men in dusty boots and wide white hats were lounging in the entrance of the store. Their talk died away at the approach of Terry. With studied care, they drew aside to let him pass. Not so long ago Roan Alford would have greeted him with jubilant welcome. Jack Turley was a newcomer in the country.

Evans waited on Terry. The storekeeper was a tall, lean man with chin whiskers and a clean-shaven upper lip that gave him a precise, almost sanctimonious appearance. He had the same dry, ageless look he had brought with him from Vermont twenty-five years earlier.

He nodded greeting. 'How are you, Cal?' he asked.

A third man had joined the two in the doorway, and all of them were watching Terry. The late-comer was Lee Hart, a heavy-set, bowlegged man of about forty. His brother Nate was sheriff of the county. All the Harts had been for a long time enemies of Calhoun Terry. Yet there was something in the steady, unwinking regard of these three men that surprised the manager of the Diamond Reverse B. No pretense of friendship existed between him and any of them, but there was a chill challenge in their silence he did not understand.

As Terry bought a bill of goods, apparently ignoring those who watched him, the deeper current of his mind was busy with the resentment beating against him almost like something tangible. He knew that the tide of hatred in the Buck River country had been rising for years, but as yet there was no open and declared war. Calhoun had lived too long outdoors in a wild country not to have that sixth sense of danger close and immediate. The feeling of peril flowed through him now, though he did not betray it by any change in his inscrutable face or by any movement in his lean, poised body.

He asked for a case of cartridges for a Winchester. Evans got the cardboard box and put it with the other supplies.

From the shadowed darkness back of the big drum stove a voice came cold as a wind blowing over a glacier.

'Going hunting again, Terry?'

The manager of the big ranch turned deliberately, slowly, toward the direction from which the question had come. If he was startled, no evidence of it reached the surface.

A man had moved forward and was leaning

against some bolts of goods on the counter. There was a catlike litheness in his tread, and the slight figure fell into a pose astonishingly graceful. The light eyes held a diamond-hard glitter.

Calhoun picked out the significant word in the query.

'Again?' he asked, stressing the syllables.

'Why, yes, that's what I said.' There were both mockery and defiance in Jeff Brand's jeering voice. 'Don't tell us they didn't let you in on the killing of Buck Hart?'

Terry looked at the man with hard intentness. 'Is Buck Hart dead?'

'You know damn well he's dead.'

'Take care, Brand,' the ranch manager warned.

Brand laughed hardily. Reckless lights gleamed in his eyes. 'You're one of the big moguls now, aren't you? They wouldn't murder Buck without yore say-so, would they?'

'Who killed him?'

'Hell, I'm not giving you information. Not none. You don't need any. Your friends the big cattlemen killed him, because he was in the way.'

'How do you know? Were there any witnesses?'

In Brand's voice was a rustle of dry sarcasm. 'Not likely. Their work isn't as raw as that. But they did it—by hired deputy.'

Terry's answer rang out sharp and dear. 'I don't believe it. Buck had private enemies. He was a man that made them.'

Lee Hart bowlegged forward from the door. 'Sure he had private enemies,' the heavy-set man broke in harshly. 'You done said it, Terry. One of them might have plugged him in the back. But he got his orders from above.'

'Buck was shot from behind,' Calhoun said, his inflection making a question of the statement.

'Drygulched from the brush.' Hart crowded on, the heat of anger rising in him. 'Maybe by one of them enemies you've mentioned, Terry. Maybe you could put a name to him.'

Calhoun's patience was wearing thin. There was a hot rashness in the man, held down by a disciplined will. It was known that he let go of his temper only rarely, but when he did someone was likely to get hurt.

'Better go home and think that over, Hart,' he advised very quietly. 'You're not quite yourself today. I'll not hold you accountable for what you say.'

The storekeeper spoke up. 'That's right, Lee. You've had a heavy blow. We all sympathize with you. Don't make a mistake before you have thought this over.'

Hart waved him aside. 'You're not in this, Evans. Keep out of it. I'm telling Mr. Terry that the man or the men who killed my brother have got to reckon with me.'

'And I'm telling you,' the ranch superintendent replied curtly, 'that you're making a fool of yourself, for all I know of your brother's death is what you've told me yourselves.'

Jack Turley spoke, for the first time. He was a big broad-shouldered man with a long reach of well-muscled limb. The nose in his leathery brown face had been broken by a pitching horse.

'The killer left a note pinned on Buck's coat,' he said evenly. 'It claimed he was killed because he was a rustler.'

'That proves nothing,' Calhoun said quickly. 'Except that the guilty man was trying to cover his tracks and put it on someone else.'

'We think different,' Roan Alford contradicted, anger riding his voice. 'The big cattlemen are bull-headed enough to let us know Buck was rubbed out as a warning to the rest of us.'

The manager of the Diamond Reverse B took his time to answer. He looked at the little weather-beaten rancher, a wrinkled, gray-haired man with quick, beady eyes. Alford and Turley had moved closer, so that the four men hemmed Terry round in a semicircle.

When Calhoun spoke there was a slurring drawl in his speech. Through the slow drag of the words a challenge lifted. 'Come clean, Roan, and say yore piece. Are you meanin' that I had anything to do with this?'

Time stood still while Alford made up his mind. Evans waited behind the counter, ashen-faced, with breath suspended. He knew the tense emotion pent up in the room. If the little man's answer called for a showdown guns would roar and men would sink to the floor through the smoke.

'I'm not claiming that,' Alford said at last, the sulky words coming thickly. He had been a friend of Calhoun Terry's father in pioneer days. Perhaps he remembered that during the long moment before he spoke. 'But I say your friends were in it, by God.'

'No,' Terry disagreed. 'They wouldn't do that. If they wanted to get rid of a rustler they would hang him openly.'

Lee Hart lifted a hand with a violent gesture. For an instant Calhoun thought the time for action had come, but he saw that the man's arm had flung out involuntarily in the stress of his anger.

'Meanin' that Buck was a rustler?' he exploded.

'Meaning what I said and no more. Don't put words in my mouth, Lee. I can say what I want to without any help from you.' He added after a moment: 'I don't want any trouble with you today, not after what has happened to your brother. Go home and sleep on your anger. If you have to get your revenge, be sure you find the right man.'

Brand said, not hiding his sneer, 'He's going to talk himself out of it.'

The ranch manager let his frosted eyes rest on the young cowpuncher. He was a Beau Brummel of the range, immaculate from the shine on his expensive boots to the fine white Stetson he wore on his curly head. Calhoun did not make the mistake of thinking Brand effeminate. He knew his reputation as a dangerous man was justified. Gay though he was, and popular among his associates, he would as lief fight as eat. There was a rumor that he had killed two men in Texas, and it was almost sure that he swung a wide loop over other men's cattle.

'I never was in it,' Calhoun said. 'You're barking up the wrong tree. If I ever want to kill a man I'll tell him so face to face.'

He turned, with arrogant contempt, and settled with Evans for the supplies he had bought. His manner told them that he had said all that was necessary and had dismissed them from con-sideration. They glared at his broad, flat back, uncertain and angry. There had been no plot to destroy him. He had walked into the picture, the most hated of all the big cattlemen, at a moment when rage at the death of Hart was boiling in them, and they had moved against him on urgent impulse. But they were not ready to wipe him out in cold blood.

Terry gathered his parcels. He let his eyes drift over them coolly, from one to another, a touch of scornful amusement in his gaze.

'If that's all for today I'll be going,' he said, irony flickering in his voice.

He pushed between Alford and Turley and

walked out of the store. They watched him go, a man strong and virile, too sure of himself to look back and make certain that one of those he had infuriated would not shoot him in the back.

II

Terry put his purchases in the saddlebags. He showed no haste, no hint that he considered himself in danger. When he had finished he stepped back to the sidewalk and sauntered down the street.

His enemies were in the doorway of the store, still watching him.

'This isn't finished yet,' Hart said hoarsely.

The Diamond Reverse B superintendent did not answer. As if he had not heard he moved forward, evenly, unhasting, a man apparently at peace with the world. Two men came out of the Crystal Palace, stopped abruptly at sight of him, and stood in their tracks while he passed. Plainly they resented his presence at Round Top. Though Terry did not let them know they were on the map for him, he was quite aware of their unfriendliness. Grimly it came home to him that this was no longer his town. He was no more welcome here than a blizzard on the range.

He passed through the courthouse grounds to the opposite side of the square and walked into the office of the *Logan County Gazette*. Nobody was in the front office, but he found the editor, Horace Garvey, setting up an editorial in the back room.

Garvey peered at him over his spectacles. The editor was a dried-up little man with a face like parchment. 'What in Halifax you doing here today?' he rasped.

'Don't you welcome visitors to your little metropolis?' Terry asked.

'You must be crazy, Cal.' Garvey snorted. 'This town is on the warpath today. Haven't you heard about Buck Hart?'

'Heard of it at Evans's store. Some of the boys crowded me a little bit.'

'My advice is for you to light out.' The editor shook his composing-stick at the cattleman. 'Damn quick. Before the boys talk this over too much.'

'I expect that's good medicine,' Terry admitted. 'I'll be going presently. What do you know about this Hart killing? Is there any evidence about who did it?'

'Assassin unknown.' Garvey stopped talking in headlines and banged a table excitedly with his fist. Goddlemighty, man! Don't worry about who killed Hart, but about who is going to kill Calhoun Terry if you don't get a jump on you. Lee Hart is here, and a bunch of his friends.'

'I've met them,' Terry said. 'We passed the

time of day. No tracks left by the murderer, you say?'

'Not far as I know. Where's your horse?'

'You've heard no talk—no names mentioned?'

'No—except that the big fellows hired it done as a warning. You don't have to decide that now. Fork your horse, Cal, and light out of town.'

'It's not quite as bad as that, Horace,' the ranch manager said. 'Lee and his friends have said their little piece for today, I reckon. But this killing of Buck Hart disturbs me. I'll not say he didn't have it coming. He was a proven thief, even if a rustler's court and jury did turn him loose. But it's bad medicine just the same. I don't know who did it. He was a bully, and plenty of people would have liked to see him dead. The point is that the big ranches will be blamed for this. Trouble will come of it.'

'They'll be rightly blamed, in my opinion,' Garvey said tartly. 'But no use going into that. You know where the *Gazette* stands in this controversy between the settlers and the big cattlemen. It's for the people.' He brushed that aside with an impatient gesture. 'I'm thinking about you, Cal. You're too bull-headed. Some low-down scoundrel will get you from the brush one of these days if you're not careful.'

'I don't think so,' Terry replied carelessly.

'You're unpopular as the devil.'

'Are you congratulating me on the enemies I

have made?' the cowman said, his smile scornful. 'They *are* a fine lot.'

'Some of them are good men, and you would know it if you were fair-minded.'

'Read the riot act to me, Horace.' Calhoun Terry put a big brown hand on the scrawny shoulder of the editor. 'Say whatever is in your mind.'

The younger man knew that Garvey was his friend, and had been ever since the day when Calhoun had stepped with a horsewhip between a hectoring ruffian and the little editor.

Garvey shrugged his shoulders. 'No use talking to you. Wouldn't do any good. All I'll say is you don't have to go strutting around as if you were God Almighty's deputy.'

'Do I strut?'

'You go ram-stamming ahead without paying any attention to the other fellow. He has rights too.'

'Not on the Diamond Reverse B range or among its cattle.'

'Well.' The editor gave up. 'No sense in arguing. But don't go too far, Cal. And right now, get out of town while there's a road open for you.'

A smile broke the hard lines of Terry's face and for the moment showed it warm and friendly. 'I'll take your advice, oldtimer. I'm on my way now.'

The cowman waved a hand in farewell and walked out of the building. As he crossed the courthouse grounds he passed the county judge just mounting the steps. They bowed to each other, stiffly, without speaking. Judge Curtis had been elected by the votes of the small settlers. The allies of Terry called him a rustler's judge. They meant that no cow thief could be convicted in his court.

That the old days of the free open range were passing forever Terry knew. For a decade and a half the cattleman had been king. His stock had ranged the plains unhampered and had multiplied exceedingly. The big ranches had paid good dividends to the stockholders in Edinburgh, London, or Boston. Then evil days had fallen on the industry. The cattle boom had collapsed.

There were several reasons for this. One of them was bad management. Those in charge of some of the large ranches had fallen into the habit of living in Cheyenne or Denver and leaving the properties mostly to the care of subordinates. In order to show profits they had overstocked the ranges and in some cases sold too many cows and calves. The grass was eaten short and the winter feed killed. Moreover, as the country opened to settlement nesters moved in and homesteaded the water-holes. There was conflict between them and the cattle kings who had up to this time possessed the land. As a result of this, rustling greatly increased. It was easy for a small outfit on the edge of a big one to increase its holdings by branding calves of the large concern. Year by year the antagonism increased until it grew very bitter. The great ranches were doomed, the managers saw, unless they could stop the stealing of their stock and hold sufficient range to feed the herds.

Calhoun Terry was particularly hated by the smaller ranchmen because he had been one himself. That was after he had ridden as a lad for the Bottleneck Ranch. From his father he had inherited a place in a bend of the Buck River that bit in and took a great mouthful out of the natural range of the Diamond Reverse B. For several years he had been a leader of the little stockman, an irritant thorn in the side of the great ranch. A man of vision, he saw that the two properties ought to be combined. At a board of directors' meeting of the Diamond Reverse B he proposed to sell his place in exchange for stock in the company, provided he was made manager. Since nobody in the territory knew cows better than Terry the directors jumped at the offer. The news of the deal shocked the small settlers. They felt that he had betrayed them. A bitter resentment wiped out his popularity.

Politically the small man dominated the county. The nesters combined with the people of the towns to elect tickets opposed to the cattle barons. As a result of this clean sweep the latter felt they could get no justice in the courts. No proof was sufficient to send a cow thief to the penitentiary. So the victims of rustling claimed.

Some of them felt that if they were to get fair play they must make it for themselves outside the law by throwing the fear of vengeance into the hearts of the rustlers.

III

Terry tightened the saddle cinch, taking more time over it than was necessary. He wanted to show the men peering at him out of the pool room and those grouped in front of the post-office that he was in no hurry. When at last he mounted and turned his back to them he held his horse to a walk. His enemies were not going to have it to say of him that he had dragged out of town on the run. Deliberately he rode out of the square into a street leading to the east.

He caught a glimpse of a face staring at him from a grimy window of the Red Triangle Saloon, one that vanished so quickly he did not have time to identify it. A moment later a gun roared. His hat tilted forward. Through the brim and the crown a bullet had torn its way.

Calhoun Terry drew his horse to the side of the road, dismounted, and dropped the reins. He walked back along the wooden sidewalk, close to the wall, and pushed through the swing doors of the Red Triangle. That this might be a foolish thing to do he knew, but the reckless heat of anger in him would not be denied. They had tried to kill him from cover. He would find out if they would dare to do it in the open.

He took three steps from the swing doors to the end of the bar and stood there, his back in the angle formed by the bar and the wall. His glance swept the room. Some men were playing poker near the back of the saloon, but there was no dry click of chips. The game was momentarily suspended and the eyes of the players turned on the Diamond Reverse B foreman. Three customers were at the bar. Alford—Turley—Brand. The gaze of Terry picked them up in turn. It observed also that the back door was ajar. He had a mental vision of somebody vanishing into the alley swiftly a moment before his entry, a heavy-set, bowlegged man with an ugly, sullen face.

A chill silence had fallen over the room. Not a chair scraped. No finger lifted. Whatever thought of pleasure had brought this group here was forgotten. For a man had walked into the room, strong and unafraid, to challenge a dozen of his assembled enemies. Most of those present were strongly individual, of wild and reckless temperaments, familiar with danger, and because of it they saluted in their hearts the cynical audacity of the man who faced them with contemptuous scorn.

'By God, you take the cake, Terry,' Brand said with a hard laugh. 'You got away with it at

23

Evans' store. Don't you reckon you're pressing yore luck too far?'

The cattleman ignored the question. The gray eyes in the lean, sun-tanned face of the man standing at the end of the bar were inscrutable.

Attempting a diversion, the bartender proposed a drink on the house.

'Didn't Lee Hart have time to shut the door when he ran away?' Terry asked, his voice gentle, almost caressing.

It was not the expected question. None the less it was a center shot, for it claimed sure knowledge of who was the attempted assassin. There was a pause, too long, before Brand spoke.

'Hart hasn't been here.'

Terry took the hat from his head and looked at the bullet holes in it. 'Hasn't he? Then perhaps somebody else wants to claim credit for this bad marksmanship.' He drawled the challenge out, low and clear.

There was another moment of silence before Turley answered: 'We heard a shot. It didn't come from here, if that's what you mean.'

The cowman stretched out his left arm and laid a forefinger on a hole in one of the panes of the window beside him. 'My mistake,' he said.

'Fellow shot that hole in the window in a row two months ago,' the bartender explained.

Terry did some swift guessing. The bullet which had passed through his hat had come from a rifle.

The sound of the shot told him that. But Hart had been armed only with a revolver. Therefore he had borrowed the saloon Winchester. Since he was in a hurry to get away unnoticed, he had not taken it with him. The weapon must still be in the room, but Calhoun's searching eyes had not found it. Probably somebody had passed it to the saloon man, who had hurriedly put it under the bar.

Terry held out an expectant hand. 'Give me that rifle under the bar,' he ordered.

The bartender's eyes grew big. 'Why, Mr. Terry, I—I don't reckon—'

'The rifle,' interrupted Terry coldly.

'You don't have to give it to him, Hank,' Brand told the man. 'This fellow ain't cock-a-doodle-doo in this town.'

Apparently the bartender was of a different opinion. He was a slack-jawed man with a receding chin, and he could not face the steel-barred eyes drilling into his so steadily. He stooped down and passed a rifle across the top of the bar.

An investigation showed that it had been fired very recently. Terry laughed scornfully and handed it back to the man in the white apron.

'Somebody may want it again to shoot me in the back when I leave,' he said.

'Like Buck Hart was shot,' Brand retorted.

'Lee thought he would square accounts,' the cowman suggested.

'I don't recollect mentioning Lee.' The light blue eyes quickened defiantly. 'Since you're so anxious to pin this on one of us I'd just as lief tell you I did it.'

'Only it wouldn't be true. You'll have to find some other cause of quarrel with me.' Terry's gaze passed to rest on Alford. 'I'm a little surprised at you, Roan. When I was your neighbor you wouldn't have stood back of a scoundrel who tried to shoot another man in the back.'

Alford shifted uneasily on his feet. A flush crept up into his wrinkled face. 'I don't stand back of anybody doing it now,' he said.

Calhoun Terry gave him a long, keen look. He could see that the little man was embarrassed and ashamed.

'I get it, Roan. Lee took you by surprise. Didn't give you time to stop him.'

'You keep harping on Lee,' Turley cut in. 'We done told you he wasn't even here.'

'But you're not good liars,' the cattleman replied contemptuously. 'Of course you didn't have time to fix up a story before I butted in. Maybe by tomorrow you'll have made up your minds who did it. I've made up mine already.'

'And do you aim to do anything about it?' jeered Brand insolently.

Terry's gaze rested on the man. 'I'll take that under consideration,' he said after a pause.

'And when you've decided you'll let us

26

know?' the flashy young cowpuncher scoffed.

'I'll let *him* know,' the Diamond Reverse B man corrected.

He let his cold eyes sweep the room again disdainfully, then turned and pushed through the swing doors. Walking to his horse, he mounted and rode away at a road gait. There was a place in the middle of his back, just below the shoulder blades, that did not feel comfortable, but he held to an even pace and did not look round to see whether his enemies were yielding to the temptation.

Past the railroad yards and the loading pens he rode, past the piles of old tin cans and bottles, to the quiet and shining plains beyond. No sky could have been clearer or more blue. Not one thin skein of cloud broke the uniformity. The air was like wine. Rays of the sun, which was declining toward the far sawtoothed mountains, streamed across the gray-green sage. The silence was deep as eternity, but the stillness lay over a scene warm and peaceful. Its restfulness did not minister to Calhoun Terry's troubled thoughts.

That the country was heading for trouble he knew. Too much hate had grown with the years to make mediation possible. The points of view of the differing factions were not reconcilable. Passions had been stirred too greatly. To his mind there flashed the words of a hymn he had sung as a small boy in Sunday School.

Though every prospect pleases,
And only man is vile.

Except for the people in it this would be a good world, he thought sardonically.

IV

Though it was not yet seven o'clock the morning sun flooded the land with light. So still was the air that even the aspen leaves did not tremble. It seemed to Ellen Carey, during that momentary impression, a country without voice and empty of life. Yet the fugitive thought had not faded from her mind before a meadowlark flung out its gay and joyous song, before she saw outlined against the horizon a file of antelope passing through the sagebrush.

She loved that about the mountains and the high plains of her homeland, the constant surprise of change. One had to know and have a feeling for them to realize how seldom they were the same. The far and shining mountains had their different aspect every hour of the day, and the sunrays streaming across the gray-green sage could still fill her with the wonder of infinity.

It was all familiar to her, yet how good to see again! For five years she had been away at school with her aunt in Kansas City, and during that time she had been at home rarely and for short holidays. She had accustomed herself to city ways, had seen plays and heard good music and learned how to dress. But she had never been quite happy away from the wide-open country where she had been born and brought up. Now a quiet content filled her. She had come back to stay in the West, where she belonged.

She turned Buck's head toward the ranch. Breakfast would be waiting for her, and Lane Carey liked to have his daughter eat with him. She guessed how lonesome it had been for him during the years she had been away.

At the top of the first rise she stopped a moment to look down into the valley where the Box 55 lay among the cottonwoods by the river. The main house was hidden in the trees, but she could see the corral with its clicking windmill, the stable, and bits of other buildings. From the blades of the windmill the sun heliographed her a welcome in swift light-flashes.

Her glance swept along the river and continued to the huddled hills lying south of it. Above one of them, from the hollow beyond, rose a cloud of slowly moving dust. She knew what that meant. Cattle or horses were on the march, traveling so steadily that she could tell they were being driven. Somebody must have got an early start.

Ellen dipped into a hollow, crossed a dry creek, and rode up the slope beyond. When she reached the summit she saw the dust of the herd closer. She and it were moving toward the vertex of an acute angle. They would not meet because she would be there long before the cattle.

A rider showed on the nearer lip of the hollow. While she watched, a second came out of the valley and joined him. One of the men rode a bay horse, the other a black. It was too far to be sure, but she thought she recognized the one on the bay. There was a lithe grace about the figure that suggested Jeff Brand. A faint pink beat into her cheeks. That reckless ne'er-do-well had been in her thoughts a great deal during the past two weeks. She found the combination of deference and audacity in him fascinating.

Apparently one of the riders caught sight of her. Both of them looked in her direction for a moment, then disappeared into the valley from which they had come.

Ellen reached the house in time not to keep her father waiting for breakfast. She told him where she had been and mentioned the riders she had seen. Lane Carey took this more seriously than she had expected.

'You think they were driving stock?' he said.

'I'm sure of it.'

'Into the hills?'

'Yes.'

'You weren't near enough to know who they were?'

The girl's answer was delayed only a fraction of a second. She told the truth, with a reservation. 'No.'

Lane frowned down at his plate, thinking this out. He was a big, powerful man in the early fifties, tanned and leathery and tough, a product of forty years in the saddle under wind and sun. His thoughts about this drive he did not put into words. There was no ranch in the vicinity that could be trailing cows to the hills without news of it having reached him. In a cattle country intentions of such moves are mentioned in advance and known to all. From where, then, had this stock come? Either they had started on the trek yesterday and thrown off for the night or been driven through the hours of darkness. If the latter, somebody was pushing the herd hard to get to the cover of the hills as soon as possible. That meant rustlers.

Carey was an honest man. He had cows himself, and no man could say he used a running-iron too freely. Though times were hard, he made a reasonably good living because he had the post-office at Black Butte and ran the stage station. But some of his neighbors were hard pressed. Low prices and short feed had kept them impoverished. Until recently they had made ends meet by work-ing part time for some of the big cattle outfits. But the large ranches, owing to the prevalence of rustling, had made a ruling not to employ any man who had cattle of his own. The result had been to increase rather than decrease thefts. A good many nesters were suspected of ranching in the day and rustling at night.

A small cowman himself, Carey knew how overbearing the large ranchers could be. His sympathies were all with the little man. While he did not hold with cattle-stealing, he did not feel that it was his business to take a hand in helping to protect the raided ranches. The less he knew about the nefarious business the better he would be satisfied.

He rose from the table and picked up a dusty, weather-beaten hat.

'Wish you'd take care of the mail today, honey,' he said. 'I got to help Jim fix the pasture fence. May not be back in time.'

'All right, dad.' She looked him over critically, as the daughter of a widower grown careless of his appearance is likely to do. He wore no coat. His vest and trousers were wrinkled, and the run-down-at-the-heel boots would have been rejected scornfully by a tramp. 'We're going to get you some new boots next time we go down to Round Top.'

He raised a protesting hand. 'Now, don't you go to ridin' yore old father. These boots are right comfortable. I got them broke in fine, and I wouldn't swap them for new ones.'

As the only woman on a ranch with half a dozen

men, Ellen had plenty to do. Black Butte was the halfway house of the stage line. The passengers and driver ate dinner at the Box 55 every day but Sunday. She watched her father ride away, then walked across to the log building he had constructed for a restaurant.

Jim Budd, the negro cook and waiter, was peeling potatoes when Ellen arrived. To keep himself company he was singing a refrain she heard from him several times each morning.

I've been working on the railroad
All the livelong day;
I've been working on the railroad,
To pass the time away.

'There will be at least five on the stage for dinner, Jim,' she told the cook. 'Mack told me yesterday there were four reservations. You had better count on two or three more.'

'Yes'm. I aim to give 'em a pot roast, potatoes, beans, and apple pie.'

'I hope there will be a piece of that pie left for me, Jim,' the girl approved. 'It melts in the mouth.'

Jim was fat and good-natured. Moreover, like all the men on the place, he liked this slim young mistress who was so friendly and yet so firm. He beamed at her praise.

'There will sure be plenty for you-all no matter how many folks come on the stage,' he promised.

Ellen spent most of the morning at the house. Her maid was a half-breed Cheyenne who called herself Jennie, though Ellen preferred to use Star Bright, the English translation of her Indian name. The girl was willing, but it was taking patience to make good help of her. Her mistress had to show the slim young Indian over and over again how to make a bed, how to iron a shirtwaist, how to cook the simplest foods. Often the work was done wrong, but Ellen rarely lost her temper with her. She knew that Star Bright was trying to function in a world totally alien to her past.

When the stage rolled up to the door Ellen was at the post-office waiting for the lean sack of mail the stage-driver flung on the table for sorting. Six passengers emerged from the Concord and streamed to the eating-house. A nester's wife, a redheaded boy, and two cowpunchers reached the office shortly after the stage arrived. Over various trails they had ridden in to Black Butte. Ellen guessed that the range riders who had drifted in were not looking for mail. They had come a few miles out of their way on the chance of seeing the postmaster's daughter.

In a country where the male population outnumbered the female four to one, a young woman as vivid as Miss Carey was bound to attract attention. Most of the young men within a radius of seventy-five miles had ridden to Black Butte on one excuse or another since her return.

Generally they were painfully shy when they did meet her. They blushed, pulled one foot back in an awkward bow, murmured 'Pleased to meet you, ma'am,' and relapsed into an embarrassed silence. Out of this she usually dragged them by asking questions that called for answers. If she could get them to say anything of their own volition she felt the meeting had been a success. They were not all so bashful. A few of them were quite the reverse. On the whole she was not sure that she liked the brash ones as well as the others. She noted an exception in her mind, a young man named Jeff Brand. Maybe she did not like him. She was not sure about that. But at any rate she was interested in him.

While Ellen sorted the mail others drifted into the office. During the hour the stage was there Black Butte was a gathering-place for the neighborhood. Men sat on the porch and exchanged gossip. Cowboys on the bread line came here to learn what ranches needed riders.

Snatches of talk drifted back to Ellen. Sometimes the voices dropped to a murmur, then were raised so that words and phrases came to her. She caught the name 'Buck Hart' once, and two or three times that of his brother Lee. They were connections by marriage of the Carey family; rather remote, but they called her Cousin Ellen. The girl had raised no objection, though she had no great interest in them.

Through the window she caught sight of a man alighting from a sorrel horse. A faint excitement stirred in her. She heard someone walking across from the big house. Her father said, 'How's everything, Jeff?'

The drawling answer was, 'Fine and dandy, Lane.'

Carey relieved his daughter and she walked out of the post-office.

Three men lounged on the porch. One of them rose lithely, the muscles flowing under his skin as smoothly as those of a panther. He joined Ellen and strolled to the house with her. The other two on the porch followed them with envious eyes. They resented the ease with which Jeff Brand had attached himself to this sweet and lovely girl, though their annoyance was more at themselves than at him. They recognized a difference between her and most of the ranch girls they knew. The years at school, building on a body made muscular and strong by the free life of the plains, had given her sheathed beauty a grace remarkably poised.

'Thought I saw you this morning while I was riding,' she said.

Brand slanted a look at her. 'Not unless you were up at Jack Turley's place,' he answered. 'I've been busy breaking a colt to the saddle.'

'No, I was out Flat Top way.'

He shook his head. 'Must have been someone else.' He smiled at her. 'I'll have to do better than that. Can't have you mistaking every bowlegged waddy for me.'

'It doesn't matter, does it?'

'A lot. Take a good look at me, young lady.'

She did not avail herself of the offer. 'I've seen you before,' she mentioned.

'And you'll see me again, any number of times.'

'Dear me! Is that a threat or a promise?' she asked lightly.

His cool eyes rested on her dark good looks. 'It's a promise, to myself.'

'You don't know how grateful I am,' she mocked, with an ironic curtsey. There was a little dancing light in her eyes. 'I have been told that Mr. Brand is the glass of fashion in the Buck River country. When he looks twice at a girl she bridles with pride.'

'Are you grateful enough to let me take you to the Sleepy Cat Ranch dance?' he wanted to know.

She considered that a moment. 'No, I don't think so.' She added, 'Of course I'm greatly flattered.'

'Why won't you go with me?'

'Must I give reasons?'

'Are you going with someone else?'

'Since you ask—yes.'

'Who?'

'Burny, burny, Mr. Brand.' She shook a finger at him reprovingly.

'Meaning you won't tell me.'

'You'll find out in time, if you are there.'

He did not like it. She saw that. There was a suggestion of sulkiness in his good-looking face. 'I hope he'll enjoy himself, whoever he is.' There was an implication in his manner that the unknown escort might not find pleasure in all of the evening.

'I do hope so. If he looks bored it will be a bad social start for me, won't it?'

'He won't be bored,' Brand predicted. 'I'll help you entertain him.'

Ellen read into his words vindictive resentment. She stopped, slim and straight, dark eyes flashing. 'I don't think that will be necessary, Mr. Brand.'

'It will be a pleasure,' he told her.

They had reached the house. The girl moved up the porch steps and turned to look down at him. She said slowly, 'I can see I'm not going to like you.'

Not at all abashed, he smiled up at her confidently. 'Oh, yes, you are. Very much. I'll take care of that.'

'You're very sure—and very bossy, aren't you?'

'Yes.'

She felt anger stirring in her. 'Some people would call it impudence,' she said, a tide of color in her cheeks.

Ellen turned and walked into the house, leaving him there.

In Jeff's eyes, as he walked back to the post-office, little devils of mischief gleamed. Long ago he had discovered that one way to stir a girl's interest in him was to arouse her resentment. It kept her mind full of him while she was devising ways of satisfying it.

His quick glance picked up another horse at the hitch-rack across the road from the post-office. It did not take him a second look to read the brand. Inside the building a man with his back to the door was talking to Lane Carey.

'A gent from the Diamond Reverse B with us this morning?' he asked one of the loungers out of the corner of his mouth.

'His royal nibs,' a young man in chaps answered. 'None other than Mr. Calhoun Terry.'

Jeff did not move as much as a muscle, yet a certain vigilance seemed to stiffen his body. 'What does he want?'

'Inquiring about some strays that jumped the reservation.'

Terry came out to the porch, let his gaze drift around slowly, and crossed the road to his horse. There was a cool arrogance in the way he ignored Brand that got under that young man's skin. Jeff could not let it alone.

'I see you are still wearing the hat that went to the wars, Mr. Terry,' he jeered. 'Did you do anything about that matter you were going to take under consideration?'

Without a word Terry swung to the saddle and jogged down the road. Jeff glared angrily at his broad, flat back, then turned and walked into the office.

'What did Terry want?' he asked abruptly.

Carey looked at him, surprised. 'Wanted to know if I had seen anything of a bunch of she stuff missing from a park where he had them herded.'

'What did you tell him?'

'I don't like the way you ask that question, Jeff,' the ranchman said quietly.

Brand corrected his manner. 'Sorry. I meant, were you able to give him any information?'

'I told him Ellen had seen a bunch being driven into the hills,' Carey said, the eyes in his tanned, leathery face without expression.

'Who was driving it?'

'She wasn't close enough to tell.'

Jeff hesitated over another question, made up his mind, and walked out of the room without asking it.

The ranchman wondered what that query, suppressed before it was uttered, might have been. His thoughts came back to young Brand several times during the day.

So did those of Ellen.

That night at supper she said to her father, 'Are you going to beau me to the Sleepy Cat dance?'

'What's the matter with the young men? Are they all asleep?' he asked.

'Not all of them. I had an invitation from a very good-looking man.'

Lane guessed right first time. 'Jeff Brand?'

'Yes. I told him I was going with a handsomer man.' Ellen smiled at her father. 'So you mustn't let me down.'

'I won't,' Lane answered. He did not smile back at her. 'I hope you're not going to—be interested in—a man like Jeff. I'm afraid he's bad medicine, Nell.'

'For girls?' she inquired.

'Yes, and for others too. He's a lawless young devil heading for trouble. My guess is that he is already a cattle thief. Don't be more than civil to him.'

She smiled reminiscently. 'He probably thinks I wasn't even that, today.'

V

Among the rolling hills to the north of the Diamond Reverse B lay the empire of the Bartlett Land & Cattle Company, familiarly known as the No, By Joe. It stretched over hundreds of thousands of acres of grazing land, over which roamed great numbers of cattle bearing the **B** brand.

The manager, Clint Ellison, rode in from watching a beef cut to hold a conference with important guests who were just arriving. He was a short, broad-shouldered man with a gray, powder-marked face in which were set eyes as cold as deep lake water just before it freezes. He cantered across the plaza around which were grouped the buildings of the home ranch. A corral, stables, barns, sheds, shops, store, and bunkhouse formed three sides of a quadrangle dominated by the big white house of the manager.

At the porch of the house he dismounted and handed the reins to a boy. 'I'm expecting visitors,' he said. 'Have they arrived yet?'

'No, sir, but I seen dust over the hill. That might be them, don't you reckon?'

'Bring them to my office as soon as they get here,' Ellison ordered sharply.

He walked along the gallery and turned into his office, a room expensively furnished with a walnut desk and comfortable padded chairs, with wall pictures, a large safe, and a cabinet well equipped with drinking supplies. Within a few minutes three men who had come in a surrey were ushered into the office.

They shook hands with Ellison, said a few words by way of greeting, and at his invitation found seats. He brought glasses and a bottle of whiskey from the cabinet, a pitcher of water from a tray on a sideboard.

'Help yourselves, gentlemen,' he invited.

John McFaddin, joint owner with his brother of the Flying V C, a very large ranch far up on Elk Creek, poured whiskey into a glass and drank it neat, after a perfunctory 'Here's how!' He was a large, rough man, built very solidly, with a thick neck, a long, drooping mustache, and shuttered eyes as dead as those of a cod.

Ellison pushed the bottle to another of his guests, a tall, thin man dressed very neatly in a well-cut, gray, tailor-made suit. He was Perry Gaines, manager of the Two Star Ranch, another important property in the cattle kingdom of the Northwest.

Gaines shook his head. 'I never drink until I'm through my day's work.'

The third guest reached for a glass and the bottle. He was a round, roly-poly man of middle age, rubicund countenance, and bright, twinkling, merry eyes. 'I drink before I begin it, during same, and after I have finished,' he announced. 'Here's to you, gentlemen. Happy days.'

McFaddin thrust into words the thought that was in his mind, that had been present with all of them for some days. 'So an accident happened to one of the gents too free with a rope and a running-iron near your range, Clint.'

Ellison passed a box of good cigars and took one himself. He puffed it alight before he answered. When he spoke it was in a manner almost casual. 'Referring to Buck Hart, I take it.'

'You take it right.'

The foreman of the No, By Joe looked at the Flying V C man, no expression whatever in his steely eyes. 'I'm told he was shot. With a rifle.

In the early morning. By a person unknown.'

Slanting a grin at Ellison, the plump, red-faced man—he was Tod Collins, manager and part owner of the Antelope Creek Ranch—offered a chuckling suggestion. 'Have to call him Mr. X, I reckon, like they do in these detective stories.'

'The less we call him anything the better,' Gaines differed. 'My advice would be for none of us ever to mention what's been done unless it is brought up by an outsider. That goes for any talk about Buck Hart too. He was a thief, and he has paid for it. Forget him.'

'I hope Mr. X don't forget Buck's friends,' McFaddin droned. 'He's made a good beginning. Let him be thorough.'

A silence followed. Nobody made any comment on this, unless the remark of Collins could be considered one. 'Since we don't know who Mr. X is, he'll have to play a lone hand far as we are concerned,' he said dryly.

Ellison looked a long time at his cigar tip. 'Like the rest of you, I've been milling this over night and day, gentlemen. We represent four out of the five biggest ranches in this part of the territory. I didn't ask Cal Terry to join us today because he isn't in quite the same position as we are. A few years ago he was a little cattleman himself, and though his old friends hate him like poison now, he may still have scruples against what I have in mind. Later we'll have to take him in, but we might as well make our plans first. John used a word a minute ago that suits me. The word is thorough. If we're going to protect our properties from wholesale thieving we must wipe the rustlers out *en masse*.'

'Listens fine, Clint,' Tod Collins assented, with obvious sarcasm. 'Now will you tell us how? The thieves own the sheriffs, prosecuting attorneys, and judges. The law won't do a thing for us. You know that well as I do, so I reckon you're not proposing for us to look to the law.'

'No. Time was when the cattlemen ran this country, as was right and proper. They developed the industry that was making Wyoming. A fine lot of men. Hardly a cull among them. Times have changed. The small man and his friend the rustler control this county and a good many others. Gentlemen, we've got to take the law into our own hands.' Ellison banged a fist down on the desk. 'Or else we're done for. It's fight or be wiped out.'

'My opinion, too,' Gaines agreed. He added deliberately: 'I'm a law-abiding citizen, as you all are. But this country's legal machinery is in the hands of outlaws. I believe in self-preservation. I'll throw in with you against the common enemy.'

Ellison looked at McFaddin, who ripped out a lusty oath. 'I'll go all the way with you, John,' he said. 'I'm not going to lie down and let scoundrels rob me right and left.'

Tod Collins grinned. 'The Antelope Creek rides to war with the rest of you. Cut loose with what's on your mind, Clint.'

'If you're going to tell us about Mr. X,' McFaddin began, and was interrupted sharply by Gaines.

'No!' he cried. 'I don't want to hear anything about him. We can do our own guessing about who he is. Let it ride at that. The fewer who know, the better.'

'Yes,' assented Ellison. 'We won't go into that matter.'

From his pocket Collins drew a wallet and counted out one hundred and twenty-five dollars in bills. He put the money on the desk. 'Now's a good time to settle that election bet we made with Clint, boys,' he said.

The managers of the Flying V C and the Two Star ranches each put the same amount on the desk. Ellison gathered it up and put the wadded bills in his pocket.

He leaned forward and in a low voice began to outline the plan he had in mind.

VI

Ellen drew up on the bluff at the edge of Johnson's Prong and let her eyes wander over the vast panorama of country that stretched to the far horizon. In the foreground, hundreds of feet below, lay the North Fork Valley, the creek winding through it like a silver snake. A windmill on Sheriff Nate Hart's place, near the upper end of the valley, caught the sun's rays and heliographed them to her. To the right she made out, half a score of miles away, the diminished outlines of Round Top's scattered buildings. Beyond the North Fork a hundred huddled hills stretched to the horizon's edge. Forests marched up the slopes of the farther ones, blue and blurred in the hazy distance.

Gathering the reins, the girl turned down the long spur which led to Box Cañon, from which she would emerge to the valley. Just before she entered the gorge the trail brought her again close to the edge of the prong. Her glance picked up a puff of smoke, and a fraction of a second later there came the sound of a shot.

Ellen thought she saw something moving among the brush close to the river, but if so what she had seen was too far and vague to identify as man or beast. It might have been a cow grazing.

Silence closed over the scene again. Ellen watched intently. One who lives in the wide spaces of the open West develops a habit of close observation. By means of it an oldtimer reads much on the terrain that is not written there for a tenderfoot. The sound of that single shot, coming in the deep stillness, disturbed the girl a little. This was not a country of friendly neighbors, had not been for some years. Though she had not been back long, it had not been possible for her not to sense the tense feeling in the district.

She dipped down into the cañon, following the steep trail winding among the boulders. It was a rough descent, one not used often. Ellen had come this way because the cañon route to town was a prettier one than the dusty wagon road usually taken. There were pines in the upper reaches of the gulch. Below she could see an aspen grove, the leaves quivering in the sun.

The path grew less steep as she came down toward the mouth of the gorge. Her horse passed into the aspens, and when it came into the clear again the cañon was opening to meet the foothills below.

She swung around a great boulder and came face to face with a man. Both of them pulled up, taken completely by surprise. For a moment, before he realized she was a woman, a brown hand moved swiftly to the dark butt of a revolver suspended from his hip. He was a lean, bronzed man, broad of shoulder, strongly built. A vague memory stirred in her. She must have known him when she lived here before going to school, but she could not fix the fugitive recollection.

Ellen said: 'Don't be afraid. I won't hurt you.'

His grim face relaxed. There was a hint of a smile on the lips, but the girl noticed there was no laughter in the eyes. He lifted the hat from his black hair.

'Good morning,' he said. 'Did you meet anybody as you came down the cañon?'

'No,' she told him.

The girl noted that his eyes were a deep blue, with little steel bars radiating from the pupil to the perimeter. His look was direct and hard. She thought that he would be a bad man to have for an enemy.

'A rider couldn't have hidden while you passed?' he asked.

'I don't think so.' She flashed a question at him in her turn. 'Why should he?'

'Are you headed for Round Top?' he said. His voice was low and resonant, but there was an imperative in it she resented a little.

'Yes, since you are interested.'

If he noticed the inflection of irony he paid no attention to it.

'Don't go,' he replied curtly.

Ellen sat a little straighter on the horse. Her chin set. 'Why not?'

49

He did not answer immediately, but continued to regard her, frowning. 'I don't believe I have met you.'

Her smile was bland. 'I didn't hear you answer my question, sir.'

'There has been some trouble.'

'What kind of trouble?'

From the first she had known that there was something on his mind. She could see that now he hung undecided, uncertain how much to tell her.

Making up his mind, he spoke abruptly. 'A man has been killed.'

Ellen echoed the last word. 'Killed?'

'Shot from ambush—drygulched.'

She stared at him, her eyes on his. 'Who was killed?'

'Man named Tetlow. Lives on Fisher Creek.'

'Who did it?'

'I don't know. I heard someone galloping away through the brush, and a little later I came across the body.'

'Just before I started down the cañon I heard a shot,' Ellen said. 'Just one. Do you think they had a quarrel?'

'No. Tetlow didn't have his gun out. A bullet from a rifle went through the back of his head.'

'Murder.' The word fell from the girl's lips in a low, shocked voice. 'The second in a week.'

'Yes.'

'What's come over this country?' she asked

unhappily. 'Are the big cattlemen starting in to kill all the settlers who are in their way?'

'No.' He spoke sharply, instantly. 'These men were both rustlers, according to common report. That's true. They lived violently and made enemies. Maybe they quarreled among themselves.'

'One of them was my cousin.' She sat slim and straight in the saddle, eyes flashing. 'I don't believe a word of it. You work for one of the big outfits, I suppose.'

'Yes,' he admitted.

She looked at him, a man strong as steel, hard-bitten, seasoned. The cool, sardonic eyes suggested arrogance. Then, as her glance fell on the rifle in its scabbard beside the saddle, there jumped to her mind a horrid thought. He might have done it himself. Why was he carrying a rifle in a country where the almost universal custom was to wear only revolvers? How did he happen to be on the scene of the crime so pat? He had not expected to meet anybody in the cañon. Discovered in flight, he had cooked up the first story that came to his mind.

'Was Jim Tetlow your cousin?' he asked.

'No. Buck Hart, by marriage.'

The girl did not move, but she felt herself recoiling from him. She was moved by shock rather than personal fear, by the repulsion a clean and healthy soul feels at contact with something foul. More than once she had known men who

51

had been forced to kill in self-defense. Instinctively she had felt they were not bad but merely the victims of circumstances. But one who laid in wait to destroy another from ambush was worse than a rattlesnake.

Yet he did not look like that kind of man. She judged him to be cold and perhaps bitter, but the ugliness of sin had not stamped itself on the face. Nor did those steady steel-blue eyes appear to mirror vileness.

'Then you live in the hills here,' he said.

'My name is Ellen Carey.'

There jumped to his mind the picture of a thin, long-legged, harum-scarum girl flying about the Black Butte country on a pinto horse. He had not ever given her a second look, but he remembered her as a dark, ugly little thing. Looking at the lovely planes of her face, at the slender fullness of her gracious body, it was amazing that such a child could have developed into such a beauty.

'Lane Carey's daughter?'

'Yes.' She frowned at him, on the verge of a discovery. 'You are Calhoun Terry,' she said. 'I knew I'd seen you before. You were a friend of my father then.'

'Before I committed the crime of trying to better myself honestly and lawfully,' he explained.

She knew those who looked at what he had done from another angle, but she did not intend to discuss it with him.

'What are you going to do with . . . the body?' she asked.

'I'll notify his friends where to find it.'

'I could tell the coroner while I'm in town.'

He shook his head. 'Better not go to town this way, Miss Carey. The killer may still be down there in the flats somewhere.'

Ellen looked at him, startled. 'You don't think he would hurt me, do you?'

'Not unless he thought his safety required it. Maybe not then. But he might fire from the brush before he realized you aren't a man.'

'You mean, thinking I might be a witness against him.'

'It's just a chance. But why take it? I daresay he is miles away now, scurrying to get out of the vicinity. But we can't be sure.'

'No,' she answered, her eyes fixed on him. 'I can't be sure.'

'I'll ride up the cañon with you as far as the Hartman place, just to be certain.'

'It's not necessary. I haven't seen anybody coming up the cañon—except you.'

Something in the way she said it, some inflection that was an unintended betrayal of her thought, caught his attention and fixed it. For the first time he understood that he was under suspicion. He might be the assassin, discovered while riding into this gash in the hills to escape.

Grimly he smiled. 'Nobody—except me. And I

came direct from the scene of the crime, carrying the rifle that may have held the cartridge. Perhaps you'd better arrest me, Miss Carey.'

She felt excitement drumming in her veins. 'I haven't accused you, have I?'

'Not in words. Would you like to examine my rifle? Maybe you'll find the empty cartridge in it.'

'No.'

'Quite right. Of course I would fling out the cartridge. Maybe it is not safe for you to ride up the gulch with me, since you're the only eye-witness against me.'

Their eyes met and held, searching for what lay beneath the surface. Into Ellen's consciousness there beat an assurance that this man was no assassin. He was stiff and very likely wrong-headed. He might have traveled far from that straight path followed by men who do no wrong to others. But to look at that lean, strong-jawed face, clean-cut and forceful, was assurance of some fundamental decency in him. Beneath that steady regard, she judged, there might be a wild rash-ness explosively violent. But unless the man's character completely libeled his appearance it would not carry him to coldblooded murder.

'I'm as safe with you as I would be with my father,' she said quietly.

He was a man not easily moved, but her words sent a little shock of pleasure through him.

'Some of your friends might not say so,' he

answered dryly. 'Haven't they told you what a villain I am?'

'They were your friends too,' she reminded him, 'before you turned your back on them and joined their enemies.'

He understood that she had shut a door between them. She stood with the nesters and the small cattlemen against whom he and his allies fought. That she had declared herself stirred no resentment in him. She made him think of a fine spirited young race horse.

Turning the head of her mount, Ellen began the climb. He fell in behind her. They took the stiff grade slowly. The muscles of their ponies tensed as the hoofs gripped new footholds in the rocky ascent. Neither of the riders spoke. There were no sounds except from creaking leather, the deep breathing of the animals, and the striking of steel shoes on stones.

Ellen did not look round. She had settled the status of their acquaintance. Nothing more needed to be said. If he had been a man who killed from ambush, the crook of a finger could destroy evidence very damaging against him. But he was not. Since her return from school she had more than once heard him cursed bitterly as a traitor who had sold out his friends. That might be true, in a way of speaking. He was a hard man, ambitious, not too scrupulous as to how he fought for what he considered his rights. But however warped they might be, he had standards that regulated his way of life. In him there burned a spark of self-respect no misguided thinking could destroy. So Ellen's quick eyes and brain had judged.

When they came out on the top of Johnson's Prong the man moved forward and rode beside Ellen. He looked across the North Fork Valley, the creek winding through it a ribbon of silver, to the forests marching up the huddled hills to the blurred horizon's edge. A snatch of Heber's missionary hymn jumped again to his mind. He laughed sardonically.

The girl looked at him. 'You are amused?'

He quoted the verse:

> . . . every prospect pleases
> and only man is vile.

Her eyes, judging him indignantly, refused to join his mockery. 'I don't find murder funny,' she said.

'I wasn't thinking of murder, but of the man who turned his back on his friends. I suppose you would call him a traitor.'

'It isn't my business to call him anything.'

'You don't need to have anything to do with him—after we reach the fork in the road just ahead. That's so. You can go back to your nice good friends, who shoot at enemies as they pass, through a window.'

'That's not true!' she cried.

'My mistake. I should have said cousin, not friend. The name is Lee Hart.'

'When did he shoot at you—if he did?'

'Wednesday a week ago, about 4 p.m., from the Red Triangle Saloon.'

She did not speak for a moment, and when she did it was to repudiate Hart. 'He isn't really my cousin. Only a distant relative by marriage. I haven't spoken to him five times in my life.'

'You should cultivate your distant-relative-by-marriage,' he advised. 'A fine character, barring some peculiarities.'

Ellen felt a tide of angry color beating up under the brown skin of her cheeks. She drew up her horse. They had come to the trail fork. The path to the left led to Black Butte, the other eventually to the Diamond Reverse B.

'I'll not trouble you any more, Mr. Terry,' she said coldly.

'It's been a pleasure,' he answered ironically, and took the road to the right.

For days Ellen's mind was full of this adventure and the man who had shared it with her. He had not asked her not to tell that she had seen him coming into the cañon, but she did not mention it to anybody. When she heard the murder discussed at the post-office she told nothing of what she knew.

Alone in her room at night, she could not

escape thinking of Cal Terry. After she had gone to bed he would stand there in the darkness, as vivid as if actually present, lean and strong and cynical, a look in his cool blue eyes that told her he would go to death if necessary with a spirit unconquerable.

VII

Excitement ran like a prairie fire through the Buck River country. When men met far up in the mountains or out on the desert they stopped to talk over the killing of Jim Tetlow. Coming as it did so quickly after the murder of Buck Hart, few among the nesters or the homesteaders had any doubt that it meant notice from the big cattlemen that they would no longer permit rustling with impunity. The bitterness was intense.

The heat of it converged on Calhoun Terry. He had reported finding the body of Tetlow, after having been seen by two men an hour or so after the killing not far from the upper end of Box Cañon. When seen, he had a Winchester rifle in a scabbard tied to the side of his saddle.

There was a sharp division of opinion as to whether Terry had himself killed Tetlow, but most of the settlers held that he was in it, either as principal or accomplice. The sheriff's posse had followed the trail of a horseman from the body to the lower mouth of the cañon. Here he had been joined by another rider. It seemed likely that the second man was Cal Terry. Probably he had been waiting there to make sure his hired killer did the job for which he was being paid.

Sheriff Hart rode up to the Diamond Reverse B to ask Terry to explain his movements. His brother Lee had suggested a posse, on which Jeff Brand and Jack Turley had offered to serve, big enough to capture the foreman of the ranch unless his men offered organized resistance. But Nate Hart decided against this.

'We haven't evidence enough on which to convict him—nothing like enough,' he said. 'No sense in going off half-cocked.'

'And what will you do if Cal starts a gun-play?' Turley asked.

Sheriff Hart was a stout-hearted man. 'Why, I reckon I would have to accommodate him, Jack,' he answered.

Turley was a newcomer to the neighborhood, compared to the others. He had homesteaded a waterhole about a year prior to this time, but his aggressive spirit made him one of the leaders of the settlers.

The broken-nosed man scowled. 'Fine, if four–five of Terry's warriors join in with him. We'd have to bring you back to town in a wooden box after they quit using you as a target.'

'Cal isn't such a fool as that,' Brand said, from the counter on which he was sitting. 'I don't like him a lick of the road. But he's game, whatever else you say about him. I'm not so doggoned sure he was in this Tetlow killing. If so, whyfor did he send one of his men to notify Jim's kin where they could find the body?'

'He's got nerve enough to sink a ship,' Lee Hart broke in. 'Thinks he can get away with anything, no matter how raw it is.'

'Well, boys, I'm going to the Diamond Reverse B alone,' the sheriff said flatly. 'And I'll come back good as new.'

'You'd better let me and some of the other boys go along,' Lee insisted. These fellows have served notice on us that they want trouble, and far as Cal Terry goes he never was a friend of ours.'

'He was a friend of mine once,' the sheriff differed. 'Before he threw in with the big fellows who want to own the whole damn country.' His eyes drifted a little scornfully over his heavy-set, bowlegged brother. 'I'm going for business, not war. If I took you along, Lee, it would be like waving a red rag at Cal.'

So Nate Hart rode alone to the Diamond Reverse B. As he came closer to it he passed cattle bearing the ranch brand. Emerging from a deep swale, he came on a wide-open valley. This was range for Diamond Reverse B stock. He presently came upon some cowboys at work. They had rounded up a bunch of several hundred cows and were branding the calves.

The sheriff rode up to the brush fire where they were heating the irons and relaxed in the saddle, shifting his weight to ease cramped muscles. He passed the time of day with the punchers, who were a little less than cordial. They considered Hart a rustler's sheriff, and they were loyal to the ranch that employed them.

'Came up to have a talk with Cal Terry,' the officer explained. 'I'd hate to miss him after riding so far. Can you boys tell me just where I can find him?'

His question met a blank silence. If Hart had not known better he might have thought they had never heard of a man named Cal Terry.

'I just want to get a little information from him,' Hart went on pleasantly. 'Maybe I had better jog on to the house.'

They offered no opinion on that. One of them went down a rope to a calf jerking at the other end of it, caught the skin close to a fore and a hind leg, and with an expert lift threw the blatting animal from its feet to the ground. Two others stretched the legs while the hot iron was applied. The air was filled with an acrid smell of burning hair and flesh. A moment later the calf struggled to its feet, shook itself, and ran bawling to the mother. The cow licked away the pain of the wound, and in five minutes both of them had forgotten an unpleasant experience.

Hart turned back to the road and jiggled down it at a road gait. In the distance he could see the windmills of the ranch, the white house, and the group of buildings that surrounded it. Bathed in the pure air flooded with sunlight, they looked miles closer than they were. He jogged on for the best part of an hour before he pulled up at the wide gallery running around the main house.

He hailed a lad walking across from a bunkhouse to the blacksmith shop and inquired for the foreman.

'The boss came in not five minutes ago,' the boy said. 'I wouldn't wonder but what he's in his office. Corner room on the right.'

The sheriff found him there looking over the ranch accounts. Terry looked up, the paper still in his hand. His eyes regarded Hart. At once he had become a man on his guard. He said nothing, waiting for the officer to speak.

Hart was in his early thirties, big and rangy and vigorous. He had a long-jawed, bony face, in which were set hard, unwinking eyes. The general opinion was that he was by all odds the best of the Hart brothers.

'I've heard a lot of talk, Terry,' he said. 'Thought I'd better ride up and find out what you have to tell me.'

The ranch superintendent rose. 'Take a chair,

sheriff. As I understand it, you are here officially.'

Hart drew up a chair 'Well, I am, and I'm not. I thought I'd better hear your story.'

'You mean about your brother shooting at me from the Red Triangle,' Terry said, on the theory that a swift attack may be the best defense.

'Don't believe all you hear. My brother didn't shoot at you.'

'I must have imagined the holes in my hat,' Calhoun said.

The sheriff did not pursue that line any further. 'What I want to talk about is the Tetlow killing. You were the first to reach the body. Were you in time to see the killer?'

'No. I heard the shot. He was gone when I found the body.'

Neither of them raised his voice. There had been trouble between Terry and the Harts, but because of it each was a little more careful than he would otherwise have been. They were studiously polite.

'What were you doing down on the North Fork at that time?' the sheriff asked, his manner obviously casual.

'I was on my way back from Jim Creek, where I had been to see the station agent about wiring for some cars I needed to make a beef shipment.'

Hart accepted the other's explanation for the present. He could confirm it later by the agent.

'After finding the body you went home by way of Box Cañon?'

'Yes.'

'Was there anybody with you?'

'No.'

'You went up the cañon alone?'

'I did.'

'We found two sets of tracks, both very recent. They must have both been made that day, because it rained the night before. You didn't happen to see anybody else?'

'I met two men on the mesa above.'

'But nobody in the cañon?'

'No. Isn't it possible that the second set of tracks could have been made by the killer while he was escaping? He may have passed up the cañon either before or after me.'

'Yes, it may have been that way. But the tracks show that the two rode side by side for a ways after they reached the prong.'

'Not necessarily. The tracks may not have been made at the same time,' the foreman suggested.

'The men who met you on the mesa say you had a rifle with you.' Hart's manner was not offensive, but the eyes fixed on the foreman were cold as a wind sweeping across a glacier.

'I always carry a rifle, sheriff, since my life was attempted at Round Top the other day.' Terry added with soft-voiced sarcasm: 'A precaution that seems necessary.'

'A Winchester?'

'Yes. I see you are about to tell me that Tetlow was shot with a Winchester.'

'That's right.'

The world is full of coincidences, isn't it?' Terry mocked. 'Maybe the same scoundrel shot Tetlow that shot at me from the Red Triangle. That might be a line worth investigating, sheriff.'

'I have another view of it,' Hart replied shortly, his politeness worn a little thin. 'Like to look at your rifle, if you don't mind.'

'Help yourself.' The ranch manager waved a hand at the weapon, which hung in its scabbard on the wall.

The sheriff broke the gun, took out a shell, and looked at it. He put the cartridge in his pocket. After examining the rifle he replaced it.

'Same size shell,' he commented. 'And a .45-70 Winchester like this.'

'Maybe the killer borrowed my gun,' Terry drawled.

'Bullets from the same rifle killed my brother Buck and Tetlow. Both bodies had notes pinned on them in the same handwriting, a warning that this was what happened to cattle thieves.'

'Want a sample of my writing?' Terry asked contemptuously.

'I have plenty of them.' The sheriff fired a swift question. 'Where were you when my brother was killed?'

'When was he killed?'

'It must have been about five o'clock in the morning of the same day you were at Round Top in the afternoon.'

'That's right early. I reckon I was in bed. It's the slack season. I don't have breakfast till about seven.'

'Can you prove you were in bed?'

'I don't think so.'

'Or that you were on the ranch at all?'

'No. I expect Jim Wong would testify I ate bacon and eggs and a plate of hot cakes at breakfast two hours later.'

'Two hours later won't help. Buck was killed, as you know, on the range where your cattle run. You might have ridden out and back.'

'Your brother must have had early business,' Terry said significantly.

'Leave him out of it,' Hart cut back harshly. 'I'm talking of you.'

'Maybe you'd like to arrest me.'

Nate Hart came back to the desk and looked down at the other, his eyes steady and hard. 'No use being mealy-mouthed, Terry. There's a killer around, and I'm sheriff. I mean to find out who he is.'

'That's what you're paid for,' the cattleman agreed blandly. 'The citizens of Sweetwater County elected you to stamp out crime.'

'You're concealing something. Come clean, Terry. You know the talk that is going round. If you didn't kill my brother or Tetlow you had better tell what you know.'

'Aren't you putting the cart before the horse, Mr. Sheriff?' Terry asked, his voice brittle but still low. 'If I understand the law I don't have to prove myself innocent, though of course in this part of the territory the courts have established new rules.'

'An innocent man would want to make the fact clear to everybody.'

'I don't give a damn what rustlers think of me,' Calhoun said curtly.

'The majority of the residents of Sweetwater County are not rustlers,' Hart retorted.

'Not thieves themselves, but friends of thieves.'

'I won't argue that with you,' the officer snapped. 'Point is, I'm looking for a murderer. Who is he?'

'You tell me,' the man at the desk said suavely. 'You're the sheriff.'

'I'm asking you if you know.'

'And I'm telling you that you wouldn't believe me if I said I did not. So why waste my breath?'

'The general opinion is that these crimes were done by a killer hired by the big cattle companies.'

'The general opinion is wrong. They were probably done by some of their own gang with whom they had quarreled.'

Hart bristled. 'I don't like the word gang, Mr. Terry, used in connection with my brother.'

The Diamond Reverse B man flung back the challenge instantly. 'And I don't like the implication, based on no evidence, that I shoot down men from ambush.'

They had come to an impasse. Neither of them were men overly patient. Each read a storm signal in the hard, unyielding eyes of the other.

The sheriff had not come for a fight. He said grudgingly; 'I'm not claiming you shot my brother and Tetlow. I think you know more about it than you have told.'

'I know nothing whatever about it.'

'All right. Why couldn't you say so? That's all I want to know—for the present.'

Hart turned to walk out of the room. The foreman let him reach the door.

'Dinner in about half an hour if you care to stay, Mr. Sheriff,' he said, with no warmth.

It was a custom of the country that any stranger who dropped into a ranch near mealtime stayed to share it. The next nearest place where food could be obtained might be thirty miles away.

The officer declined. 'Thanks, no. I brought a snack along with me. I'll be hitting the trail.'

He stepped down from the porch, unhitched his horse, and swung to the saddle. From the doorway Terry watched. He did not like Hart, but his sense of hospitality was not satisfied.

'Some of the boys are branding down the road two–three miles,' he said. You'll just make it in time for a cup of coffee and a steak. They will be glad to have you join them.'

'They acted right cordial when I asked them a question on the way in,' Hart answered dryly. 'I don't reckon I'll trouble them.'

He swung his mount round and started down the road.

VIII

Owing to a broken axle caused by an upset, the stage was nearly two hours late at Black Butte. Sheriff Hart arrived about the same time, and after he had eaten joined the usual forum on the porch of the post-office. A cowboy whittling on a piece of soft pine asked him whether he was in this neck of the woods on business or for pleasure.

Ellen moved a little nearer the window to catch the answer of the sheriff. She was giving out the mail, but just at the moment nobody was inquiring for letters.

'I been over to the Diamond Reverse B to have a talk with Cal Terry,' he explained.

'What does that curly wolf have to say for himself?' growled Jack Turley.

'What you'd expect him to claim, that he knows nothing about the killings.'

'Just happened to be on the scene by accident

with a rifle loaded for bear,' Turley said with a jeering laugh. The man had an ugly, lupine face, not improved by the disfigured nose.

'He gave a reason for being there. I aim to check up on it.'

'Would that reason cover the fellow he had with him too?' the cowboy inquired, pausing in his whittling.

'Says there was nobody with him,' the sheriff replied.

'I reckon he thinks nobody in this country can read sign,' commented Turley acidly.

Roan Alford spoke. 'Cal didn't used to be a fool, not when I knew him. How does he explain the double tracks, Nate?'

'Suggests the killer may have come up Box Cañon either before or after him, and that the hoofprints just happen to run a parallel course on Johnson's Prong.'

'Too thin.' It was Turley's harsh voice again. 'The tracks ran side by side quite a ways.'

'I wasn't satisfied,' the sheriff assented. 'I'll not say Terry was in on the killings, but he knows more than he will tell.'

'Unless he's changed a heap from the Cal Terry I usta know he wouldn't stand for drygulching a man,' Alford contributed, chewing a quid of tobacco thoughtfully. 'When I was a kid I wrote in my copybook about touching pitch and being defiled. But even so I don't reckon a man teetotally changes after his mind is old enough to get jelled, as you might say.'

Out of sight but close to the window, Ellen listened intently. This was not a private conversation, but talk in an open forum for all to hear. It was public opinion in the process of formation, and she was vitally interested in knowing how it ran.

Turley's bullying voice took up the thread. 'You fellows are too soft. Facts talk, I claim, louder than a killer's unbacked alibis. Terry hated Buck Hart. It's known he accused Jim Tetlow of being a rustler and warned him to keep away from the Diamond Reverse B range. He was on the ground right after the killing and found the body. Later he rode up the cañon with another guy, probably the fellow who fired the shot, and claims he was alone because he dassent give his side-kick's name. When seen on the mesa he was carrying a rifle. Put those facts together and it spells guilt.'

The whittling cowboy closed his jack knife and threw away the piece of pine. He rose and stretched himself. 'I'll say this, boys. Mr. Terry can't get away from that double set of hoofprints. They tie a rope round his neck, or leastways they had ought to. I never did like him. He's too high and mighty for me.'

He walked toward the hitch-rack to get his horse, but pulled up in his stride to listen to a new

71

voice which had cut into the talk, a clear contralto throbbing with indignant scorn.

Ellen had come out to the porch and was standing in the doorway.

'Since you don't like him, Yorky, of course he ought to be hanged. He must be the assassin because he didn't want Diamond Reverse B stock stolen and was the man who discovered Jim Tetlow's body. And if somebody rode up the cañon with him that is sure proof he shot Jim. What more do you need?'

Their astonished eyes fixed on her. She was not a bouncing, round-breasted girl blooming with color like the other daughters of the ranchers with whom they had danced and perhaps flirted. The dark-tempered beauty and quick, animal grace of her slender person were alien to their experience. They had been shy of her because they did not understand her. Though they appreciated the impetuous gallantry that challenged them, they were puzzled for a cause sufficient to have stirred it.

'I didn't know you liked him, Cousin Ellen,' the sheriff said. 'Fact is, I hadn't heard you had met him since you came back.'

She turned on the sheriff eyes bright with resentment. 'I don't like him. What's that got to do with it? Isn't there such a thing as fair play? Must he be guilty of murder just because you want to think he is?'

Roan Alford defended himself, a propitiatory smile on his wrinkled, weather-beaten face. 'I don't want to think any such a thing, Miss Ellen. I'd hate to believe it of him, even if he is tied up with a mighty overbearing bunch of land-grabbers. Just the same, if he wants folks to think he's innocent he has got no right to be so doggoned biggity about holding back facts. Now take those tracks—'

Sharply Ellen cut in on him. 'All right, take them. He didn't tell who he was with because he thought it might embarrass a girl to be dragged into a killing like this. He thought—'

Hart interrupted her as abruptly as she had done with Alford. 'A girl,' he repeated. 'What girl you talkin' about?'

Her eyes did not falter, though the color had flooded into her cheeks. 'I'm talking about myself. I was going to Round Top, and I thought I'd take the Box Cañon way to see the flowers. We met below the lower entrance, just after the shot was fired.'

'How long after?' the sheriff asked.

'Oh, soon. I don't know how long.'

'Three minutes—five minutes—ten minutes—half an hour?'

'I tell you I don't know. Only a few minutes.'

'Just long enough for him to have made sure he had done a good job and then got to the cañon for his getaway,' rasped Turley.

'He didn't kill Jim Tetlow,' Ellen answered hotly.

'Maybe not. But how do you know?' insisted the sheriff. 'If you were in the cañon you couldn't have seen the shot fired.'

'Mr. Terry didn't act like a guilty man. He wanted me to examine the rifle to make sure it hadn't just been fired.'

Hart jumped at that like a terrier at a rat. 'Why did he do that? Unless he was covering up—building evidence for himself.'

'Because of something I said.'

'And the rifle—could you tell if it had just been fired?'

'I didn't look.'

'You didn't see anybody else there at any time?'

All of the men were watching Ellen closely. She could see that their interest was keen-edged. This would be talked over at every ranch in the county. There would be discussion of it at the corrals and stores of Round Top. People would wonder what she was doing alone with Calhoun Terry in a cañon so little frequented. Rumors would start that would do no good to her reputation.

'Nobody else,' she said. 'Before I came out of the cañon the killer had slipped away in the brush.'

Turley laughed unpleasantly. 'So you say. It will take a heap of proving.'

Ellen paid no attention to him. She continued to look at Hart. 'I'm telling you this because it has to be told. Mr. Terry rode up the cañon with me because he thought the killer might have slipped into the gorge and he was afraid to have me go alone. He felt I might be in danger, since the assassin couldn't know I had not been a witness.'

'Well, some folks like fairy tales,' Turley jeered.

'Cut that kind of talk out, Jack,' Alford told him sharply. 'Miss Ellen is telling us a straight story.'

'It knocks out the theory of his having an accomplice there with him,' the sheriff added. 'I'm much obliged to you, Cousin Ellen, for saving me a lot of work. I won't have to try to run down a fellow that doesn't exist.'

'And it proves that Cal Terry was right there on the scene,' snarled Turley.

'He admitted that from the start,' Alford corrected. 'That didn't need any proving.'

'There's a point there that tells against Terry, though,' Hart said. 'When he reported finding Jim Tetlow's body that looked like the action of an innocent man. Now we know he was discovered close to the spot and had to frame a story to protect himself.'

'We don't know any such thing,' Ellen differed. 'If he is innocent he didn't have to frame a story. All he had to do was to tell the truth. Which is what he did.'

Smiling at her, Alford said, 'He's got a mighty fine champion, Miss Ellen.'

The girl said impatiently: 'I'm not his champion. He isn't my friend. I've only met him once since I was a little girl, but I don't like him. That's no reason for not telling what I know about this.'

She turned and walked swiftly into the post-office. As she thought of it later, she did not know whether her story had done him harm or good. At any rate, it had done away with the talk that he had ridden up the cañon with an accomplice whose name he dared not tell.

Perhaps it was true she did not like him. Certainly she resented the importance he was taking in her thoughts. She made up her mind to take herself in hand and try to forget the whole affair. Now she had told her story to the sheriff it probably would not disturb her any more.

IX

Half an hour after Sheriff Hart had declined to stay at the Diamond Reverse B for dinner another visitor arrived in a buckboard. Terry came out from the office to meet him.

'Hello, Clint!' he called out. 'Just in time for dinner. If you had been a little earlier you might have met the law here.'

The superintendent of the No, By Joe turned the reins over to a boy and walked into the office with Terry.

'I met it down the road a bit,' he said. 'What did Hart want?'

'Wanted to arrest me for killing Jim Tetlow, but he was afraid his evidence was a little too thin even for a rustler's court.'

'No judgment,' pronounced Ellison. 'You'd think Hart would realize that if we wanted to get rid of these thieves we wouldn't do it personally that way.'

Terry offered his guest a drink. Ellison helped himself and lit a cigar.

'Hart does not seem to be sure whether I did it myself or we hired a gunman.' The Diamond Reverse B man leaned back in his chair indolently, his gaze fixed on the other.

Ellison was busy getting his cigar started. He said, between puffs: 'Tell him to look nearer home. Tell him to check up on which of the thieves have quarreled with his brother and Tetlow.'

'I did.'

'Buck Hart was killed on your range. What was he doing there? Who was with him? Why were they out so early in the morning? On nefarious business, I'll guess. If one of your riders killed him, he killed a thief caught on the job. He had it coming to him, didn't he? Why all the kick?'

'None of my boys shot him,' Terry said. At least I don't think so. I'd feel it in the air that they were keeping a secret from me. Of course Hart was a bully. He whipped a couple of my boys not long since. But I don't believe either of them killed him.'

'Probably not. Anyhow, he's better dead. I'll not do any mourning for him. Maybe there will be a little less night-riding than there has been of late.'

'I wish this could be cleared up, Clint,' his companion replied, frowning at a quirt hanging on the wall. 'We can't afford to have people think we are shooting down men on suspicion. I grant you both of these men were dyed-in-the-wool thieves. We were sure of it. I wouldn't have objected to stringing them to a tree openly. But I don't want Wyoming to think we approve of drygulching men we don't like.'

'You think Hart and Tetlow would rather have been hanged than shot?' Ellison asked with a quizzical grin.

'I'm not thinking about them but about us. I hope Hart finds the assassin in order to clear our skirts.'

The No, By Joe superintendent shrugged his shoulders. 'The fellow isn't likely to be caught, unless he gets drunk and talks. You are giving this too much weight, Cal. Nobody is going to care if a few rustlers are rubbed out. They asked for it. . . . But you said something a minute ago that will bear discussion.'

Ellison walked to the door, looked around to make sure nobody was near, and decided not to risk speaking of what was on his mind just now.

'After dinner we'll stroll out into the open where there can't be any eavesdroppers and do our talking there,' he said.

Jim Wong shuffled into the room and announced that dinner was ready. The cook was middle-aged and fat. He wore felt slippers and a queue wound tightly on his head. The rest of his clothes were American.

'Cold loast bif,' Jim said in a sing-song voice. 'And vlegtables and glavy.'

'Just what I would have ordered, Jim,' Ellison told him.

The midday dinner finished, Terry and his guest strolled out to a corral and leaned against the fence. Inside there were a few horses, but no human being except themselves within fifty yards.

'Cal, unless we take the law in our own hands the big ranches are through,' Ellison began abruptly. 'We've all lost money this year, and we'll lose more next. You know the reasons, well as I do. Short feed, hard winter, and too many rustlers who call themselves ranchmen preying on our stock.'

'Yes,' agreed Terry. 'And you named the worst last.'

'I did. We're through, unless we can wipe them out.'

'How?' asked the Diamond Reverse B foreman. 'We range over so big a territory and the thieves are so slick we hardly ever catch them.'

'We know pretty well who they are, don't we?'

'A good many of them. That is, we're pretty sure, even when we haven't proof.'

'Isn't that enough? Are we going to lie down and let the thieves put us out of business?'

'I'm listening,' Calhoun said quietly.

'What I propose is to bring in a little army of warriors, round up the known rustlers, and hang them as we sweep through the country. Those we are not sure of we could give orders to leave.'

Calhoun Terry drummed with his fingertips on the top rail of the fence. 'There must be several thousand settlers in this district where we operate,' he mentioned, 'the big majority of them on the side of the little fellow. How big an army are you thinking of bringing in?'

'Maybe a hundred men. We would have to keep our plans absolutely secret. My idea is to drop off the train at Jim Creek, where we would arrange to have horses to meet us, then come up through Box Cañon.'

'If we were seen—and eventually somebody would be bound to meet us—word would be rushed to Round Top and to every nester within seventy-five miles. They would be down on us like swarms of bees.'

'I would hold prisoner every traveler we met, no matter who he might be, until we had done the job. The friends of the rustlers would not know until too late. By that time the fear of our vengeance would be in all their hearts. They would accept the situation as a fact accomplished.'

'We couldn't ask our own riders to go with us. They would be marked men the rest of their lives. Besides, they would not join us to destroy men with whom they have ridden the range and gone to dances. Fact is, as you know, though we no longer employ riders who have stock of their own, a good many of our boys are related to the small ranchers or are friends of some of them.'

'We would leave them out of it. My idea is to bring in men who have been United States deputy marshals in Texas and Oklahoma. They are tough fighting men, crack shots, and used to running down outlaws.' Ellison flung out an impatient gesture of protest. 'I don't like this any better than you do, Cal. But it's neck meat or nothing. Things have come to such a pass that we have to make our own law. It's forced on us, unless we want to move out and let the thieves control the country.'

Without knowing it, Terry played 'After the Ball' with his fingertips on the top fence rail. He noticed that his cowpony Blaze was walking a little lame as it moved around the corral. Better have it turned into the big pasture for a few days to rest. Which reminded him that he had seen a bunch of Diamond Reverse B horses on Bailey Flats yesterday. Good idea to have them rounded up and brought in for inspection. His surface mind considered these details of ranch business, just as it had flung out to Ellison difficulties in the way of executing his plan. Beneath, his deeper thoughts brooded over the proposal itself.

Unless conditions could be changed the big ranches faced disaster. They were too easy prey for the light-fingered gentry who surrounded them. He could name a dozen settlers whose calf crops were amazingly fertile. They were building up herds by theft. There was no legal way to touch them as long as they elected the county officers. Ellison was right. The honest cattlemen had to fight or quit, and there was no way to fight except outside the law.

For more than a year now the big ranches had employed stock detectives to check up on the rustlers. Some of these were local men. Others had come in as cowboys and settlers. Their reports implicated many scores of nesters, drifters, and men on the dodge.

Owing to their immunity from punishment, the rustlers had grown very bold. Threats would not stop their depredations. But if a number of them were caught and hanged it would throw a fear into the thieves that would have an effect. Terry did not dodge the logical consequences of such an invasion. The plan proposed by the manager of the No, By Joe meant war, a private extra-legal war of the stock association against the rustlers, and not only against them. The nesters and the small cattlemen would throw in with the thieves, not because they liked them but as a choice of evils.

They felt that the big outfits were their chief enemy. A great many men would lose their lives, and he was not sure a clean-up would solve the range troubles. He doubted whether the large cattle companies with absentee ownership were any longer economically feasible. But his thoughts about this were not clear, and he did not care to discuss them yet with Ellison.

He shook his head slowly. 'I don't believe it can be done, Clint. You can't keep a secret with that many men in on it. Before we had traveled forty miles there would be hell to pay. Besides, we're not ready yet for anything as drastic as that. We may win the elections this fall. At any rate, we ought to wait and see. We must do everything in the world to protect ourselves legally before we start a civil war.'

Ellison brushed this aside impatiently, the frozen eyes in his gray, powder-marked face fixed on the manager of the Diamond Reverse B.

'We've tried everything we know already, and they are robbing us blind. Not a chance for us to win the election. You know that. Why fool yourself?'

'I don't think we'll win,' Terry agreed. 'But we'll have made our fight. After that, my suggestion is, the first time we catch a rustler red-handed we go to court with it. When we don't convict him, I'd get the story in Cheyenne, Denver, and Salt Lake papers, with a review of the whole controversy. I think then that public sentiment in the West would back us in fighting back the only way we can.'

'It's ready to back us now if we have the nerve to act,' Ellison said bluntly. 'If we wait we'll be just that much poorer and weaker, and the thieves will be stronger. I say strike now—and strike hard.'

'Not the way you propose,' Terry differed. 'We don't want the Governor calling out the militia against us, or government troops being sent in to stop us.'

'No chance of either. The Governor is a cattleman himself. We have a big pull with the Administration. We'll be looked after. Don't worry about that. I've talked with John McFaddin. He's with me. So are the Antelope Creek and the Two Star ranches. All the decent cowmen will throw in with us.'

'Not many of the little fellows,' Terry disagreed. 'Lane Carey won't, for one.'

'Why won't he? The rustlers have gone after his stock the same as they have after ours.'

'Not as much. Some of the thieves won't touch a poor man's stuff.'

'You've got them wrong, Cal. A lot of the small cattlemen are afraid to say anything now because the thieves are in the saddle, but they will be with us when they find out we're going to stand up on our hind legs and fight. They don't like this condition any better than we do.'

'Maybe not, but they would oppose us if we tried armed insurrection. The time isn't ripe yet, Clint. Let's give the rustlers a little more rope to hang themselves with.'

'No,' Ellison said grimly, bringing his closed fist down on the top fence rail. 'Let's hang them now, while we still have a chance to win.'

'It would be a mistake,' Terry insisted.

Ellison smiled thinly, his cold eyes on the other. 'Don't think I'm blaming you for holding back, Cal. Probably in your place I'd do the same. Some of these rustlers who ranch on the side used to be your friends. You hate to move against them. If you feel that way, go on a little visit to Chicago while we're pulling off our little invasion.'

Terry looked at the No, By Joe manager dourly. 'I represent the Diamond Reverse B. I'm not throwing down on it. If men who used to be my friends have turned rustler—and I don't believe they have, with maybe one or two exceptions—it is too bad for them. I won't lift a hand to help them. Point is, the plan you suggest can't succeed. Your warriors would kill some decent man and rouse the whole country against us.'

'I say it can and will succeed,' Ellison retorted. 'There's nothing else we can do.'

Terry knew his mind was made up. He meant to sweep away opposition and carry on as he had planned.

X

Calhoun Terry went to the meeting of the Western Cattlemen's Association at Denver knowing that after the convention adjourned a decision would be reached as to the best way of dealing with the rustlers operating in his territory. There would be much talk about the cattle thieves in open meeting, but it would be a small group in secret session who would determine how to protect the ranches against the outlaws.

The manager of the Bartlett Land & Cattle Company met Terry as he and two other stockmen were going into Tortoni's Restaurant at noon. Ellison drew him aside for a private word.

'Tonight at the Windsor—eight o'clock—room 424,' he whispered.

When Terry knocked at the door of the hotel room he found ten or eleven men present, all of them representatives of big ranches. Most of them the Diamond Reverse B foreman knew. He was introduced to the others.

'You know why we are here, gentlemen,' Ellison began. 'It is very important that what we say should be and should remain secret. I have taken the rooms on each side of this one, so that nobody can overhear what is said.' He pointed to the connecting doors, which were wide open.

'One of my men is in the corridor to prevent eavesdropping. I suggest, however, that all of us talk in low tones. . . . We'll hear from Doctor Porter first.'

Doctor Porter had been an army surgeon during the Civil War, and later had moved West and gone into the cattle business. A slim, well-dressed man, with black hair and iron-gray goatee, his keen dark eyes swept the room before he said a word. Several of the cattlemen had taken off their coats, for the night was warm. The blue smoke of their cigars filled the room and drifted out of the open window. On a dresser were glasses, ice water, and two bottles of whiskey.

Briefly Doctor Porter outlined the situation. The honest stockman had to go out of business or fight, he said. No redress was possible in the courts. He had to rely on himself. All those present knew what was planned. A list of more than a hundred names of rustlers had been submitted by their field detectives and by individual ranchmen. He proposed that before the meeting adjourned this list be gone over name by name and voted on by such of the men here as knew the rustlers.

'All this has been talked over with each of you individually,' Porter explained. 'But it has seemed best to decide this in a larger group. That's why we have met. At the present time Sunday Brown, whom some of you know, a famous deputy United States marshal from the Indian Territory, is busy enlisting about sixty fighting men in Texas and Arizona. He is choosing tried men, all of them officers who have fought as marshals or sheriffs against desperadoes. In the course of two or three weeks Brown and his men will reach this city. From here they will be sent by special train to the scene of action. In addition to these, there will probably be fifty cattlemen and their friends in our party. Our intention is to move fast and secretly, so that nobody will know what we are about until too late to stop us. We expect to meet no organized opposition. The rustlers whom we trap will fight if they get a chance, but that is to be anticipated. If everything goes well we ought to be able to sweep through the country, wipe out scores of rustlers, and get back to the railroad with our identities unknown.'

A big wide-hatted stockman named Kinnear took the floor. He was an oldtimer, of large experience, a Texan who had driven his own herd north and settled in the territory.

'Fine,' he said, 'if everything goes right.' His gaze swept the room leisurely. 'But hell, boys, chances are you can't pull it off. Don't get me wrong. I'm with you till the cows come home. Still, a hundred armed men on horseback can't go galumphing through the country without plenty of people getting wise to it. I don't say we can't make our clean-up, but make up yore minds to this: You're going to have to fight yore way out.'

Terry was of the same opinion. 'We'll meet a dozen men not on our list. What do you aim to do with them? If we let them go they'll stir up the country. If we keep them prisoner they will know every last one of us.'

There were a lot of questions, suggestions, explanations. Most of the cattlemen present were inclined to brush aside the difficulties of the undertaking. Somebody wanted to know what the authorities would do about such an invasion.

'Nothing at all,' Ellison answered. 'The Governor will give orders to all the local militia company commanders not to assist the county civil officers unless a call to that effect goes out from headquarters. Our representatives at Washington are pledged to see that the President gets the right angle on this and does not send government troops.'

'If we're bringing up a bunch of gunmen from Texas it is going to cost a lot of money,' Gaines of the Two Star Ranch said. 'How is this to be financed? Are we all to be assessed in proportion to the number of cattle we run?'

This was discussed at length and a method of raising the money decided upon.

Two or three of those present objected to bringing outside gunmen in to deal with the rustlers. Terry was one of these. His judgment was that once they started killing they would not be careful enough in differentiating between outlaws and honest citizens. He did not see how it was possible they could be, since they did not know personally any of the men with whom they had to deal. It was explained that some of the stockmen would be with them all the time. Terry was still opposed to the plan, and said so bluntly.

The names of those on the list to be rubbed out were taken up for consideration. All the men at the meeting felt the tenseness when Ellison rose with a paper in his hand. They were about to condemn scores of men to death.

Ellison read the first name. It was that of a notorious bad man known as Black Yeager. Nobody had anything to say in his favor. His name went on the black list. The second one read was unknown to Terry.

'He's only a kid,' John McFaddin said. 'After we string up a few he'll light outa the country *pronto*. I say, let him go.'

It was voted not to include him.

'Jeff Brand.' The No, By Joe manager waited for comment.

'A bad man from Texas,' explained Tod Collins of the Antelope Creek Ranch. 'One of the worst of the Hart gang.'

Others corroborated this. Brand went on the death list.

'Roan Alford.'

'No'—Terry spoke with sharp decision. He's a rancher, not a rustler. I've known him all my life.'

'Two of our detectives have turned his name in,' mentioned Gaines of the Two Star outfit.

'He doesn't come in the group we want to get,' Terry insisted. 'Roan has two daughters about sixteen and seventeen and a son of ten. His wife is always ready to nurse anybody in the neighborhood who is sick.'

'Question is whether he is a calf thief,' Ellison said dryly.

Calhoun Terry took issue with him. 'Maybe he branded a calf sometime without being too sure it was his. But he is no rustler by profession. I would call Roan a pretty honest man.'

'Friend of yore father, wasn't he?' suggested the No, By Joe superintendent, his smile suggestive.

'Yes. He'll tell you he's no friend of mine. That's not the point. We want to rub out the rustlers who are making a business of robbing us, not those who have just slipped over the edge sometime.'

'Give Alford the benefit of the doubt,' McFaddin voted. 'He used to work for me. A top roper, and a pretty good scout. He's too thick with the Harts to suit me, but maybe he'll learn his lesson.'

'That satisfactory, gentlemen?' Ellison asked. 'I'll scratch Roan off the list if there are no objections.'

A score or more of names were read and discussed. Some were put on the black list, and others pardoned because of insufficient evidence or extenuating circumstances.

'Lee Hart.'

'We all know where he belongs,' a redheaded cowman replied. 'Put him on the list to be hanged and pass on to the next.'

No voice was raised in his behalf. The next name was read.

'Sheriff Nate Hart.'

Terry broke the long silence that followed. 'It's known that the Harts are enemies of mine. I don't get along with Nate any better than I do with the rest of them. But that doesn't make him a rustler. Folks in the Buck River country do not consider him one.'

A dark brown man sitting on the bed in his shirtsleeves let the match with which he had intended to light a cigar die out. 'Not a rustler himself, but a politician who uses cow thieves for his advantage. He's worse than they are. I say, rub him out.'

McFaddin ripped out an oath. 'He and two of the county commissioners are the leaders of the whole mess of thieves. They organized the opposition to us—got the nesters and the scalawags to throw in together against us to elect officers who won't give us justice. If we're going to let them go we might as well not start.'

'The way I look at it too,' somebody else said.

The cool gaze of Terry swept the room slowly.

'Gentlemen, you are proposing to take in too much territory. Maybe we can round up most of the known thieves and get away with hanging them. I think we will be lucky if we do. But we can't kill the duly elected sheriff and commissioners of a county and expect not to pay too high a price for it. Right then we would lose the support of the public all over the country. If we are going to do a crazy thing like that we might as well be thorough and hang Judge Curtis too. He's as much a political leader of our enemies as the other three.'

'The scoundrel ought to be hanged!' McFaddin cried angrily.

'Not quite so loud,' Ellison urged. 'Whatever we do, gentlemen, has to be kept a close secret. If word of our intentions reaches the thieves we are defeated before we move a foot.'

Doctor Porter gave his support to Terry. 'I think Cal is right. When we invade the Buck River country we are going to raise a rookus that will get headlines in every city paper in the States. Don't make any mistake about that. Reporters from New York and San Francisco and Chicago will hotfoot for the scene. After we get started there won't be any secret about what we are doing, and if we wipe out officers legally elected—even with the help of thieves' votes— we are going to make a fatal mistake. These fellows may be as much enemies of law and order as the man who puts his brand on my stock, but we can't afford to lay a finger on them.'

'Nate Hart is a pain just the same, one of these slick talkers who stir folks up to make trouble,' Gaines complained. 'He has his county organized so as to hold political control.'

A smile creased the plump face of Tod Collins. 'He has it sewed up tight, sure enough. No range thief can be convicted. It's a case of the vote being mightier than the pen. Judge Curtis tried a fellow called Roberts last week. We had found three of our calves in his barn. Fellow who used to work for the Antelope Creek outfit, one I had kicked out because we suspected him of playing in with the thieves, testified that we trained our calves to break into folks' barns to get the grain in them. I'm damned if the jury didn't acquit Roberts.'

This brought a shout of laughter that released the tension a little.

'I hadn't finished making my point,' Gaines continued. 'Though I think Nate Hart more dangerous than his brother Lee, I'm in favor of striking him off the black list. We don't want to play with any more dynamite than is necessary.'

'His name goes off,' Ellison answered. 'The understanding is that our vote must be practically unanimous.'

The roll call went on. Morgan—Dennison—Tolman condemned. Vallery reprieved. Bill

Herriott given a Scotch verdict of not proven, at the urgent insistence of Terry. The two lads had ridden their first roundup together, and Calhoun could not believe that he was beyond reclaim.

Ellison read the next name a little reluctantly. It had been handed in by one of the stockmen present. Jack Turley, the name was.

The No, By Joe superintendent ran a pencil through it. 'Known not to be a rustler,' he said.

'Who knows it?' Terry asked. 'He spends most of his time with Lee Hart and Jeff Brand. If he isn't a rustler, why does he run with thieves?'

'I'd like to know that too,' the redheaded man said.

Ellison hesitated. He was secretary of the territorial stock association and was on the inside of certain matters that could not be discussed publicly.

'I can give him a clean bill of health,' he said at last.

'How can you do that?' the redheaded man persisted. 'I probably know him better than you do, and whenever I see him he's hanging around with some of the Hart gang.'

'All right'—Ellison threw up a hand in surrender. 'He's a detective for the association. We sent him into the Buck River country two years ago to get information about the thieves' activities. I don't need to tell you, gentlemen, that if anybody here talks, if a hint of this reaches the miscreants

95

with whom he trains, his life wouldn't be worth a plugged dime.'

Those present pledged themselves to secrecy.

After the list of suspects had been disposed of there was some discussion as to what the attitude of certain influential citizens, in no way connected with the rustlers, would be toward the invasion of the Texans and the clean-up.

'Garvey and the *Gazette* will be against us,' Collins said. 'Unless Cal can influence him to be neutral. How about that, Cal?'

'Not a chance,' Terry replied. 'Horace Garvey will do what he thinks is right, and it is his opinion that the small settlers have a prior claim to the country over the big ranches.' He added, to forestall the indignant protest he saw on the lips of several: 'Not a priority in time but in equity. Horace thinks the homesteader and the small cattleman have a title to the range far superior to ours. I don't agree with him, of course. This is a cow country, and the plow is going to ruin it. But plenty of people don't see that.'

Somebody mentioned Lane Carey. Ellison summed up his position in a sentence.

'A small cattleman, absolutely honest, no friend of rustlers and no friend of ours.'

The meeting broke up late. Before anybody had left the room the man on watch outside came in with a telegram just arrived for Doctor Porter. The ex-army man ripped open the envelope and read. He considered the message a moment before speaking. His voice lifted above the noise of talk that had been suddenly released among the groups into which the meeting had separated.

'Just a moment, if you please,' he said. 'I have a message with important news sent me by my secretary.'

The hum of conversation died down. All eyes turned upon the slender Civil War veteran who faced them, eyes flashing with excitement, waiting for silence to convey his news.

'Jackman wires me that yesterday a meeting of small cattlemen, including rustlers, no doubt, was held at Round Top to form an independent ranchers' and stock-growers' association. They voted to hold their roundup about the middle of May, three weeks before the legal one set by us. Other branches of this association are to do the same.'

A stunned silence followed this announcement, succeeded by a babel of voices. Every man present knew what this meant. By means of these roundups the enemies of the big ranches would collect and brand the mavericks before the wagons and men of the large outfits could get into action. All calves not following their mothers closely would be assigned to the small cowmen and to the rustlers who had started herds of their own. To let this pass without effective protest would be ruinous.

Doctor Porter waved his telegram for a cessation of talk.

'There's another piece of news in my wire, gentlemen. Jackman says that early this morning the body of Pete Tolman was found in front of his cabin. He had been shot through the forehead by a bullet from a rifle.'

Again the lift of excited voices. Snatches of words broke above the rest: '. . . saves us the trouble . . . had it coming to him . . . bound to be war after this . . . wonder who could have done it.'

Calhoun Terry said nothing. His mind was full of doubt. One killing, or even two, might be due to private quarrels among the rustlers. But when it came to three, all of them assassinations from ambush, it began to press home on him that there was a system behind these murders. All the victims were notorious cattle thieves. The most likely explanation was that a hired killer had shot them. If so, he was probably employed by some of the ranches whose stock was being lifted.

XI

At the Sleepy Cat Ranch dance very little was talked of except the murder of Pete Tolman and its relation to the other two killings which had preceded it. All over the Buck River country there was great excitement and anger. If there had been any doubt as to who had shot Hart and Tetlow, the death of Tolman resolved it to the satisfaction of most of the settlers. It was not known whose finger had pulled the trigger, but few had any doubt that the crimes had been done by a paid gunman of some of the big ranches. The victims had all been active and flagrant rustlers. Nobody but the large cattle outfits had any interest in destroying them. These had a double motive to rub them out: to prevent future raids by the men themselves, and to throw the fear of death into their associates.

That fear, though generally concealed, was plainly in evidence at the dance. Ellen read it in the nervousness of those she met, in the lowered voices and furtive whisperings. It lay back of the hot anger which cried out against the crimes. There were a score of rustlers present. Some of them were with wives and others with sweethearts. None knew where the bolt would strike next.

Jeff Brand asked Ellen for a dance. She rose at once and took her place with him in the quadrille. Lane Carey had brought her to the dance, and she remembered the little passage at arms she and Jeff had had when he asked her to go with him.

Her eyes danced with mocking laughter. 'You promised to help entertain my beau, and I haven't seen you say a word to him yet.'

He laughed. Whoever else might be worried,

Jeff Brand was not. She had never seen him more gay and carefree. That he thrived on danger was an easy guess. Two out of the three killed had been close associates of his. It might very likely be his turn next. He was not alarmed for himself, any more than he was mourning for them.

'You chose the wrong beau, honey. I don't reckon I'd better entertain him the way I figured I would.'

He was a graceful scamp, and he danced as no other man in the room did. There would be a waltz later, and she was sure he would ask her for it. Though she did not intend to give him any more squares, she did want to join him in a light-footed twosome when the waltz was played.

The caller sang out the directions.

Lady down the middle, an' the gent solo;
Swing her when you meet, as of course you
    know.
Grapevine twist on an emigrant car,
Lady back to gent—and there you are.

Bill Herriott was the caller. He stood on a bench, unconsciously picturesque after the manner of his kind. In deference to the ladies, he had hung his pinched felt hat on the horns of an elk's head attached to the wall. But he still wore the chaps, the flannel shirt, the high-heeled spurred boots which were part of his usual equipment. His legs were bowed from much living in the saddle, and hands and face were coffee-brown from the wind and untempered sun of the high plains.

Brand returned to Ellen after an 'alemane left' which had taken him round the circle.

'I'm asking you for the first waltz now,' he mentioned. 'The two best dancers in the room ought to give a little exhibition, don't you think?'

She nodded. 'Even if we elected ourselves the two best. It's nice of you to count me in, though of course any girl who dances with you can't help being the best at the moment.'

The light shallow eyes in the bronzed face smiled at her. 'I'm good, and so are you. We both know it.'

Her gaze held to his, interested and a little puzzled. She was not thinking about what he had said. 'Everybody else is worried and unhappy about what happened today. You seem to be on the top of the world. Wasn't Pete Tolman a friend of yours?'

'We rode a lot of trails together,' he said.

'Well?'

'I ought to be pulling a long face, you think. My idea is different. Pete did a lot of living in his twenty-four years. Maybe he wandered off the reservation considerable. He made his own laws, and he had a lot of fun doing it. I've heard him say he didn't want to live to be an old man with creaky joints, that he'd rather go out high, wide, and handsome. I'm gonna miss him. But when I think of him it will be as I saw him last, waving a hand at me as he went over the top of a hill at a gallop.'

Ellen said, 'I understand now.' She added gently, 'Pete would not want you to act solemn.'

'Not Pete. If I'm ever blue about him, it won't be when I'm with other folks.' His brown jaw tightened. 'Don't think I'm forgetting how he was killed.'

She still was not quite satisfied to drop the subject. 'You know what is worrying everybody.'

'I reckon I do,' he answered, not at all disturbed.

'That we haven't seen the last of this. A killer is loose in the land. It's a dreadful thing, isn't it?'

'Say it plain.' His face creased to a smile. 'They figure I'll be next.'

Gravely she replied: 'Of course you think it won't be. I expect Pete Tolman thought that too.'

He glanced around the room. When he spoke, there was mockery in his sardonic face. 'I reckon some of the boys would like to know for sure the next would be me. They don't feel any too safe their own selves. I'll bet they don't do any more riding than is necessary, and they will stick to the brush and the ridges when they can.'

'Why don't you leave this part of the country—start tonight for Montana?' she asked impulsively.

His cool eyes rested on her. Again a smile

parted his lips and showed white flashing teeth against the brown of his face. 'Why, I like this country, and my girl lives here,' he drawled.

She felt excitement quickening in her at his reckless audacity. He would not sneak away. He would stay and face whatever was in store for him.

They had strolled to one of the benches placed along the side of the room. She was seated, and he was looking down at her.

'I didn't know you had a girl,' she mentioned, her voice light.

'Oh, yes. She doesn't know it yet. I think she's just beginning to find it out.'

'How interesting for her! She'll be dreadfully unhappy until she is sure of you.'

'I wish I was certain of that,' he drawled.

'Let me know when I'm to congratulate you, Mr. Brand.'

'Yes,' he promised. 'You'll know.'

Herriott clapped his hands. 'Partners for a quadrille.' It was perhaps just as well for his peace of mind that he did not know twelve men in the room of a Denver hotel were at that moment voting whether he should live or die.

A red-faced, perspiring young man came up to claim Ellen for the dance. During the changes of the dance she caught sight of Jeff Brand several times. There was always, she observed, gaiety and animation in the group around him.

Most of the dances were squares, since many present could not waltz. It must have been nearly an hour later when Ellen found herself in Brand's arms in a round dance. There were only two other couples on the floor, and one at least of these was making hard going of the steps. Most of those present watched Miss Carey and her partner. His lithe figure was a picture of grace, and she followed his lead light as a feather. When the music stopped he led her out to the porch to get a breath of air.

'I enjoyed that dance,' she said.

'Two of us did, then,' he replied.

They moved to the end of the porch beneath the shadow of a morning-glory vine. It was a glorious night of moonlight, a myriad of stars in the sky. For a time both were content with silence.

Ellen spoke at last, harking back to the subject discussed earlier in the evening. 'If you won't go away, you will be careful, won't you?'

'I never threw down on myself yet,' he told her carelessly.

The audacity of her next question surprised and delighted him. 'You *are* a rustler, I suppose?'

'My goodness, you go right to the point. Nobody ever asked me that before. You're supposed to say that with a smile or with a gun in yore hand.'

'I'll withdraw the question, since it's none of my business. But I should think that girl you were telling me about would want to be very sure you weren't.'

'Maybe she would rather have a man who just plowed and dug,' he said scornfully.

She might. 'There is another name for rustling.'

'I've heard it. The big cattlemen like to use it when they speak of their small neighbors, but I don't expect they like the word applied when they fence land that doesn't belong to them or homestead public domain by using their own riders as dummy entrymen.'

'Two wrongs don't make a right,' Ellen reminded him.

'Or when they hire killers to shoot down men never convicted of any crime,' he added. 'Nothing wrong about that, since they are big fellows.'

The reckless gaiety had been washed from his face and left it grim and bitter.

'I can't understand men like that!' she cried. 'I've met some of them. They seemed very nice and pleasant.'

'As long as they have their own way and everybody steps aside for them,' he added.

'What's the matter with them? Don't they think straight? Or are they just heartless?'

'They have been running the show so long in this territory that they hate to see their power vanish. Naturally they think the little fellow's rights don't count.'

'The big ranches claim they can't keep going

unless the stealing of stock is stopped. There *is* a lot of rustling, isn't there?'

'Yes.' He added cynically: 'Why make any bones about it? You have danced with two–three tonight of the suspected gents.'

'So that the Diamond Reverse B and the other big outfits really are fighting for their lives, in a way of speaking.'

'They are fighting for dividends to pay to absentee owners, most of them. Who ought to own this country—rich men in Edinburgh and New York, or settlers right here on the ground?'

'Isn't there any way to stop this terrible condition?' Ellen asked.

He looked at her, eyes hard and bleak. 'We have guns too. I reckon this war won't be all one-sided. We'll find out who this guy is with the Winchester. One thing is sure. He's mighty familiar with the habits of the men he killed. How did he know where Pete would be staying last night?'

'You think—'

'I'll do my thinking in private for a while. If the guy is too slick for us one of his bosses will make a good substitute.'

'But you don't know who hired him.'

'We can guess, the way they guessed about who did the rustling.'

'At any rate we know that Calhoun Terry didn't do this, since he is in Denver at the convention.'

'How do we know he is there?'

Ellen looked at him, startled. 'He took the train at Round Top.'

'Maybe he got off at a station thirty miles away and came back. It might have been a blind.'

'No,' she said instantly. 'I don't believe it. You don't either.'

He took his time to answer, frowning out at the night. From inside the house came the shuffle of feet and the sawing of the fiddles.

'No, I don't reckon he did. Terry has hell in the neck, but what shooting he does will be done in the open. Just the same he belongs to the group that is paying for this drygulching.'

A leather-faced man with a broken nose peered out of the doorway and looked around. Ellen moved quickly back of Brand.

'Don't let him see me,' she whispered.

Turley went back into the house.

'Why don't you want him to see you?' Brand asked, amused.

'He has been asking me to dance with him, and I'm not going to do it.'

'You don't like him?'

'No, I don't. Is he one of your friends?'

'He isn't anybody's friend, not even his own. Turley is one of those fellows who have a grouch at the world. I'll save you from him and dance the next with you myself.'

'Very generous of you, but I won't let you sacrifice yourself. . . . Time we went back.'

At midnight coffee, sandwiches, and cake were served. Two or three hours later the older settlers gathered their sleeping babies from the bedroom where rows of infants lay and departed in wagons, buggies, and buckboards. The younger guests did not leave until day was sifting into the sky.

Ellen and her father left while the dance was still in full swing.

'Have a good time, honey?' he asked after they had started.

'Yes, I did. Everybody was troubled at first, but they seemed to wake up and enjoy themselves.' She yawned and snuggled down into a more comfortable position on the seat.

'I noticed that Jeff Brand did,' Lane said dryly.

'Did I dance with him a good deal?' Ellen asked demurely, coming at once to the point she knew was about to be raised.

'Didn't you?'

'Maybe I did. He was the best dancer there. Besides which, he is interesting.'

'But not safe.'

She laughed. 'No, I wouldn't call him safe. By the way, he made some kind of proposal to me. Well, not exactly that, but a promise to be kind to me later. I think I'm to be his girl, whatever that means.'

'He's an impudent scoundrel,' her father growled.

'Isn't he? I'm not sure his intentions are honorable. You'd better ask him about that, Mr. Carey.'

Her gaiety reassured Lane. 'Just remember that he is bad medicine for any girl. The less you have to do with him the better.'

'If I let all my prospects get away I'll be an old maid,' she said.

Her father grunted. His opinion was that there was no chance of that.

XII

As soon as Ellen's head touched the pillow she slept, and did not wake until the sun was high. She came drowsily to life, lying on her back in that pleasant state of relaxation which is reluctant to recognize urgent duties. There was a little smile on her lips. She was thinking of Jeff Brand, the picture of him very clear in her mind, a graceful, virile scamp who could walk unafraid into desperate peril. Snapshots of him jumped before her when she dropped her lids to keep out the untempered light. He was crossing the dance floor, jauntily sure of himself, the well-packed muscles rippling beneath the skin as he moved . . . Or he was flirting with her, little gay devils of mischief bubbling in his light eyes . . . Or his ivory teeth were flashing in that impudent grin so provocative of either pleasure or resentment.

She was finding it difficult to draw sharp lines between good and bad. Jeff Brand was an example. Her interest in him was growing, and with it a reluctance to condemn him utterly. No doubt he was a thief, but she guessed he stole not for profit so much as for the thrill of it. If rumor was true, he had killed men in Texas and found it wise to leave suddenly. Yet he was human, with unsuspected loyalties. He was making wreckage of his life. None the less the gay courage with which he did it was fascinating.

And there was Calhoun Terry. Most of those living near Black Butte would call him traitor because he had changed sides. But was that judgment final? Could one dispose of him so definitely? The deep blue, steel-barred eyes with which he looked at one so steadily were hard and cold but honest. If appearances counted for anything, he was the last man in the world to kill another furtively from the brush or to hire a substitute to do it. She did not doubt he could be overbearing, could ride ruthlessly over the rights of others. But by his own standards he would first find justification.

It was a puzzling mix-up. Right and wrong existed, of course, yet there was a borderland of conflict where the differences ran thin. Ellen brought the more impersonal aspect of the difficulty to her father. The time was after supper when he was reading one of Horace Garvey's editorials in the *Gazette*.

'Garvey takes a strong line about these assassinations,' he said. 'He sure enough hits out right from the shoulder. Just what he should do, too. Tells the big ranches they can't sow the wind without reaping the whirlwind.'

'Does he say the big ranches had these killings done?' Ellen asked.

'Not in so many words. But you can see who he is pointing a finger at.'

'You feel sure they did it?'

'Either they did, or else there's a crazy man loose on the range.'

Ellen was silent for a minute. A frown puckered her forehead. 'Isn't there any way to stop this dreadful bitterness? I mean, couldn't there be a compromise of some sort, the way there was in the sheep and cattle war over on the South Fork?'

Lane Carey shook his grizzled head. 'Not so easy as that, honey. Over on the South Fork it just happened there was a country sheep could graze that was no good for cattle. Different here. There's a direct conflict of interests. The big cattle outfits want a wide-open free range for their stock. They don't want the land plowed up or the country along the creeks fenced. They have grabbed what they can, one way and another, by using their riders as dummies for homestead and pre-emption rights. But that isn't enough if they are going to run herds as big as they have been doing. So there you are. If the little fellows fence and plow the land the big ranches can't have it for range. Cattle came here first. The large concerns feel the nesters and homesteaders are interlopers, and they have gone some farther than the law allows to let them know it.'

'You think the Diamond Reverse B and the No, By Joe, with the other big outfits, are to blame, then?'

'They made it mighty hard for the small fry to earn a living in these lean years when they quit employing men who had places and stock of their own. But there is another side to it. Rustlers have been very active, and I'm afraid a good many of the nesters have helped themselves to calves to build up their herds and to steers for food when they got hard up.'

Lane began to look around for his pipe, and Ellen brought it to him from the mantelpiece. She stood there while he packed and lit it.

'So everybody is wrong and nobody is right,' she said.

He drew on the pipe for a few moments to make sure it would not go out. 'I wouldn't say that. You might put it that there are conflicting rights hard to reconcile, and of course some people have kept out of this row. Plenty of them have branded only their own stock.'

'Lane Carey for one. I don't have to look far for an honest man.'

A deprecating smile broke the lines of Carey's tanned and leathery face. 'I haven't been in the same position as some of these poor devils. We've done pretty well. I haven't been pinched for my next meal and known that we had already scraped the bottom of the barrel. I haven't had to watch my children go hungry. So we won't brag about my honesty for a while yet.'

Ellen brushed tobacco from his coat. 'You don't see any hope of peace, then?'

'I wish I did,' he said at last. 'But all the talk is the other way. Fact is, war is already with us. These killings are a challenge, and the rustlers are going to strike back. You can be sure of that. I heard that fellow Jack Turley say at the dance he was going to carry a rifle with him when he rode after this. The men he was talking with seemed to agree.'

'I don't like the man,' Ellen cut in, deflected from the main thought. 'He has been hanging around me a little.'

'Not a pleasant fellow . . . This new ranchers' and stockmen's association the little men formed at Round Top the other day will certainly make trouble. The big ranches aren't going to let them round up range stock and brand whatever they please in a gather of their own.'

'What will they do?'

'I don't know. But you may be sure they will do something.' He added uncertainly, 'I've a good mind to send you back to Kansas City until things quiet down.'

'Oh, no, father!' she protested.

'No more riding about the country alone,' he told her sharply. 'The killer might make a mistake and think you were a man. You'll have to stay close to the house.'

'I won't enjoy that.'

'I reckon not, but I would be uneasy every minute you were away.'

'What about you? Are you going to stay out of the saddle too?'

'Any riding I do will be necessary. Of course nobody wants to get me. If I were shot at it would be because I was mistaken for some other man.'

'You would be just as dead if they hit you, wouldn't you?'

'If I go into the brush after stock it won't be alone. I'll have two–three other men with me.'

Ellen kissed her father good night, lit a lamp, and went upstairs to her room. It was some time before she could get to sleep. Into her mind trooped thoughts connected with ambushings and sudden death, and even after she slipped into sleep her dreams were wild and turbulent. She saw Jeff Brand and Calhoun Terry stalking each other in the sage. A gun would crash, but before her flying feet could take her to the scene the protagonists had changed. It was her father lying wounded, and Jack Turley was straddling his body rifle in hand.

Strangely enough, Ellen saw next day at Black Butte all the four men of whom she had dreamed. Terry came up on the stage, on his way back to the Diamond Reverse B from Denver. Brand and Turley dropped into the post-office shortly after the stage had arrived. The ranch foreman was eating dinner at the restaurant, but after he had finished he strolled across to the post-office to wait while the fresh horses were being hitched.

Brand was sitting on the porch, his back against a post. At sight of Terry his lids narrowed. Though he did not change his position, the hard glitter in his eyes suggested that he was every instant very much aware of the Diamond Reverse B man.

To Turley he said aloud, with a sneer, 'Look who's with us.'

Terry's first glance had identified them both, but he crossed the porch and went into the post-office as if he were not aware of their existence.

He asked for his mail. Ellen made a pretense of looking, though both of them knew this was not the office to which his letters came.

She came back to the window. 'No mail for you, Mr. Terry . . . May I see you a minute . . . alone?'

He was surprised at her request, but scarcely more than she was. For it had been born of a sudden urgent impulse.

'Of course,' he replied. 'Here?'

Her father came into the building.

'At the house—if you don't mind.' To Lane Carey she said: 'Will you take care of the mail a little while, please?'

Carey glanced at her, at Terry, and back at his daughter. 'Why, yes,' he agreed. He did not know what was back of this, and he did not quite like it.

The two young people walked out of the room together. Ellen spoke to Brand, including Turley in a general bow to a couple of others present. She could see that Jeff was astonished at what she was doing, and she knew as they walked to the house, even though her back was toward him, that his gaze was fastened on them. The Diamond Reverse B manager, she observed, had walked through the group as though oblivious of their presence.

Ellen did not take Terry into the house. She stopped with him in front of the porch, coming swiftly to what was in her mind.

'Isn't there any way, Mr. Terry, of stopping all this killing that is being done?' she asked. 'Does it have to go on, building up hate, making this country an awful place to live in?'

A little breath of wind had modeled the girl's dress against her slender limbs. Calhoun Terry got an impression of vivid youth. The small, high, pointed breasts, the faint flush in the clear-cut, delicate face, suggested immaturity as much as

116

did the parted lips and shining eyes. If he was moved by her indignant appeal his immobile face gave no evidence of it.

'I think the trouble will go on, in one way or another, until stealing cattle is stopped,' he said.

'You favor murder?' she cried.

'Did I say so?' he countered.

'You said—' She cut off her own sentence. 'It doesn't matter what you said. Your friends are hiring murder done. Can you deny it?'

Terry had not at first believed this. Hard though he was, assassination from ambush was too cold-blooded for him. It was not consistent with the hot rage that could boil up against the barrier of his disciplined restraint. But doubts of his associates had seeped into his thinking until they had become almost a conviction. These murders looked like a hired killer's work. If so, the fellow was employed by some of the big ranches.

The Diamond Reverse B manager replied to her question with another. 'Can you prove it?'

'Of course I can't.' Stormy-eyed, she pressed the attack. 'But you know it's true. I don't know what part you have in it, but your friends are trying to stop theft by murder.'

'I don't know any more about it than you do,' he answered, anger and obstinacy in his steel-blue eyes. 'If you want this trouble stopped, go to your father and his friends. Get them to persuade the rustlers to move out. What do you expect? Do you think we'll let these scoundrels steal wholesale from us and laugh in our faces when we take them to court? If you do, your ideas are different from mine. We are going to protect our property.'

'By killing men from ambush?'

'No.' A dull flush of rage beat into his face beneath the tan. 'By hanging known thieves by the neck to trees when we have enough evidence. Is there anything else you would like to know, Miss Carey?'

She stood, very erect and proud. 'No, Mr. Terry. I know all I want to know—about you.' Turning, she walked into the house.

Calhoun Terry walked back toward the stage. It was in front of the post-office. The horses were being brought out to hitch. He saw Jeff Brand move forward to meet him. There was a light, rhythmic ease in the way the man walked. Most of his life he had spent in the saddle, but he had none of the bowlegged roll common to cowboys.

Though Terry's hand did not shift a fraction of an inch toward his hip, he was aware without looking exactly where the butt of his revolver could be found.

Brand stopped squarely in front of him. 'Like a word with you, Mr. Terry,' he said, drawling the words so that they seemed almost to drip from his nearly motionless lips.

Terry said nothing. He waited, his chill gaze meeting that of the other man steadily. There is sometimes a force in silence more potent than any speech. When it goes with strength a patient stillness is disconcerting to a jittery man who sputters talk.

But Jeff Brand had no jumpy nerves. Also, he had come to talk and not to listen. When he spoke his voice was cool and even, but there was a bite to it.

'You and yore crowd have been cutting a lot of mustard. Rubbing out our friends without giving them a chance for their white alley. Not like rattlesnakes. They give warning. I always did claim there was vermin lower than a sidewinder. Now I've found them.' Brand followed this with a string of scabrous epithets, not once raising his voice or showing the slightest heat.

'Are you quite through?' the ranch manager asked coldly.

'Not yet. I'm mentioning now that we'll take a hand in this game. Two can play it as well as one. From now on there's an open season on Diamond Reverse B men and on those of the other big outfits. We'll be trying for the bosses, but when we don't find them handy a plain lunkhead waddy will do. The brake's done bust. We're off, and hell and high water can't stop us.'

'I wouldn't talk that way if I were you, Brand,' Terry advised quietly.

'I'm talking. You're listening. This is a message to you and to all the other damned rascals you're sleeping in a bed with. I'm making war talk. Understand?'

Calhoun Terry understood perfectly. The rustler was offering him a chance to draw if he wished. For a flash of time no longer than two heart-beats the cattleman felt a roar of blood in his veins. But he crowded down imperatively the impulse to take up the challenge. If he killed Brand, even when goaded to it, another black mark would be drawn against the cattlemen in the ledger of public opinion. The account that went out would be distorted. Moreover, Terry understood the bitter rage burning in the heart of the man. His friends had been destroyed by an assassin. There was justification for his anger.

Terry shook his head. 'No dice, Brand. I don't know who killed these men, and I'm not going to make myself responsible for it. I won't let you hang it on me by forcing it as an issue. You can't put me in the wrong that way.'

The cowboy jeered at him. 'What do you wear that gun beside you for, Terry? Or don't you draw it unless a man has his back to you?'

They were close to the porch. Terry knew the other two men could hear every word Brand had said. Again he felt that tumultuous boiling up of the blood, the recklessness ready to break out in him explosively.

Lane Carey came out on the porch, a big weather-beaten Westerner who had fought his way through the rough and tumble of frontier life.

'Don't be a fool, Jeff,' he said, no excitement in his even voice. 'Can't you see that Mr. Terry doesn't want to fight unless you goad him to a showdown?'

'I see he doesn't want to fight whether I goad him or not,' Brand answered, a bitter derision riding him.

Terry said coldly: 'I choose my own causes for a fight, and I won't be maneuvered into defending assassins. But I'm not overly patient when bullies try to run over me.'

'Jeff isn't a bully, Mr. Terry,' the postmaster explained placidly. 'He's some excited, and kinda went off half-cocked. We can't rightly blame him for that, after his friends have been drygulched. But since you're no party to these killings nothing he has said applies to you.'

Carey had walked down from the porch and stood almost between the two men. He was determined not to have any difficulty here.

'You make it quite clear, Mr. Carey, that he couldn't possibly have meant me,' Terry said, with a thin, ironic smile.

'That's right, isn't it, Jeff?' Carey persisted, his quiet urgency crowding the cowboy toward some withdrawal of his attack. 'Since Mr. Terry isn't the guilty party, you could not have meant him.'

Though not a wealthy man, Carey's character and personality gave him much influence in the community. It was important for the group to which Brand belonged not to drive him into the camp of the enemy.

Jeff grudgingly gave ground. 'What I said goes for the murderers, whoever they are.'

'I'll join you in condemning them,' Lane Carey agreed. 'But I reckon we'd better not jump to conclusions. As yet we don't know who this killer is.'

'We know who is backing him,' Brand said bluntly.

'No. That's guesswork too.' Carey turned to the stage-driver. 'Ready to take off, Hank?'

'Y'betcha.'

Terry followed the other passengers into the stage. Hank kicked the brake loose. The horses swung into the road and went down it in a cloud of dust.

Turley laughed unpleasantly. 'Mr. Terry certainly took meek the worst cussin' out I ever heard.'

Headed for the post-office, Carey stopped in his stride.

'Don't make a mistake about Calhoun Terry, boys. He's game as they come, and he'll be standing at the gate with a gun out whenever he figures that is the proper play. He was giving Jeff straight goods. If there had been a killing just now the story would have gone out that he was standing up for the drygulchers, maybe because he was one of them. Since he didn't want that, he didn't fight. Seeing that I have got started, I'll tell you something else. Unless Cal Terry has changed a lot from the young fellow I used to know, he isn't hiring anybody to rub out his enemies. If it's to be done, he'll do it himself in the open.'

'You're quite an orator, Lane,' sneered Turley. 'Ever think about going to Congress?'

Carey's heavy eyebrows met in a frown. 'I say what I think, Turley, and anybody can like or lump it as he pleases.'

With which he walked into the office.

XIII

For hours Calhoun Terry had been riding across territory ranged by stock of the Bartlett Land & Cattle Company. He had been following, as far as was possible, the wooded ridges above the valleys, but his quick eye had picked up a dozen times little bunches of cows bearing the J B brand.[x] His sorrel was not traveling fast. Since he wanted to reach the journey's end safely, the cattleman's roving eye searched every hill and hollow for any sign of motion or for any stationary object that might be a man lying in wait.

[x] **B**

From a high ledge he looked across the rolling uplands to the buildings of the No, By Joe ranch where Jesse Bartlett had built his first house before the Indians and the buffalo had been entirely cleared from the land. The blades of a windmill flashed him greeting. He could see little checkerboard squares of green, fields of alfalfa or grain watered by the irrigating ditches fed from a tributary of the Buck River.

Dropping down from the ledge, Terry wound his way across a sage flat to the rising country beyond. A coyote skulking through the brush brought his rifle up from its position across the saddle. He laughed at the start it had given him. 'You're liable to be a goosy man right soon, Cal,' he murmured, 'if you've got to spend most of your time dodging bullets from guys that aren't in the landscape.'

He rode down a lane between barbed-wire fences. On the right was a pasture of unbroken land, miles square; on the other side a field of lush alfalfa. From this lane he debouched into a wooded grove that brought him to the plaza formed by the buildings of the ranch.

Ellison was at home, and presently Terry found himself in a comfortable padded chair, his dusty boots sinking into an expensive Aubusson carpet. The luxury with which some of the big ranches were equipped always annoyed a little the Diamond Reverse B manager. His forthright view was that raising cattle was an outdoor man's job. He did not drink champagne at the Cheyenne Club himself, and there seemed to him a touch of flabbiness in those who did. There was nothing wrong about it, but it did not fit in with his conception of a cowman's attitude toward life.

His host got out a bottle and pushed it toward Calhoun, who waved it aside with a gesture almost impatient.

'I've brought a message for you from Jeff Brand,' he said.

'From Jeff Brand? What is that scoundrel sending me a message about?'

'He is serving notice that he and his friends are going to make reprisals for the rustlers who have been murdered.' Terry's gaze rested steadily on the No, By Joe manager. 'They are going after the bosses, but if they can't get them, riders for the big outfits will have to do.'

'The nerve of him!' Ellison cried. 'It shows what this country has come to when a known outlaw can send such an impudent message to honest men.'

'We didn't need that to show us,' Terry answered bluntly. 'To have three men shot down from ambush in two weeks is evidence enough.'

Ellison did not follow that lead. 'Where did you see Brand?' he asked. 'Or did he send you a message?'

'I saw him at Black Butte on my way back from

125

Denver. He tried to drive me into a fight with him right then.'

'Probably he had two–three others waiting for the signal to draw.'

'No. He's ready to fight at the drop of a hat. I wouldn't have it that way.'

The Bartlett outfit manager leaned back in his chair, drumming on the desk with his fingertips. The cold eyes in his gray powder-marked face watched the visitor closely. 'Why?' he asked. 'I've seen the time when you didn't have to be deviled into a fight.'

The Diamond Reverse B man told him why. 'Because his anger was justified, and I wasn't going to let him make me draw in defense of drygulchings that I think damnable.'

Over Ellison's eyes there seemed to drop a shutter, which left them hard and blank. They are asking for trouble,' he said. 'I reckon they will get it.'

'Yes, they will get trouble and so will we.' The eyes in the lean, sunburned face questioned Ellison. 'I expect we have asked for it too—considerable. I would like to know how much.' Terry stopped, still searching the other's gray countenance for an answer. 'When outfits throw in together to play the same hand, Clint, it ought to be played above-board for all of them to see.'

The other man said, after a moment's hesitation, 'Some things are better not talked about, Cal.'

Terry had his answer. He had found out what he had come to learn. 'You will have to count me out,' he told the No, By Joe manager, and rose to go.

'Wait!' Ellison got up and paced the floor, talking as he walked, stopping to stress his points. 'You're too soft, Cal. These men were thieves, robbing us wholesale. The law wouldn't touch them. When we took them to court they jeered at us. The rustlers are growing stronger. Weak lads are joining them, because it is an easy way to make money without working. Is there any other way, except to make examples of the worst of these scoundrels?'

'I thought we settled that in Denver, though not to my satisfaction or best judgment. I thought we were going to hang them openly, standing back of the job the way men ought to do. This shooting from ambush is assassination, whether we do it or the rustlers.'

'Not the way I look at it,' Ellison replied harshly. 'I would say they were executed.'

'Without a trial.'

'They had the same kind of trial we gave that list in Denver. Each one of them was a hardened thief, and two of them were known killers. . . . But I'll say this, since you're worried about it: There won't be any more of it. In two weeks—three at the most—we'll be ready for the big drive. Until then we'll rest.'

'Have you arranged it with the rustlers to rest too?' Terry asked bitterly. 'I don't think so. Before forty-eight hours we'll hear of one or two of our riders shot out of the saddle. When we do we'll know that we murdered them just as surely as if we had used our own bullets.'

'That's no way to talk, Cal,' his host reproved. 'You and I know there always has been a lot of violence connected with the cattle business. It had to be so, since ownership could be transferred by the simple process of driving away another man's property under its own power and blotting out a brand. There were thousands of rustlers in Texas before we ever began operating in this northern country, and there are hundreds in Wyoming, Montana, and Colorado. The only way to stop them is to put fear in their hearts. Now about our cowboys. When a rider joins up he knows he isn't going into something safe and sane like selling drygoods behind a counter. In my time I've known a lot of punchers killed one way and another—in stampedes, swimming rivers, bucked off and trampled, caught in blizzards, shot down. A considerable percentage die young. That's the risk they take.'

'No use talking about it,' Terry said. 'If we argued till Doomsday we wouldn't see this alike. The point is, I won't stand for drygulching. It stops, or I walk out. That's short and plain, Clint.'

'I heard you before,' Ellison answered coldly. 'I've already told you there won't be any more of it on our side. Do you want me to sign a bond?'

'I want you to know exactly where I stand. You can tell the others too. I haven't been given a square deal, and I don't like it. All over this country I'm suspected of being at the bottom of this. I'm telling you now that if there's any more monkeying with the cards I leave the table.'

'You're not looking at this the way you should,' Ellison told him.

'I'm looking at it the way a decent man has to look at it,' Terry answered.

He turned and walked out of the house.

XIV

It had come on to rain, a soft, fine rain that blurred the landscape. The mountains were no longer visible, and the foothills were vague and shadowy. Calhoun Terry had untied his slicker from the saddle and put it on. He judged from the sky that there would be no more sun before night. This was not a summer shower. There was a lot of moisture in the clouds, and the downpour would last until morning. Presently it was going to rain harder.

He had been in the saddle nine hours—five on the way to the No, By Joe, and four on the return journey. Now he was back on Diamond Reverse B territory. In another hour he would reach the ranch house and Jim Wong would set about preparing him a good supper. At thought of Jim he smiled. The Chinaman was devoted to him. He showed it by the way he fussed over and scolded him. When he thought it for his good he ordered his boss around plenty.

Terry descended a long slope at a walk, forded a trickle of a stream winding down the draw, and put his mount at the slope. The rim above was fringed with bushes, and back of these rose a small grove of aspen.

A bullet whistled past him. There was a puff of smoke from the aspens. Terry swung his horse swiftly and raced for the wild cherries on the bank of the little creek he had just left. Every instant he expected to feel the shock of lead tearing into his body. There was another shot. A slug tore through the arm of the slicker he was wearing. After this, scarce three seconds later, two more explosions sounded. But before the echo of the last had died away Calhoun was in the bed of the stream, crouched behind a screen of wild cherry tangle. He had freed the horse and let it wander down the draw, but not before he had withdrawn the rifle from its boot.

All his senses were keyed to tension. He could see no movement in the aspens, nor did any sound come to him except the drip of the rain in the foliage. His gaze swept the slope, to make sure his enemies were not circling the hillside for a flank attack.

For there were at least two of them. The first two shots were from a rifle, the others from a revolver. There was something strange about this. The man with the revolver had waited until Calhoun was practically out of range. Nor had Calhoun seen the bullets strike on the hillside.

While the foreman waited there came to him news on the breeze. Back of the rim and out of sight a man was riding from the aspens. He heard the swish of bushes and the clink of a hoof against rock. A vague, distant rumor told Terry that the horseman was still going. There might be two of them. He could not tell that.

The ambushed man did not intend to make any mistakes. This might be a trap. There were three possibilities. Those who had lain in wait for him, having failed to get him, might be hurrying away to escape detection. That was very likely. Or one of them might be making a wide circuit to take him in the rear. Or two or three of them. Still another thought to consider was the chance that one of the attackers had ridden away to draw him from his cover, and had left a confederate to deal with him when he came into the open.

Terry did not intend to come into the open, nor did he mean to wait there for a possible rear attack. He slipped along the bed of the little creek and reclaimed his horse. Leading the animal, he came to the end of the draw and circled a hill, taking care not to let himself be seen by anyone who might still be watching from the aspens. He mounted, but still kept to the low country until he had made a circuit which brought him back of and below the grove from which the shots had come.

This had taken time. Twenty-five minutes or half an hour, Calhoun guessed. He tied the horse and began a slow approach to the rock rim. Before he left he meant to find out all that could be learned about this attempt on his life. He did not see how it could have been planned with any advance information. What was more likely, he thought, was that the rustlers had come to pick off any stray Diamond Reverse B rider they could find.

Terry took no unnecessary chances. The heavy clouds and the rain had darkened the day, so that visibility was not good. The bad light was in his favor. He availed himself of every bit of sage and of every bush that would give cover. Before he moved from one point of safety to another he scanned the terrain vigilantly. As he approached the aspens his progress was slower. He did not think he had been seen, but there was always a chance somebody might have him covered and be waiting for a better shot.

Every minute made him more certain that his enemies had gone, but he took nothing for granted.

When he edged into the grove at last he had made sure nobody was lurking there to pick him off.

Darkness was beginning to fall. He found the tracks of two horses—cut the sign of them where they had come in and again where they had left. A few moments later he came on a discovery that shocked him. The body of a man lay face down on the mold formed by last year's leaves. To his back a paper was pinned. On it was written, 'This is what happens to rustlers.'

The body was still warm, though the heart had ceased to beat an hour ago. Calhoun turned it over. The man was Black Yeager, a notorious bad man, the first one to have his name put on the black list at the meeting in Denver. He had been shot twice. One bullet had torn into his stomach. A second had struck him between the eyes. Evidently the revolver had been fired at close quarters, for there were powder marks on the face. Yeager's rifle lay beside him, still clutched in one hand.

Terry tried to reconstruct the scene. Two men had ridden into the aspen clump together. They had dismounted and tied their horses. Whether they had been quarreling, or whether there was an old animosity between them, he did not know. At least there had been no open enmity which would have prevented them from siding each other on this ride. He could see where at the edge of the rock rim they had lain down side by side.

To guess the details of what followed was not

possible. Yeager had taken two shots at him. The empty shells showed that. Had the other man protested? There had been hardly time for an exchange of words after Black had fired. Moreover, the dead man's face was a witness to the contrary. Fixed on it was a look of shocked surprise, as if the impact of his companion's slugs was entirely unexpected.

It smelled to high heaven of treachery. Yeager had been killed by an accomplice. But why? Calhoun could see no need of it born of the circumstances. They had not been trapped. No spur of danger had prompted this crime, as if for instance there had been a desperate urge to escape, with only one horse available for two men. The murder was deliberate.

The Diamond Reverse B foreman read again the message on the paper. The meaning of it was perfectly plain. Though the words of the warning varied, a note of similar context had been found attached to the body of each of the four slain rustlers. Terry knew the cattlemen's association had stock detectives living among the settlers and gathering information. Ellison had admitted as much when Turley's name had come up for voting at the Windsor Hotel in Denver. Some one of these spies must be the assassin. It was possible that in this case the detective had killed Yeager to prevent him from firing again.

If the two men had ridden out together publicly

from Black Butte or from some ranch, the survivor might find himself in trouble. Perhaps he had grown bold from previous immunity. The powder marks would not bear out a story of having been set upon by Diamond Reverse B riders. Of course the likelier chance was that the two men had happened to meet and that nobody knew they were together.

Terry left the body where he found it and rode to the ranch. He wrote a note to Lane Carey and sent it by a messenger. After supper he lay down on his bed and rested. Presently he would take the saddle again, and he had learned to snatch an hour's sleep when he could.

About eleven o'clock Jim Wong woke him. 'Two men want see boss,' the Chinaman said.

Terry rose, put on his boots and coat, and went downstairs to meet his guests.

XV

Ellen was playing a game of checkers with her father. Usually he could beat her, but after two or three games in the evening he would get sleepy and relax his vigilance.

He yawned, made a move and considered it, without lifting his fingers. 'All right,' he said, removing his hand.

Ellen promptly took three men.

'Hold on! Wait a minute!' Lane Carey protested.

The shiny face of Jim Budd appeared in the doorway.

'Man to see you, Mista Carey,' he drawled. 'Brought this here note along.'

Carey drew a sheet of paper from the envelope. He spent so much time reading it that his daughter grew curious. She observed that he went back and gave part of it a second consideration.

'What is it, father?' she asked.

Carey told Jim to ask the messenger to wait. After the colored cook had gone he passed the letter to his daughter.

'More trouble,' he said.

Ellen read two or three lines of the letter, then turned back to the signature. 'From Calhoun Terry,' she murmured, surprised.

I am writing from the ranch [the girl read]. If possible, will you come here at once? An hour ago I found the body of Black Yeager about four miles from my house. He had been killed shortly before under very peculiar circumstances. While he was firing at me from ambush a companion of his shot him at close quarters. Please withhold judgment until you realize the facts.

If Jeff Brand is within reach will you bring him with you? He may be able to get a clue as to who the killer is from studying the *situation. Until you have seen me, better not discuss this with any others.*

'It's terrible,' Ellen said in a low voice. 'I don't understand it. Why would a companion of Black Yeager shoot him? But that's what he says.'

'Yes. I don't understand it either.' He had risen and was buckling a belt around his waist. 'I suppose I'll find out when I get there.'

'Do you think it's safe to go, father?' she asked. 'Let me go with you.'

'No,' he vetoed. 'You'll stay right here.'

'I don't like to have you go alone,' she protested. 'It may be a trap. Maybe the letter isn't from Mr. Terry.'

'It's on Diamond Reverse B stationery. And I'm not expecting to go alone. Jeff Brand will be with me.'

'Why does he want Jeff to go with you?'

'I don't know. Perhaps because he wants to clear himself with Jeff's crowd.'

'Will Jeff go? He may think this is a plot to trap him.'

'Will he go?' Lane Carey laughed dryly. 'You would have to rope and hog-tie him to keep him away. I thought you knew Jeff.'

'Let's have the messenger in here where we can see him in the light,' Ellen suggested. 'You ought to make sure the letter is from Mr. Terry.'

'A good idea.'

The man who had brought the letter was a Diamond Reverse B cowboy called Slim. Both of the Careys knew him. He said that Calhoun Terry himself had put the letter in his hands. Slim had no idea what was written in it. But the boss had told him to be sure the letter reached Carey, and that he was to wait and ride back with him.

It relieved Ellen to know that her father would not travel alone in case he did not find Jeff. She did not know why anybody would wish to harm her father, but anything was likely to happen in a country so wrought up as the Buck River region was now. Though she tried not to be demonstrative, she could hardly keep her fluttering hands away from Lane while he was getting ready to go.

'I don't know why he sends for you anyhow,' she fussed. 'You haven't anything to do with it. You're not on either side.'

'Maybe that's why he's sending for me,' her father suggested.

Ellen could guess the real reason. There was nobody in the district who did not give weight to Carey's character and judgment. He was a man to whom people brought their troubles, one whose advice was often sought and followed.

'You will be careful, won't you?' she said, standing at the stirrup after he had swung to the saddle. And put that slicker on. It's still raining a little.'

Lane laughed. 'This girl of mine bosses me like

she was my wife, Slim. I reckon you would call me henpecked.'

The cowpuncher's gaze rested on the slender girl standing beside her father with lifted head. He could name a good many men who would not mind being bossed by her for the rest of their lives. Slim was a realist, and he knew that her vivid beauty, so delicate in appearance yet as vital as that of a spirited young thoroughbred, was not for him or any other run-of-the-brush cowboy. None the less he had lain awake under the stars more than once and let his thoughts drift around her. When Terry had picked him to ride in to Black Butte it had pleased him immensely.

Ellen smiled at the young fellow. 'Will you tell Mr. Terry that I'm loaning him my father on condition that he is returned safe and sound under escort?'

'Nonsense!' her father demurred promptly. 'I've looked after myself quite a spell unassisted, and I expect I'll make out to do it for a while yet.'

'But you'll tell him just the same, won't you, Slim?'

'I sure will, Miss Ellen.' It occurred to Slim that it might be a good idea to leave the impression with the boss that she had asked him personally to come back with Lane. No use making two bites of a cherry and sending another man.

The two men vanished at a road gait into the darkness.

'We're going to pick up Jeff Brand,' explained Carey. 'He's up at Roan Alford's place. Been gentling some horses for Roan.'

Slim, astonished, looked at his companion. 'Did Terry say for us to get Jeff?'

'That's what he said.' There was a gleam of satiric humor in the older man's eye. 'Maybe the lion and the lamb are going to lie down together.'

'Would you tell me which one is the lamb, please?' Slim asked, chuckling.

'Maybe I'd better have said the lion and the tiger.'

'What's up, Mr. Carey? I could see by the way the boss talked that it is something serious.'

'It is,' Lane answered. 'I can't tell you more than that because Terry asked me not to talk. But you'll know right soon.'

Brand had gone to bed in the little bunkhouse and was sound asleep when the two riders arrived. Carey was careful to call from a distance before knocking on the door.

'Hello the house!' he shouted.

After he had repeated the call several times a voice answered sleepily. 'Who's there?'

'Lane Carey. I want to talk with Jeff Brand.'

They heard the man speak to somebody else in the room. 'Wake up, Jeff. Guy wants to speak with you. Claims he is Lane Carey. Another fellow with him.'

Presently, after a moment of low-toned talk,

Brand's voice took up the conversation. 'If that's you, Lane, move forward alone where I can see you. Let the other fellow stay back.'

Carey rode a little closer and drew up a dozen yards from the bunkhouse. 'It's Lane, Jeff. No trick about it. Want to see you out here a minute.'

After Brand had pulled on his trousers and boots he walked out to meet the man from Black Butte. 'Didn't know you'd taken to night-riding, Lane,' he drawled. 'Honest, I'm wore out busting Roan's broncos. Even if you are raiding the Diamond Reverse B range I'll have to beg off tonight.'

'Have your little joke, Jeff,' Carey answered. 'But that's exactly where I'm going—to the Diamond Reverse B—and I'm taking you along.'

The friendly derision went out of the rustler's face as a light does from a snuffed candle. 'What's in yore mind?' he asked.

Carey took from his pocket the letter received from Terry and handed it to the other. 'Read that.'

Jeff read, by the light of several matches, a dark flush of anger pouring into his face as he did so. He began to curse Terry, his voice low and bitter.

The owner of the Box 55 raised a hand in protest. 'Don't push on the reins, Jeff. My idea is that Cal Terry is telling this the way it happened. Anyhow, I'm taking him up on his offer to go to his place and talk this over. It's up to you to go along with me or to refuse.'

'What in Mexico does he want with me there?'

Brand asked. 'I don't get it. The thing doesn't make sense.'

'I don't know what he wants, but I've got a sort of notion. He wants us to hear his story and look the ground over with him. My opinion is, and you can take it for what it's worth, that Cal hasn't had a thing to do with these killings. Naturally, if that's so, he would like to clear himself from blame.'

'And if it isn't so, he'd like to whitewash himself just the same,' Jeff jeered.

'That's so. He would. But say he could convince us of his innocence in this case. We would be two pretty good witnesses in his favor. I'm supposed to be a neutral, and you are strong for the small man.'

'Mr. Terry wouldn't put it just that way about me,' the outlaw said. 'He'd go quite considerable stronger.'

'Anyway, I'm convinced he's not setting a trap to get you. But if you think so of course you had better not—'

'Hell! I'm going with you, Lane. I'll take my chance of any shenanigan. I want to see what the fellow is up to. Be with you soon as I've caught and saddled.' He walked back to the bunkhouse and finished dressing, after which he joined the others at the corral.

They rode across-country through the sage until they cut the trail to the Diamond Reverse B.

Slim led the way. There was no conversation after they got into territory close to the ranch, except an occasional word or two. It lacked only an hour of midnight when they filed into the plaza.

Jim Wong shuffled out to the porch and took the two visitors into the room the ranch manager used as an office. Here Terry joined them shortly.

'Better sit down, gentlemen,' he said.

Brand looked at him, hostility in his hard eyes. 'I'll stand.'

The ranch manager's gaze met his coldly. 'Better take a chair, Mr. Brand. This isn't a social occasion. After we get through with our business you can shoot at me just as properly as you could have before. I haven't called you here as my friends. I'm not so dumb as that.'

'Is it straight goods that Black Yeager has been killed?' blurted out Jeff.

'Yes. That's why I sent for you.'

'Who killed him?'

'I don't know. It looks as though he had been killed by a man supposed to be his friend.'

Brand sat down. 'All right. Spill it. I'll listen.' He kept his eyes on the Diamond B man. Anger had boiled out of him into his face. His jaw was set in an obstinate refusal to accept any explanation his enemy might offer.

Calhoun Terry told the story of the attack on him and what he had later discovered in the aspen grove.

XVI

Jeff Brand said bluntly, 'That's *your* story.' His bitter laugh was skeptical. 'Sounds likely, doesn't it? Black and this friend of his were trying to drygulch you, then suddenly the side-kick turns on Black and blasts him. I reckon almost anybody would believe that yarn.'

Carey leaned back in his chair, frowning at a pair of spurs hanging on the wall. It was not a convincing story, but that was one reason for not rejecting it too hurriedly. If Terry had wanted to invent one to exonerate himself he could have done better than that.

'Don't get on the prod, Jeff,' the owner of the Box 55 suggested. 'Mr. Terry could have buried the body if he had been minded that way. He didn't have to send for us and tell a yarn so improbable that I reckon it must be true.'

'How could it be true?' demanded Brand angrily. 'Why would two guys waylay this fellow and then one of them gun the other? It don't make sense. Who was the bird that did it? Have you got any friends who would go out with you to do a job and right when you were doing it pour slugs into you?'

'I hope not,' Carey said. 'But I'm not Black Yeager. He was a tough, surly *hombre*, and there might be one of his so-called friends waiting to get a chance at him.'

'So he rode with Black for a couple of hours and didn't crack down on him till he knew there was a witness in the neighborhood to testify against him later maybe. Too thin, Lane. I'm not that easy.' The rustler swung round on the Diamond Reverse B manager sharply. 'What was the idea in sending for me?'

The frosty blue eyes of Terry met those of the outlaw steadily. 'The idea is to have you examine the ground and see for yourself. I don't enjoy the reputation of being a man who kills from ambush.'

'Queer you have a habit of being around when these murders take place. You're mighty unlucky, or else . . .'

'Did you bring the body in, Mr. Terry?' Carey asked.

'No, I thought it better for you to see it on the ground.' He added: 'Two of my riders are camping out in the grove to keep off wild animals. We can't read sign till morning. You had better turn in and get some sleep. We'll have breakfast early and take off by daybreak.'

'That's good medicine,' Carey agreed. 'How about it, Jeff?'

'No obligations on either side, Mr. Brand,' his host said. 'As I mentioned before, a strictly business transaction. There will still be an open season on me.'

Jeff took his sarcasm sulkily, but he made no protest. There was no sense in sitting out in the rain all night because he did not like the ranch boss or its policies.

Brand and Carey followed Terry to the dining-room. Jim Wong had set two places. There were sandwiches on a platter and a pot of coffee beside some cups. A bottle of whiskey and glasses were on the sideboard.

'You've had a long ride in the rain,' the foreman said. 'Jim Wong fixed you up a little refreshment. I'll have your horses looked after while you eat.'

He left his two guests to themselves.

'Terry is no more guilty than I am,' Carey said. 'At least I don't think so. But we'll know more about this tomorrow.'

'So you're swallowing hook, line, and sinker the fairy tale about Black's own partner bumping him off,' sneered the younger man.

'I'm reserving judgment about that.' Lane leaned forward and spoke, almost in a murmur. 'Has it ever struck you, Jeff, that the big cow outfits may have stock detectives right in our midst?'

'You mean some of their own cowboys.'

'No, I don't. Somebody closer to the rustlers. One who sees them oftener and maybe rides around with them. A nester, perhaps.'

Brand thought it over. 'Might be so. If I could prove it on one I would sure give him a quick

146

ticket to Kingdom Come. But what has that got to do with this affair?'

'Might have nothing to do with it. Might have a lot. A spy like that who could be hired to give away his friends would not stop at murder from ambush.'

They kept their voices low.

'You mean that this spy, whoever he is, may have been the man who put the slugs in Black.'

'Not only in Black. All these killings were probably done by the same man. If he was a spy, posing as a friend of Black, it would explain how he could get close enough without suspicion to turn a gun on him suddenly.'

'That's so, and it would explain why he killed Black right then,' Jeff said, an exultant gleam in his eyes. 'He had to stop him from bumping off his boss. He didn't have to be afraid Terry would tell on him, seeing as his money was paying for it.'

Carey shook his head. 'I won't go that far. Somebody connected with one of the big outfits is paying him. But I don't think it is Terry.'

Jeff was not sure that he did either, though he did not care to admit it. He did not like Calhoun Terry, and he was not a man to give up his preconceived opinions easily.

The three men breakfasted early and were on their way before sunup. They took with them a packhorse to bring back the body. During the night the rain had spent itself and there was now not a cloud in the sky. The two ranchmen chatted a little as they rode, but Brand did not join in the talk. He was making no gestures that might be construed as peace overtures.

Terry pointed to the aspen grove in the draw leading up to the rock rim. The smoke from a campfire drifted above the low tree-tops.

'That's the place,' he said. 'We'd better go up the draw so as not to disturb the tracks. The men rode into the grove along the ridge from the right, and the one who didn't stay among the aspens went back with both horses the same way.'

The Diamond Reverse B riders joined them at the edge of the grove.

'Tracks of the horses are still showing,' one of them said. 'I was scared the rain might wash them out, but it didn't come down hard enough.'

Carey and Brand examined the body. It told a story of unexpected death. The powder burns on the face showed that the revolver had been fired very close to the victim. The Diamond Reverse B men stood back and let them make their own investigation and later check up on the tracks of the horses. After they had finished they returned to Terry and his men.

'Lemme see that note the fellow pinned to Black's coat,' Jeff said.

Calhoun took it from his pocketbook and handed it to the rustler. Brand studied it for several minutes. 'I've seen writing like that somewhere, but I can't just remember when,' he mentioned to Carey. 'Look how he makes his s's with the tails flying away.'

The Bar 55 owner shook his head. 'Can't prove it by me. Maybe I've seen it, but I wouldn't remember it.'

Brand put the note in his pocket. 'Mind if I keep it?' he said to Terry insolently. His manner suggested that he intended to keep it whether the foreman minded or not.

'Not at all. Nate Hart may want to keep it, but you fix that up with him.' Terry's voice was scornfully polite.

On the way back to the ranch Carey rode beside Terry and Brand with the two cowboys.

'I reckon we have come to the same opinion as you did, Cal,' the man from Black Butte told his companion.

Terry was surprised at the use of the Christian name. Until the past few years Carey had always used it, but since the younger man had allied himself with the big ranch a certain stiffness had entered their relationship.

'What opinion?' Terry inquired.

'That this killing was done by a cattle detective hired by some of the big outfits.'

'That's my opinion, is it?' the Diamond Reverse B manager asked sarcastically.

'I think so. It explains the facts better than

anything else I can figure out. My notion is you wanted to put us on our guard against this fellow.'

'Even if I was employing him.'

'I don't believe you are in this at all, but I expect you can give a good guess who hired this killer.'

Terry said tonelessly, 'I don't know anything about it.'

'You might even have an idea who the gunman is,' Carey went on evenly. 'I would say that he is no stranger here. He knows too much about the movements of the men he rubbed out. Might even be one of your own riders.'

'No,' Calhoun denied sharply.

'More likely he's a spy hired by the big outfits to live right among the fellows they suspect of being rustlers,' the Black Butte man went on placidly, slanting a look at the man beside him.

The manager of the Diamond Reverse B made no answer. The steel-blue eyes in the bronzed face were as expressionless as jade. He sat at loose ease in the saddle, apparently relaxed, but vigilant enough not to betray anything he wanted to keep secret.

'If you knew such a spy I wouldn't expect you to mention his name,' the older man continued. 'I don't reckon he would last long if some of the night-riding gentry got wise to his treachery. But maybe you could have him called off before he depopulates the country.'

Again Terry had nothing to say.

'Well, I'll leave it there, Cal,' Lane Carey concluded. 'A wink is as good as a nod to a blind horse. I've a notion you don't like this state of affairs any better than I do.'

'I don't,' the ranch superintendent agreed. 'I hate being blamed for it when I'm not guilty. I would like the word passed out that if I ever help to get rid of cattle thieves it will be in the open.'

'I've already told the boys that.'

'You may tell them too that it may be soon if they don't mend their ways,' Terry said bluntly.

They came to a fork in the road. Brand and Carey turned to the left, taking with them the packhorse, the body lashed to its back. The others followed the right branch, which brought them presently within sight of the ranch buildings.

XVII

Black Yeager was buried at Round Top, and his funeral was the largest ever held in the county. The feeling was very bitter, and it was almost unanimous against the big ranches among those at the graveyard. Even the people who did not justify rustling resented this high-handed destruction of suspected men who had not been found guilty by a jury. Among the rustlers themselves, a mounting fear lay back of their furious rage. A killer was loose in the land, and he might strike at any one of them next. They lived in a country of open spaces, and no matter how carefully they guarded them-selves it was not possible to make sure he would not find an opportunity to kill.

Several men without property slipped away quietly, not advertising their destination. They crossed the line into Montana or Colorado, or eastward into one of the Dakotas.

The loungers at the Round Top corrals and those at the Black Butte post-office discussed these matters guardedly, mentioning facts rather than opinions. A good many men were no longer quite sure of their neighbors. They talked less, even though they gathered more often into groups, as if they felt a safety in numbers.

'Bart Dennison pulled his freight last night,' Lee Hart said, chewing tobacco stolidly as he watched the stage-driver kick the brake loose. 'Left on the train for Cheyenne.'

Jeff Brand's laughter was brittle. 'Some folks scare easily,' he said.

There followed a long silence. A cowboy rolling a cigarette answered. 'Maybe it was time for him to get scared.'

'It's never time for that,' Jeff replied hardily.

Through the window his words reached Ellen. She had no doubt he was a thief, but she applauded the spirit of his defiance. What he had told her about Pete Tolman was even more true of himself. He had lived fully, physically at least. There was in him a deep capacity for enjoyment. But though mere existence was a delight to him, he would not buy it at too big a price. He would not run away. He would stay and fight it out to a finish.

The girl shifted her position a little, to see him out of a corner of the window. This graceful, curly-headed youth was a scoundrel, she supposed, by the standards of civilized society. He had strayed beyond that borderland which is the limit for honest men. At least he had the virtue of courage. His cool, sardonic eyes did not know fear. There was a quality in his superb arrogance that fascinated her.

'I dunno,' Turley said. 'All right to fight back when you know what to fight. But it's too late when you got a bullet in the belly. I'm not blaming Bart none. When I'm out on the hills I feel right goosy myself.'

'If a fellow hasn't got sand in his craw he's got no business living here,' Brand retorted, scorn etching his voice. 'He'd better get a job at a livery stable washing buggies and watering horses.'

'Staying here didn't work out so good for Yeager and Tolman,' a bald-headed man in chaps suggested, mopping his shining crown with a bandanna.

'Like Turley says, a fellow can't fight what he can't see,' Hart said.

'What we have to fight is plain for all of us to

see,' Brand replied contemptuously. 'We can tackle it, or we can lie down like yellow coyotes.'

Nobody took up the challenge. A rider was dismounting at the hitch-rack. They watched him walk across the dusty road to join them. The man was Roan Alford.

He said 'Howdy!' and nodded at one and another. Casually, as if it were of slight importance, he gave them news.

'Cuth Rogers got in from Elk Creek an hour or so ago,' he mentioned. 'Says Jim McFaddin of the Flying V C was shot yesterday.'

'Shot?' demanded the crook-nosed Turley. 'You mean, on purpose?'

'Yep. Some of the riders of his ranch heard the shooting and came a-running. They found him dead. He had his six-gun out and had fired it twice. Fellow had sent a revolver bullet right spang through the heart.'

'What fellow?' Lee Hart asked.

'Nobody knows. He lit a shuck *pronto*.'

Brand asked a question. 'Was McFaddin shot from behind?'

'Cuth Rogers says not,' answered Alford. 'He saw the body. Says it musta been a duel. The bullet came from directly in front and there was no brush for several hundred yards.'

'That's funny,' commented Turley. 'Looks like it may have been one of his own men bumped him. They got into a quarrel, maybe.'

'Both Jim McFaddin and his brother were bully-puss overbearing fellows,' Lee Hart mentioned. 'Well, I don't aim to wear any crêpe.'

'The story is that it wasn't one of the Flying V C men did it,' Alford said. 'They are all accounted for. And the man was tracked for several miles.'

'Something queer about this,' Turley cut in, frowning. 'I don't get it. If the fellow who did it was—one of our friends, say—he wouldn't of shot it out in the open that-away. He would of waited to get a crack at him from the brush.'

'Would he?' Brand asked. 'Maybe not. Maybe he wanted to show the big outfits that we had the nerve to do our killing in the open.'

Ellen felt a fluttering heart beat against her ribs. She was watching Jeff. He had spoken carelessly, as if his suggestion were a guess sent at a venture, but in his slurring drawl she had read an undertone implacable and deadly. She knew, as well as one could know without evidence to back it, that he had been the other party to that duel. A strange, breathless dread filled her being. This was not the Jeff Brand who had flirted with her gaily at the Sleepy Cat dance.

'Don't sound reasonable to me,' Hart objected. 'Nobody would be crazy enough to go on to the Flying V C range to get McFaddin in the open, with his men close enough to hear the shooting. No sense to that.'

'But that's what the man did, if Rogers' story is

true,' Brand insisted. He gave McFaddin an even break. It would have to be that way, if McFaddin got two shots before he fell.'

'I reckon this guy wanted to commit suicide, then,' Turley barked.

'Nothing like that. He was looking for one of the McFaddins and he found Jim. Likely he did not know how near the ranch hands were. He called for a showdown, and they fought it out. Of course I'm only guessing, but I'd bet my stack of blues it was that way.' Jeff added contemptuously: 'Why not? Oughtn't an even break to be good enough for any man?'

Ellen looked quickly at Lee Hart. She saw furious anger struggling with caution in the ugly face of the short, bowlegged man. He did not like to be reminded that he had fired at Calhoun Terry from cover and had bolted when his enemy had dismounted to come back for a settlement.

'The way you talk sounds dumb to me, Jeff,' he snarled. 'What you expect a fellow to do? Buck didn't have any chance, did he? Not on yore tintype. They rubbed him out when he wasn't expecting it. Why shouldn't I do the same with one of them?'

Hard-eyed, Brand looked at Hart. 'I'm not telling you what you ought to do. I don't give a damn. What I'm pointing out is how a white man would want to settle a difficulty.'

Alford nodded. 'Personally I would feel the

156

same way Jeff does. I don't reckon I could get my finger to pull a trigger of a gun pointed at a guy who didn't know I was there, not even if I was sure he was a wolf who hired out as a paid killer. But there's something to be said on the other side, too. If you're in a poker game and play fair you haven't much chance against a tinhorn who is cheating.'

Dark blood mantled Hart's flat-featured face. 'If you claim I'm not a white man—,' he blustered, and choked off for lack of adequate words.

A faint expression of contempt kindled in the narrowed eyes of Jeff. 'I wouldn't be interested,' he said, his voice insolent and dry.

'Quit beefing, Lee,' snapped Turley. 'Unless you're lookin' for trouble to boil right damned now. There's no sense in picking at words. Jeff wasn't hinting at you.'

Brand's laugh was openly insulting to Hart. 'Now we've got that all settled I feel a heap easier in my mind,' he drawled.

Lane Carey came out of a pasture on the other side of the road and tied at the rack. He was told the news.

'That's bad,' he said very gravely. 'It means more trouble coming up, and we've had enough already.'

'Yeah, we have,' Brand agreed. 'But what about them? They haven't had any till now. Let 'em taste their own medicine, I say. Already they have driven several men out of the country. Maybe they'll get the idea that Buck River isn't so safe for them either.'

There was a faint, sardonic grin on his reckless face, a diamond-hard glitter in the eyes. Ellen felt a shiver run down her spine. She wondered if her father and these other men guessed that this graceful, graceless scamp was the one who had struck so fierce a blow at his ruthless enemies.

Carey looked at him and shook his head. 'No use my saying a word, Jeff. You won't listen to it.'

'Then don't say it,' Brand advised.

The ranchman shrugged his broad shoulders and walked into the post-office.

Ellen had work to do at the house, and as soon as she had turned over the office to her father she left. Jeff Brand was waiting outside. He rose to join her, reaching his feet in one swift movement of rippling ease.

'You're certainly the workingest girl I ever saw,' he told her. 'There's a proverb about that. All work and no play makes Jeff a dull boy.'

'So you think I'm dull,' she said.

'No, no, I'm dull when you work too long. Have you ever thought that maybe in sixty or seventy years we may be too old to play? We have to leave some time for love and kisses, you know.'

She was not up to nonsense today. It was not worth trying, not while she had this queer feeling of suffocation in her breast.

'Why do you go out of your way to insult men who are dangerous—men like Lee Hart?' she asked.

He looked at her, surprised. 'So you heard?'

'I couldn't help hearing.'

The girl moved beside him, slim and straight, a pulse of excitement beating in her throat. She knew it was dangerous to show an interest in him. He was a man likely to take an ell if you gave an inch. But she pushed that knowledge from her, as much as she could with his amused eyes resting on her and drawing a rose bloom to her cheeks.

'You pack a lot in one little question,' he said. 'First off, I didn't go out of my way to insult Lee Hart. I wasn't thinking about him when I spoke, though he is sure welcome to take it personal if he likes. For the fact is, I can't stand the fellow. He's low-down mean. As to his being dangerous, I don't reckon he is—long as he is in front of you.'

He spoke carelessly, as if the matter were not important.

'Do you expect to keep him in front of you all the rest of your life?' she asked tartly.

'I'm not giving that any thought. Why worry about that kind of cattle on a day like this? Hear that meadowlark whooping up his little song just for us. See the sun throwing a million sparkles from the waves of the lake.'

He liked the curl of her sweet, derisive lip. 'So you're just a fool boy not grown up. I wonder if you'll ever be anything else—if you'll live long enough.'

'I feel right healthy,' he drawled. 'But a fellow can't always tell. Do I look peaked?'

'You look to me like a man who is dooming himself,' she said soberly, with a kind of proud defiance. For she knew young girls were not expected to talk that way to wild, reckless men who held their interest. 'You frighten me, as if— as if you were walking on your own grave.'

'Would you feel badly if you knew I were?' he asked in a low voice.

She did not look at him. Her long, slender legs moved rhythmically toward the house. But the blood was beating stormily through her heart.

'I would feel sorry for any young man condemned to death,' she said.

'I see,' he said dryly. 'Yore Christian duty. I would want a girl to give me more than that.'

She turned on him, courage in her eyes like a banner. 'What would you expect to give her in return?' she demanded.

'If she was the right girl I might give her a lover.'

'A lover,' she said scornfully.

He surprised himself in his answer. 'A husband, then.' It was the last thing he had expected to say.

'That would be a fine gift,' she told him. 'What kind of a girl could keep step with you? Do you think a wife would be happy waiting at home in terror for fear you were being shot or hanged?'

'Aren't men supposed to settle down when they marry?'

'You aren't even thinking of it. Your mind is full of revenge and hatred.' Excitement was carrying her much farther than she had intended. It had lit an explosive spark in her breast. 'Where were you yesterday afternoon? What were you doing? But no—don't tell me! I don't want to know.'

She flung out a hand in a gesture of hopelessness and turned away, running up the porch steps swiftly into the house.

XVIII

Clint Ellison read the note a second time. He frowned, his gray, powder-marked face set rigidly. He was a dominating man, and he did not like to have his plans disarranged.

> I hope you are satisfied [so the note said]. Well, you can't drag me into trouble with you. I am sticking by what I told you the other day. Count me out of the whole business. I'm through before you start on any plans you have.

The name signed at the bottom was Calhoun Terry.

Ellison helped himself to a drink, paced the floor, and returned to his desk. He picked up a pen and wrote. The burden of his message was told in two lines.

Since I am going down to Jim Creek station tomorrow I will drop in at the ranch and have a talk with you.

He sealed the note and took it out to Slim, who was waiting at the bunkhouse for an answer.

After the cowboy had ridden away he went back into his office and walked the floor again. Irritably he admitted to himself that he had made a mistake. His gunman had moved too fast for him. Before he could get to the fellow and call him off he had destroyed Black Yeager. Ellison cared nothing about that, except for its repercussions. Black was a rustler, and he had got what was coming to him. But it looked now as if the price for his death would be too high. The rustlers had retaliated by shooting Jim McFaddin. If Terry walked out on the invasion that would be another blow. Perhaps it would have been better to have waited for the wholesale clean-up without first picking off individual offenders.

But with or without Terry he meant to carry on. The No, By Joe lay in a country peculiarly favorable for thieves. The percentage of loss was so great of late that the margin of profit had been completely wiped out. The Bartlett Land & Cattle Company must either stop the rustling of its stock or fold up. Ellison was not the type to give up without a fight.

When he dropped in to see Terry he defended what he had done, on the ground that it was a necessity. He made the further point that in wiping out the thieves the big ranches would be doing a service to the territory. It would be a place where honest men could live and feel their property was safe.

Terry shook his head. 'I've been thinking this over, and I have changed my mind about some things . . .'

'Wait a minute,' Ellison interrupted. 'You think I haven't played fair with you. I want to say that I couldn't have prevented the killing of Black Yeager. It happened on your way home, right after our talk.'

'I understand that,' the manager of the Diamond Reverse B agreed stiffly. 'We'll leave Yeager out of this. Point is, I don't enjoy being shot at myself. If Yeager had fired a hair's breadth straighter I would be where Jim McFaddin is now. To think that you can ambush rustlers wholesale without having them play the same game is criminally foolish. There is no stopping that kind of business. It is like those Kentucky feuds. They go on forever.'

'So will this thieving, if we don't do something about it,' the Bartlett manager said curtly.

'I'll do what I can about it,' Terry answered. 'If we catch a man stealing our stuff, or if we find it in his possession, I'll hang him to a tree. That's as far as I'll go. I won't join in an organized drive to wipe out suspicious characters.'

Then the Diamond Reverse B outfit is through, unless it changes its manager.'

'It's through, whether it does or not. There's no other answer, Ellison. The day of the big ranch is past. Settlers have homesteaded along the creeks and on choice bits of range. More are coming in every year. We can't buck the law. Some of the large outfits are fencing land that isn't owned by them. They can't get away with it. They are licked before they start. Like it or not, the cattle empires are going to vanish. I've tried not to believe this, but it stands out as plain as Old Baldy there.'

'So you're quitting,' Ellison said, scorn in his voice.

'I have advised my people to sell at a profit while there is still time.'

'Sell to whom?'

'To settlers. My idea is to break up the ranch into twenty or more small ones. It can be divided so that the land will sell like hot cakes.'

From Ellison's gray face the color seemed to drain. 'By God, you take the cake, Terry,' he said, restrained anger riding in his voice. 'First you are with the small fry. Then you throw them over and join us. Now when we have a fight on our hands you are deserting us to go back to them.'

Terry felt the rage boiling up in him. 'You're too bull-headed, Ellison, and too smooth in your work. We were supposed to be allies, and you double-crossed me by ordering these men dry-gulched. Do you think you are God Almighty, with the power of life and death in your hands? These Texas gunmen can't be trusted not to run wild, with you giving them their orders. I'll have none of it.'

'I suppose you'll fix yourself up with your new-old friends by warning them,' Ellison jeered, bitterness in his voice.

The superintendent of the Diamond Reverse B restrained himself with difficulty. 'I ought not to take that from you,' he said quietly. But I will. It's time you went, Mr. Ellison.'

White spots pinched into the nose of the visitor. He too was holding his temper in by sheer will. 'It's one way or the other,' he flung back contemptuously. 'Either you rat on us, or you keep your mouth shut and get the benefits of our drive without taking any of the risk. You may have your choice, sir.'

Ellison picked up his wide Stetson and walked out of the room, his flat back as stiff as that of a drum major.

Calhoun Terry stood at his desk, salient jaw clamped tight. What Ellison had said was true.

He had either to warn the rustlers or let the drive go on. There was no middle ground. In any case he was now a man without a party. The rustlers and small cowmen hated him and would continue to do so. As soon as they heard his decision he would be detested by the big outfits. He would be held a traitor to both sides, and he would have to walk alone.

XIX

John Q. Powers descended from the train at Round Top and was met by Calhoun Terry. The two men walked to the Holden House, where the ranch foreman had taken rooms. Powers was a heavy-set, middle-aged man of a precise habit of mind. He wore square-toed shoes, a double-breasted coat, and a silk hat. His home was in Philadelphia, and he had never before been farther west than Chicago. The Powers family had bought for themselves and some business associates the Diamond Reverse B ranch at a time when capital was being poured into the cattle industry. So far it had been a good investment. There had been bonanza years when the ranch had returned more than thirty per cent on the original cost. But those boom days were past. The profits had dwindled, and the books showed for two years a balance in the red. A letter from the foreman had brought him out here in person. A shrewd investor, John Q. was moving to the opinion that it might be time to sell out.

As they walked to the hotel, Powers noticed that Terry did not exchange greetings with the men he met. The glances that fell on the Philadelphian were merely curious, but when they shifted to the foreman they held unconcealed hostility. There was a tensity in the atmosphere that John Q. did not like. His ideas of the West were vague. He thought of it as a wild country where there were possibilities of making money in spite of Indians, rustlers, droughts, and blizzards. Bad men, cowboys, and cattle filled the foreground of the picture.

They talked casually about the trip from Chicago until the door of the hotel room closed behind them. Then, without waste of time, Powers came to the business that had brought him here.

'You think we ought to close out the ranch?'

'I feel sure we ought,' Terry replied. An outfit as large as ours can't be run profitably under present conditions.'

'We can get a good price?'

'I think so. If the property is cut up wisely into small ranches. There would be no difficulty in disposing of the land.'

'I'd like to go out and look the situation over. You have made arrangements, I presume, to get me out to the ranch.'

'Yes. We can drive out. But I ought to tell you that there will be some danger.'

'Danger! What do you mean?'

'I have been shot at several times in the past three weeks, once as I was riding out of Round Top. A few days ago one of the owners of the Flying V C, James McFaddin, was killed while he was rounding up a bunch of stock.'

Powers stared at his foreman. 'Good God! Isn't there any law in this country?'

Terry smiled grimly. 'Plenty of it, and all on the side of the rustlers. Our enemies elect the sheriff and the judge, who try thieves before a friendly jury which acquits them.'

'As bad as that?'

'Just that bad, no matter how convincing the evidence we offer.'

'Then there is no way of stopping cattle-stealing?'

'Yes. There are ways.' The steel-barred eyes of Terry held to those of the Easterner. 'If we catch a rustler we stop him . . . permanently.'

The Philadelphian did not ask the question almost on his lips. He guessed the answer, and he did not want to get it in plain English. This method of justice was too stark for him.

'Do you catch many?'

'No. The ranch covers hundreds of miles of brush country. The thieves are smart and careful. Often they operate at night.'

'So we are really at the mercy of these rustlers.

There is nothing to do about it. This seems incredible, in the United States.'

The manager of the Diamond Reverse B decided not to spare the feelings of his boss. He had to know the truth before he could make an intelligent appraisal of the situation.

'It has been the law of Cattleland ever since the early Texas days that a horse or a cow thief forfeits his life if caught,' Calhoun explained. 'That was necessary then, because the law hadn't reached the brush country. It is necessary now, because the law has been taken over by the thieves. You are shocked because I have been shot at and McFaddin killed. These attacks were reprisals. Inside of a month four men suspected of rustling have been shot down from ambush.'

'But—but—'

'I don't know who killed them, but I can guess who ordered it done. You need not let this worry your conscience, Mr. Powers. The Diamond Reverse B is not guilty. I wasn't consulted, because those who did it were afraid I would oppose it.'

'But this is terrible. A suspected man has a right to his day in court. Maybe some of these men were innocent.'

'No. They were all outlaws, some of them killers. They deserved what they got. That is not the point. It was bad medicine. When we punish a thief it ought to be done openly before the world.'

John Q. Powers felt himself surprisingly helpless. He was a hard business man, and more than once he had driven a rival to the wall, but he now found himself in a world altogether too ruthless for him.

'Dear me!' he explained. 'I didn't realize it was like this. Of course you have written me about the rustlers, but I supposed you put them in the penitentiary when you caught them.'

'We would if we could. But we can't.' Terry judged it was time to let the Pennsylvania man have the other barrel of the gun. 'The worst is ahead of us, and coming very soon. I cannot go into particulars, or tell you how I know it. But there are plans for action soon that will make headlines in every New York paper.'

'I don't know what you mean, Mr. Terry. Please be more explicit.' The city man watched this hard, brown Westerner in fascinated alarm. Do you mean more . . . bloodshed?'

'Yes. Plans to rub out scores of men. In spite of ourselves we shall be dragged into it, unless we move fast. That's why I asked you to come at once.'

'How can we be dragged into it, if we refuse to be a party?'

'Because this country is in two camps. Everybody in this town is for the small fry against the big ranches. The rustlers and nesters and most of the little cattlemen are pooled against us, the honest men and the thieves alike. The Diamond

Reverse B is one of the large outfits. If we say we are out of this fight nobody will believe us. We'll suffer just the same. The only way to be out of it is to let it be known we are going out of business, to offer the ranch for sale in small blocks.'

Reports from Terry had kept Powers informed of increasing troubles in the Buck River country, but the Easterner had not realized how serious they were. Even the last urgent wire had not mentioned particulars. He could still hardly believe the foreman was not exaggerating the situation.

'Wouldn't it put us in the clear if I went on record publicly pledging the Diamond Reverse B to join in no lawlessness whatsoever?' he asked.

'No.' The foreman took out of his pocket clippings from a newspaper. 'Read these, Mr. Powers. They are from the *Logan County Gazette*, edited by Horace Garvey. He's against us and for the small settler. But he is an honest man, a first-class citizen. I cut the stories out so that you may see what the feeling of the average man here is in this fight.'

Powers settled himself back in his chair to read. The stories covered the five killings and the attempts on the life of Terry. Among the clippings were also editorials dealing with conditions in the district. Though Garvey tried to be fair, he was very plainly on the side of the plain rancher and homesteader and opposed to the big outfits. His editorial on the killing of

McFaddin was entitled, 'They have sown the wind, and they shall reap the whirlwind.' It did not condone the shooting of the Flying V C man, but it stressed the point that the policy of the 'cattle kings' had made such crimes inevitable.

'He makes out a case for our opponents,' Powers said thoughtfully after he had finished reading. 'I don't think he is right, but he seems to be honest.'

'No doubt of that. I thought you might like to meet him and asked him to call here. Not that I agree with what he thinks.'

Half an hour later Garvey arrived. After preliminary greetings the Philadelphian said dryly, 'I have been reading your editorials, Mr. Garvey.'

The near-sighted little editor peered over his spectacles and twisted his parchment-like face into a wry smile. 'And haven't liked them, I'm afraid, Mr. Powers.'

'It doesn't matter whether I like them or not,' the capitalist retorted. 'Question is, how true are they?' Powers waved aside the answer on the lips of the newspaper man. 'I don't care about your opinions, and I take it for granted that the facts of these stories are approximately correct. What I want to know is how closely you represent the majority feeling out here. Is this trouble likely to grow worse instead of better?'

Garvey said he thought he shared the views of

nine-tenths of the people in the district. It was his opinion the bitter feeling was likely to continue as long as the big ranches dominated the range industrially.

'I understand that your friends control the county politically,' Powers said.

'Yes.'

'A combination of townsfolk, small ranchers, and rustlers,' the Easterner snapped. 'Is that right?'

'Politics make strange bedfellows,' Garvey answered. 'The rustler vote supports our candidates, because the outlaw is naturally opposed to the large outfits.'

'Quite so. Opposed to the men they rob. Mr. Terry tells me we can't get justice in the courts when we present a case against a rustler.'

'That is correct,' the editor admitted. 'I'm sorry it is so, but there is a very strong feeling against the big cattle outfits.'

'Which you help to propagate.'

Garvey did not like the newcomer's manner. He hit back in self-defense. 'I am against a few non-resident cattle-owners monopolizing the range, if that is what you mean, to the exclusion of thousands of homesteaders.'

'The big ranches are here lawfully, aren't they?'

'That is debatable. Their cowboys homesteaded thousands of acres and turned the land over to their employers, quite contrary to the spirit of the law. All over the territory you find large tracts fenced by the cattle kings to which they haven't the slightest claim.'

Powers turned silently to his manager for verification.

'That is true of some ranches,' Terry admitted. 'Not of ours.'

'No,' assented the editor of the *Gazette*. 'But I have heard plenty of stories of Diamond Reverse B riders driving the stock of small owners from open range you wanted to use.'

'You'll hear anything, Horace,' his friend answered, neither assenting nor denying.

Powers leaned forward, tugging at his grizzled imperial. 'What would you think is the chance of disposing of the Diamond Reverse B at a good price, Mr. Garvey?'

'I don't know. Not very good, I should think. It would take a lot of money to buy it, and I don't suppose large interests are looking for investments in the cattle country these days.' He added as a rider: 'But I am not in touch with monied people. You should know much better than I do.'

Powers gave the editor the surprise of a year. 'I am not talking of large interests. We are thinking of dividing the property into small ranches and selling to individuals of moderate means. We would accept down payments for part and take a mortgage for the balance.'

Into Horace Garvey's dried-up face there came a curious expression of amazed delight. 'If you mean that, you will be doing a fine stroke of business for yourself and a great service to the territory, Mr. Powers,' the little man cried, his voice hopping up and down with excitement.

'We can find purchasers, you think?'

'No doubt of it, if your price is reasonable.'

'It will be.' Powers rose briskly. 'I'm ready to leave for the ranch whenever you are, Terry.'

'May I announce in the paper that you are going to divide the ranch and sell it?' Garvey asked.

'You may, sir. The sooner the better.'

'This is great news,' Garvey beamed. 'I believe it will be the beginning of better days than we have had for a long time.'

He left hurriedly, to write a front-page story.

XX

Calhoun Terry took no unnecessary chances with the safety of his passenger. He had brought to town with him three Diamond Reverse B riders. One of these he sent to the corral to hitch a horse to the buckboard. Another one took care of the horses. The third was a lad named Larry Richards.

At a nod from the ranch manager Larry bow-legged along the plaza past Pegleg Jim's pool room, the Crystal Palace, and the Evans store. He crossed the dusty road, spurs trailing, and strolled down a street leading from the square. Through the swing doors of the Red Triangle saloon he passed, drawing up to the bar.

There were half a dozen men in the room, and the quick eyes of the cowpuncher passed from one to another. Several of those present were inoffensive loafers. The two upon whom his gaze fastened were Lee Hart and Jack Turley. They were playing a game of seven-up.

Hank, the bartender, said, 'What'll you have, Larry?'

He was surprised to see a Diamond Reverse B man in the Red Triangle, a place largely patronized by those hostile to the ranch.

Larry did not want a drink, but he ordered one. He was here only to make sure that nobody made a hole in another pane of glass while the boss and his guest were passing.

Hart glanced up and stiffened. 'Important customers patronizing you these days, Hank,' he said offensively. 'Better get out yore best.'

Young Richards was a cool, daring man, with more than a streak of recklessness. He was a close personal friend of his boss.

'If it isn't Lee Hart,' he drawled, enthusiasm in his voice. 'How's everything with you? Good calf crop this year?'

The rustler started to jump to his feet, but thought better of it. He recognized an insult when it was addressed to him. But he knew too that Larry Richards was always ready to accommodate anybody who wanted to pick a fight with him.

He said, 'I'm not lookin' for trouble.'

'That's fine,' Larry answered. 'Neither am I. You had me scared for a moment, Lee.'

The rustler glared at him, an ugly look on his face. But it was Turley who answered.

'Did you come here to get a drink, Richards?' he growled. 'If so, there's your whiskey waiting for you.'

'Why, so it is,' Larry agreed in mock surprise. 'Much obliged to you for telling me, Jack.'

'You can't come in here and hurrah us, if that's your idea.'

'Don't you know I wouldn't try to get funny with the great Turley?' the Diamond Reverse B cowpuncher said reproachfully.

Hank polished the top of the bar with a towel. 'Now, gents,' he pleaded. 'Let's not have any difficulty.'

'Better tell this young squirt to finish his drink and get out,' Turley advised the bartender.

'On account of me having the smallpox?' Larry inquired.

'Men from your outfit are not welcome at Round Top,' Hart growled.

Richards recalled his instructions. He was posted here as a guard, with definite orders not to get into a fight. It would be better for him to sing small, but not small enough to encourage these men to jump him.

'I just dropped in for a last-chance drink on my way out of town,' he mentioned in a placatory voice. 'No offense meant, gents. I didn't know there was a deadline on our riders here.'

'Not exactly a deadline, Larry.' Hank polished vigorously. 'But you know how things are.'

'Sure . . . Sure.'

Larry grinned down into his drink and refrained from further amenities. His fool tongue would get him into serious trouble one of these days if he didn't look out. Why had he made that unnecessary crack about Lee Hart's calf crop? It was not supposed to be safe to monkey with that surly gent, though Larry was of private opinion it would be more healthy to tangle with him than with his quieter brother Nate, the sheriff.

The swing doors opened, to let in Slim.

'Dog my cats! Where did you drop from, Slim?'

Larry's expression of pleased surprise did credit to his ability as an actor, considering the fact that the arrival of the other Diamond Reverse B man was according to program.

'I been around,' Slim said. 'On my way back to the range now. How about you keeping me company?'

'I reckon I'll have to do that. Never saw it fail. When a fellow gets with a bunch of nice friendly guys someone comes along and drags him away. Well, *adios*, gents! Been nice to meet you.'

Larry flashed a derisive smile at the seven-up

players and turned his back to them. He rolled and lit a cigarette, then treated them to an amended snatch of a popular song.

> Oh, see the boat go round the bend,
> All loaded down with Diamond men,
> Good-bye, my lover, good-bye.

The legs of a chair in the back part of the room scraped against the floor. Somebody was getting to his feet hurriedly. Larry did not look round. His guess was that he had annoyed a seven-up player. He heard Turley's voice order harshly, 'Sit down, Lee, you damn fool!'

Blandly he said to his friend, 'Yeah, I reckon we better be hittin' the trail, Slim.'

The cowboys sauntered out of the Red Triangle, mounted the two horses at the hitch-rack, and cantered up the street. They caught up with the buckboard before it had reached the cattle chutes by the railroad tracks. From the driver's seat Terry slanted an inquiring glance at Larry.

'Everything all right?' he asked.

'Fine as silk.'

'See anybody you know at the Red Triangle?'

'Lee Hart and Jack Turley were there.'

'Either of them say anything?'

'Nothing important. Lee mentioned he wasn't lookin' for trouble.'

The foreman looked at Larry suspiciously. 'How did he come to say that?'

Larry was a picture of innocence. Just declaring peace intentions, I reckon.'

'Did Turley declare any?'

'He asked me if I came in to get a drink, and I said "Sure!" '

Terry asked no more questions. They were in the outskirts of town now, and the gray-green sage stretched away on either side of the long ribbon road. Calhoun guessed that there had been an exchange of verbal fireworks, but since there had been no casualties it did not matter. Larry had done what he had been sent to do—make sure that nobody from the Red Triangle would draw a bead on those in the buckboard.

'Do you always take a cavalcade of armed riders with you to town?' Powers wanted to know.

'Never before this trip,' the foreman answered, with a dry smile. 'This is an escort of honor for a distinguished guest.'

'To make sure he reaches the ranch safely?'

'Well, yes. I didn't want him to get a rustler's welcome.'

The party ate lunch at the Box 55 restaurant. Terry introduced Powers to Lane Carey and his daughter.

'They don't approve of me or of the ranch,' he explained to the Easterner. 'But since you are only the owner and not responsible for the way it is run, perhaps you will escape criticism.'

Powers had come West to find out all he could

about local conditions. 'Why don't you approve of the Diamond Reverse B, Mr. Carey?' he asked bluntly.

'I think it is one of the finest ranches in the West,' the cattleman answered. He was a little embarrassed at their directness.

'But you don't like the way it is managed.'

'I don't think you can find in the territory a young man who can handle stock better than Mr. Terry.'

'He's dodging,' the foreman said to Ellen, a gleam of laughter in his eyes. 'But it won't do him any good. Mr. Powers will keep asking questions till he finds out what he wants to know.'

They adjourned to the porch of the house. Carey talked plainly, as soon as he discovered that to do so would not be offensive to this stranger. Powers listened, fired more questions, learned the point of view of the small settler. It was not one with which he agreed, since he had been associated with big business all his life. But he was a man who faced facts. What Carey said confirmed the wisdom of the decision he had made, to sell out as soon as it could be done.

Ellen sat in silence, taking no part in what was said. Powers turned to her.

'What do the women think about this trouble?' he asked.

'They think it is terrible,' she said. 'What else can they think, Mr. Powers, when they see such awful things going on? Some of them are frightened to death for fear their sons or their husbands may never come back to them alive.'

'Because their men are thieves?' he went on, an edge of irony in his dry voice.

'I suppose they are.' Ellen carried on, impulsively. 'But what of that? The women aren't to blame. Some of them try to hold back their husbands and their sons, but they can't. If they lose them, it doesn't make them any happier to know that they brought it on themselves.'

'With the law in the hands of the thieves, honest men are not likely to have much chance.' Powers added, a satirical smile on his thin lips: 'If there are any honest men here. Your father seems to put us all in the same category.'

'My father is honest,' Ellen said stoutly. 'And there are plenty of others. Some of those who once in a while brand a calf not their own are good men in a way—good to their families, kind neighbors, generous to those in need.'

'Generous with other people's property,' the Philadelphian suggested. 'Well, no need threshing that out . . . I am going to step out of this feud before we get into it any deeper.'

A moment of silence followed his announcement. Lane and his daughter were puzzling out its meaning. The postmaster was not one to push into another man's business, but some answer seemed expected of him.

'I don't quite see how,' he said.

'You and Miss Ellen will have to transfer your disapproval to some other ranch and some other manager. We are going to cut up the Diamond Reverse B into small tracts and offer them for sale at attractive prices.'

Ellen felt a glow of joy beating up into her breast. If the Diamond Reverse B was broken up into smaller units, it was because under present conditions so large a ranch could not be made to pay. The No, By Joe and the other big outfits would have to follow the same course. The bitter feeling in the country would automatically disappear.

'I'm so glad!' she cried.

Her eyes were on Calhoun Terry. She was speaking to him, perhaps asking him to forget the hot anger with which she had turned away from him at their last meeting. He understood her words as an apology.

XXI

As Terry and Powers were leaving, Lane Carey noticed a newspaper sticking out of the Easterner's pocket.

'Is that a Denver paper, Mr. Powers?' he asked.

'The *Denver Republican*. Like to have a look at it?'

'At the cattle quotations, if you don't mind. I'm shipping next week.'

Carey took the paper, but he never got from it the information he was seeking. A front-page story caught and held his eye. The headline was:

RUSTLERS WAR IN WYOMING

The body of the story was not so definite as the headline, but it was alarming enough to Carey. The lead said that forty Texans had just reached the city and expected to leave within a day or two for some unknown point in the northwest. The Texans, the story stated, were rough-looking customers armed with revolvers and .45-70 Winchester rifles. Most of them had been sheriffs or deputy United States marshals in Texas or Oklahoma. None of them knew exactly where they were going, and there was an air of mystery about their arrival, heightened by the rumors to be heard around the railroad yards. The famous Sunday Brown was in charge of them, a man celebrated as a man-hunter in frontier days when the Indian Territory was a sink into which sifted most of the bad men of the Southwest. It appeared that Brown had been seen talking with Clinton Ellison, secretary of the Wyoming Stock Association, but Ellison in an interview denied any knowledge of the Texans. He had heard a Wild West Show was being organized. As to this, he had no positive information. One of the Texans, who asked not to have his name given, had admitted to the reporter that they were heading for the cattle country to clean up the rustlers who had been stealing so flagrantly.

Carey passed the newspaper to Terry, pointing to the story.

Calhoun read it, not a flicker of expression on his face. It disturbed him even more than it did Carey, since he knew and the Box 55 man could only guess.

'Maybe a reporter's yarn to fill space,' he said evenly.

From their manner Ellen judged that what they had read was serious. 'What is it, father?' she asked.

'I don't know as it is anything important, honey,' he answered. 'The *Republican* has a story about a bunch of Texas gunmen arrived in Denver, but likely that doesn't mean a thing to us.'

'May I see the paper, please?' she said.

Swiftly her eyes ran across and down the column. She pumped a question at Terry. 'Do you think they are coming to the Buck River country?'

'There's something in the story about a Wild West Show,' the foreman evaded.

'That doesn't mean anything,' Ellen replied impatiently. 'That's just something Mr. Ellison told the reporter. If they are coming here, what do they intend to do? One of the Texans said they were going to clean up the rustlers. Did he mean . . . kill them all?'

Carey watched Terry, the oldtimer's narrowed eyes a network of wrinkles at the corners. He waited to hear what the Diamond Reverse B man would say.

'I had a disagreement with Mr. Ellison,' replied Terry. 'When I told him I was urging Mr. Powers to cut up and sell the ranch. He felt I was deserting the big outfit group. I am no longer in the confidence of the association. Naturally they wouldn't tell me their plans.'

'But what do you think?' Ellen insisted. 'You must have an opinion.'

'I think that if I were a rustler I would be hitting the trail for parts unknown,' Calhoun answered, looking directly at her.

Ellen thought of the poor settlers she knew, some of them men with large families of small children. Perhaps some of them killed an unbranded calf when the little ones were hungry. Surely that was not a very serious crime. There were outlaws, too, bad men who had drifted in to prey on the cattle barons. Between these classes the girl drew a sharp line in her mind.

She worried about what she had read in the *Republican*, even after the foreman and Mr. Powers had left for the ranch. When Jeff Brand dropped into the crossroads stage station she lost no time in telling him the news. It was Ellen's opinion that the less she saw of Jeff the better. He was too good-looking, too insouciant and debonair and reckless, and his gaiety was too contagious. When a girl was with him she was likely to forget that he walked the wild and dangerous paths of an outlaw. So she had been avoiding him. But she thought he ought to know that the Diamond Reverse B was going out of business and that the Texas gunmen were gathered in Denver on some mysterious mission.

The second bit of information he dismissed lightly. He would not believe that they were heading for the Buck River country, and if they came the invaders would find the district too hot for them. The news about the Diamond Reverse B interested him more.

'It's the beginning of the break-up of the big ranches,' he told her excitingly. 'I'll say for Terry that he is smart. He sees that the large outfits are through. They can't buck the homesteader. The Diamond Reverse B will get out in time and save its hide. Some of the others are so stubborn that they won't.'

'Yes, they are stubborn,' she agreed. 'I'm glad Mr. Terry has broken with them. I never did believe he had anything to do with the killings.'

Brand slanted a quick look at her. 'Did he ever give you any hint who he thought the drygulcher was?'

'No. I'm sure he doesn't know, and if he did he wouldn't tell me. We're not friendly.'

He frowned down at the ground, drawing a line in the sand with his boot. 'I've spent a lot of time milling that over, girl,' he said. 'It's someone who knows our habits mighty well. He must have known Buck was going to be where he was the morning he shot him. The same goes for Tetlow and Yeager. Not many men would know that. I've been over the list of men in my mind forty times, but none of them seem to fit. Some of them are guys I would trust with my life. I have a specimen of his writing in my pocket now.'

'Let me see it,' she suggested. 'I've seen the writing of lots of people. When they send mail out, you know.'

He showed her the slip. Ellen read, 'This is what happens to rustlers.'

'Notice how the tails of his s's fly away,' Jeff said.

'Yes. I've seen the writing. At least I think so.' She looked up at him, the light in her eyes quick. 'I'm not sure, but—'

Silently, his gaze on her, Brand waited.

'Did you ever suspect that man Turley?' she asked.

'Yes, and knew it couldn't be Jack. He's too bitter against the big ranches.'

'That would be the play he would make, to protect himself.' She added: 'I believe this is his writing. I'm not sure, but it looks like it.'

He put the slip in his pocket, his eyes diamond-hard and bright.

'I'll have a talk with Mr. Turley,' he said, his voice low.

'You won't—get into trouble with him,' Ellen said, repenting of what she had said.

'Of course not.' His laugh was brittle. He changed the subject. About those warriors in Denver. I don't believe they are looking for us.'

'I asked Mr. Terry what he thought about these Texas gunmen,' she said. 'I mean, whether they were coming here. He said he had quarreled with Mr. Ellison and wouldn't know about any plans. But he looked straight at me, Jeff, and said that if he were a rustler he would light out and keep going.'

'He'd like to throw a scare into some of us he thinks are his enemies,' Jeff replied derisively. 'I don't scare that easy.'

'I'm telling you this so that you will let others know about it,' Ellen told him. 'Some of them may feel different from you about leaving.'

'I'll pass the word for those without nerve to light a shuck,' he answered lightly. 'Personally, I hope the Texas gents come. We'll try to be waiting at the gate for them.'

Ellen did not know whether she had been wise to warn him. It might only make more trouble. She wished too she had not mentioned Turley.

XXII

It was a special train consisting of two day coaches and three box cars. Light was beginning to seep faintly into the eastern sky. For hours the click of the wheels had lasted without a stop. Most of the men in the seats were asleep, slumped awkwardly in the confined space allowed them. Their booted legs sprawled out into the aisle.

They were a rough-looking lot, these Texans. Some were bearded, and a good many of the others wore long, drooping mustaches. Seasoned man-hunters, they were cool, tough specimens who had ridden hard and far into the brush after the men on the dodge wanted by the law. Many a desperado they had dragged out of the chaparral to justice. Others they had left there in shallow graves, later to turn in the report, 'Killed while resisting arrest.' Their leader, Sunday Brown, had been a noted deputy United States marshal in the days when train and stage robbers lived in the *bosque* and emerged only on nefarious errands.

At Jim Creek the engineer ran the train onto a siding. Sunday Brown passed through the cars, waking up his men and shouting 'All out . . . All out.' Sleepily the Texans came to life. They gathered up their baggage and their weapons, then filed down the aisle and dropped from the steps of the coach. Eight or ten men in chaps awaited them there. They were cattlemen and foremen of various outfits. Others would join them as the invaders moved deeper into the territory they meant to comb.

Sunday Brown was a big broad-shouldered man moving on toward fifty. He stood six foot in his shoes and weighed two hundred pounds of solid bone, gristle, and muscle. His weather-beaten face was hard and yet wary, as if years in the brush had dried out sympathy and sharpened suspicion.

He superintended the unloading of the box cars. From one the men took out blankets, saddles, bridles, food supplies, and ammunition. The mounts were led out of the other two, reaching the ground by a gangplank of heavy timbers.

Out of the brush three wagons emerged, Studebakers recently bought to carry the supplies. Into these the provisions, bedding, and ammunition were loaded.

Clint Ellison and John McFaddin led the cavalcade. They were familiar with the terrain, which was part of the country covered by their spring and fall roundups. The party followed a winding, narrow road through the sage to a ford on the North Fork. Through this the riders splashed to the bank beyond. One of the wagons, swinging too far to the left, went deep into the swirling water and almost overturned. Unable to get good footing among the slippery rocks, the horses could not budge the load. Riders looped the tongue with their ropes, the other ends attached to their saddle horns, and dragged the wagon from its precarious position.

The sun was beginning to show over the horizon edge, and far away its rays slanted on the blades of a windmill lower down in the valley. Startled antelope, moving down to water, bounded away as if on ball-bearing feet. A coyote crept its furtive way through the brush. On the side of a hill the riders caught a glimpse of startled cattle branded with the ◁B▷ .

Reminded of Calhoun Terry by the brand, Clint Ellison made bitter comment to his companion. 'We're risking our lives for that turncoat as much as for our own stuff. He sits tight and says he won't have any part in this, but his outfit shares the profits with us.'

'If any,' McFaddin amended. 'Too bad, Clint. You must of rubbed him the wrong way considerable when you had yore rookus with him. Thought you weren't going to tell him about the five hundred a head you were paying yore killer for gents designated. How come you to make that mistake?'

'He knew it had to be some of us. I didn't think he would go crazy and upset the apple cart.'

'Cal is a queer combination,' McFaddin said. 'Hard as nails, but with a soft streak runnin' through him. I was comin' up the street when that trouble blew up between him and the two bad men from Cheyenne. You never saw the beat of his coolness. They had their guns out first. It didn't last more'n six or eight seconds. They were whangin' away at him when his .45 got going. They plugged a hole in his arm. Well, sir, he shifted his six-gun and got them both, as you know. That's one side of him. Then there's the soft streak. He can't be thorough. My idea, rustlers are like wolves. Rub 'em out. But Cal thinks you got to give them a fair break like you would a white man. They done taken a couple of cracks at him from cover, but he is too stubborn to fight back their way.'

Ellison's gray face was set obstinately. 'The trouble with him is that he has too many friends among the rustlers. He used to be one of that crowd.'

'No, sir,' denied McFaddin promptly. 'He came of good, clean stock. His father, Barton Terry, was a fine citizen. Cal is all right, for that matter. Plenty of the small cattlemen are square shooters, Clint. They don't like rustlers any more than we do. I'm disappointed in Cal. But that's the way he is made.' He added after a moment: 'By the way, who is the bird who bumped off Buck Hart and his friends? Seeing it's all over now, you might as well tell me. I've got a guess, and I'm wonderin' if I'm right.'

The No, By Joe manager took his time to

answer. 'You paid your share, John, and I reckon you have a right to know,' he said at last. 'The fellow's name is Jack Turley. Do you know him?'

'I've met him. That's all. I don't want to know him any better. Fact is, Clint, we have to employ scalawags like him sometimes, but we don't have to like them any more than we would a sidewinder.'

'I'm expecting him to meet us somewhere in Box Cañon before we get to Johnson's Prong. Turley has been thick with the rustlers for some time. He knows where they roost and he is to guide us to them.'

'Damned spy!' the owner of the Flying V C spat out.

'We couldn't get along without inspectors,' Ellison said.

'He's no inspector, but a double-crossing son-of-a-gun. I'm not blaming you for using him, but don't you blame me for despising the rotten skunk.'

They passed the spot where Tetlow had been ambushed and rode up the draw leading to Box Cañon. Here the wagon road swung sharply to the right and followed the edge of the hills to find a way to the uplands. Ellison halted his little army to give instructions.

'We separate here,' he said. 'The wagons can't go up the cañon, of course. They'll follow the road past Renaud's homestead. If anybody makes inquiries, you are hauling supplies to the Becker coal mines. Don't get excited. The tarps cover the wagons and nobody will suspect anything unusual. We'll meet tonight at Packer's Fork. The rest of us have some clean-up jobs to do today. We're going up the gulch, and when we reach the prong are cutting across the hills. If anybody sees us they have to be stopped, no matter whether they are honest settlers or thieves. In case they try to run, shoot down their horses. Be careful not to hit them. We could easily make a serious mistake by getting the wrong men. We are hunting certain individuals known to us. It has to be made evident by us that decent citizens have nothing to fear. Is that clear?'

There was a murmur of assent.

McFaddin cut in to stress this. 'Get this right, men. If we should kill just one wrong man the jig would be up for us. We are rounding up thieves and outlaws, and nobody else.'

'It's easier to hit a horse than a man,' Sunday Brown contributed. 'But if any of you boys are standing where you can't be sure, don't take a snapshot. Let some other fellow stop the horse.'

'That's the idea,' Ellison said. 'If everybody is ready we'll take off.'

He led the way through the aspen grove and up the steep, crooked trail beyond. The path twisted among the boulders and climbed to the stunted pines above. It brought them to a long spur, at the upper end of the gorge, which ran out from Johnson's Prong.

Here Gaines, Collins, and several other stockmen joined the party. Two of them were small cowmen who felt they would be ruined if rustling was not stopped. One was a foreman of an outfit running cattle fifty miles away. Turley was not with them.

The leaders consulted together. They decided it would be better to wait for Turley. Without him as a guide it would be difficult to find the hideouts of the outlaws. If he did not arrive in half an hour they could start anyhow. They knew the general region they had to comb.

XXIII

As Jeff Brand rode back into the hills his mind brooded over the suggestion let fall by Ellen. He never had liked Turley. The man was ugly and mean. There was no generosity in him, and Jeff would not have bet two bits on his loyalty. But the fellow's animosity toward the big ranches had shielded him from suspicion. Yet his bitterness might be, as Ellen had said, merely a protective maneuver to cover his treachery.

Jeff tried to think back to the times when the killings were done, in an attempt to see if he could find an alibi for the crook-nosed man. His memory could not fasten on one. He was sure that Turley had not been with him at any of the periods when the assassinations must have taken place. Little things began to fit together. Jack owned a .45-70 Winchester, the weapon used by the killer. That in itself was nothing. Brand could name a dozen men who had one. It only showed he had the weapon handy. Turley had a habit of occasional absence. The boys had joshed him about it, hinting at an unknown woman, and he had smiled wisely, in effect pleading guilty to the indictment. Moreover, he was a comparatively new settler in the district. He could easily have been planted by the big outfits as a detective.

Brand drew off the trail for a few minutes to examine his gun. He was carrying the hammer on an empty chamber for safety, and he slipped in another cartridge. It was not likely he would need it, but if he did he would be needing it very badly. He made sure the weapon could be drawn from the holster without a hitch. Once he had seen a man wiped out because his revolver caught on a flap in the draw.

When Jeff rode up to the cabin on Turley's claim he found two other men there with the home-steader. One was Dave Morgan and the other Bill Herriott. Morgan had spent the night there, but Herriott had dropped in a few minutes earlier.

'What's new?' Bill asked after the first greetings.

Jeff dropped the bridle reins to the ground. 'A heap of things,' he drawled. 'You'll be surprised. First off, the Diamond Reverse B is quittin' business. Sellin' out lock, stock, and barrel.'

'Who to?' Herriott inquired.

'To Tom, Dick, and Harry. The big boss is on from Boston or somewhere. He was at the Box 55 with Terry, and he told the Careys they were cutting it up into small tracts to be offered for sale.'

They talked that over for a few minutes before Brand spilled his next piece of news.

'This guy from Boston had a copy of the *Denver Republican* with him. There was a piece in it about a big bunch of Texas warriors all garnished with guns ready to take off somewheres to clean out rustlers. Clint Ellison was seen with them. Chew on that awhile, gents.'

Jeff's eyes had not lifted from Turley as he told this bit of news. He thought the man's surprise was a little too pronounced to be genuine. But he was not sure of it. All three of them were excited by the possibilities.

'You think they are headin' this way?' Morgan asked.

Dave Morgan was a dark youth with a brittle manner and a face upon which time had etched the evidence of a fierce and uncontrolled temper. A twisted scar disfigured his forehead, souvenir of a brawl in a Mexican *tendejón* where knives had flashed.

'I wouldn't know. Do yore own figurin'.' Brand's hard, shallow eyes still held fast to Turley. 'What would you say, Jack?'

Turley was disturbed by the steadiness of that regard. 'Why, I wouldn't know, Jeff. Chances are there's nothing to it. It doesn't sound anyways reasonable. But maybe I'm wrong. What's your idea?'

'I haven't made up my mind for sure. Thought I'd wait till I heard from you.'

'From me?' Turley's startled face showed more than astonishment. 'Why, how would I know?'

'I expect you know a lot we don't, Jack,' Jeff answered, his voice ominously gentle. He pulled a piece of paper from his pocket and handed it to Herriott. 'Take a look at that, Bill, and pass it on to Dave. It was found pinned on Black Yeager's coat. The gent who killed him left a sample of his handwriting. I don't reckon you recognize it.'

Herriott frowned down at the paper, shook his head, and passed it to Morgan. He did not understand what Jeff was driving at, nor how it fitted into the present situation.

Morgan said, 'Can't prove a thing by me,' and passed the slip to Turley.

As Turley looked at it, a gray-green pallor spread over his swarthy face. He knew his Day of Judgment was at hand. Snatches of thought raced through his mind, but he could not organize them because of the rising fear in him. Brand could not know for certain. How could he? And yet . . .

'I . . . don't know . . . who wrote it,' he mumbled, and looked at Brand, despair in his eyes.

'I do.' Jeff's voice rang out crisp and hard. 'We've found the killer, boys. He's standing there with the paper in his hand that he left on Yeager's coat.'

'No . . . no! It's not true.' Turley gulped down his terror, to fight back. 'He can't prove it. Everybody knows how I hate the big ranches.'

'Everybody knows you have kept saying so,' Jeff replied coldly. 'The game's up, Turley. You've come to the end of yore crooked trail.'

Watching the trapped man's fear-filled face, Morgan realized that Jeff had found the guilty man. He did not know what his evidence was, but the completeness of Turley's collapse betrayed him.

'Better talk, Turley,' he advised ominously. 'Talk fast, if you don't want us to believe Jeff.'

'While he is talking you and Bill search the cabin, Dave. You might find money. A lot of it. He's been playing poor. Let's get wise about that.'

From a chalk-dry throat Turley offered an explanation. 'My folks sent me some money, boys.'

The two men walked into the cabin and began rummaging among its contents. They tossed out of the door boots, chaps, shirts, a coat and vest, and various other things. In a straw tick they found a rip, through which their exploring hands brought a canvas sack. In the sack were four packages of greenbacks.

'Count 'em,' Jeff said.

Not for an instant did he move his gaze from the face of the killer. The man's shock of terror, sweeping over him in the first surprise of the crisis that had leaped at him, was giving way to a cold desperation. Soon, now, when he knew for certain that he could not dodge or twist out of the trap, Turley would reach for his gun. Brand meant to be ready for that moment.

'Must be nearly two thousand dollars here,' Herriott said.

'Five hundred apiece.' Jeff's voice was cold as a mountain stream fresh from a glacier. 'They pay fine, don't they, Turley?'

'You've got it wrong, Jeff,' the killer croaked hoarsely. 'I wouldn't do that to boys I had bunked with. Don't you know I wouldn't?'

'Come clean,' Morgan snarled. 'Who hired you?'

'Nobody. That money came from my folks, like I said. Boys, I been your friend. You wouldn't—'

His voice died away in a quaver.

'You're bucked out,' Jeff said evenly. 'You're going on a long journey. Starting right damn now.'

The man looked round from one to another. His glance slid back to Jeff. 'Thing to do is . . .

talk this over,' Turley began, and stuck. There was no mercy in these implacable eyes.

'You didn't give Buck or Black or the other boys a show for their white alleys,' Jeff told him. 'You don't deserve one either. But I'm giving you one. Bill and Dave will keep out of this till I'm through. It will be one of us at a time. Don't keep me waiting, you—'

The guns came out together. The roar of them was almost simultaneous. But not quite. Jeff was the quicker by a fraction of a second.

Turley spun round from the shock of the bullet, clutched at his heart, and pitched forward full length. His finger twitched and a bullet plowed into the ground. A shiver went through his body. He lay still.

After a silence, Morgan said, 'That will be all for Mr. Turley.'

Herriott looked at Jeff admiringly. On the frontier, when occasion came, a man had to be thorough. Good or bad, he had to stand on his own feet and carry on with no law to back him except that he found in his holster.

'One shot was enough, Jeff,' said Bill. 'He's done gone on that long journey you mentioned.'

'Yes,' agreed Brand quietly, watching the prone figure. His arm had dropped so that the revolver pointed to the ground. From the end of the barrel a thin trickle of smoke came.

Morgan too looked down at the body of the

man caught in his treachery and snatched so swiftly from life. On his thin, fierce face there was a rancorous satisfaction. 'I wish I had done it instead of you, Jeff.'

'Two–three times I thought it might be Turley,' Brand said. 'But it didn't look reasonable. I reckon nothing could be lower than for a human to murder his friends for money. He must of known punishment might jump out at him, but some fools will do anything for profit. Well, he'll never spend his pay.'

'No.' Herriott looked at the greenbacks in his hand. 'What will we do with this blood money? I wouldn't want to spend a nickel of it.'

'Jim Tetlow left a wife and three children,' Brand said. 'Take it up Fisher Creek to her, Bill, when you head for home. Part of it is the price of her husband's death. The other boys weren't married. It will come in handy to feed the kids.'

'That satisfactory to you, Dave?' asked Herriott.

'Sure. It's coming to her.'

'Tell her to put it in the bank where it will be safe.' Jeff thrust the revolver back into its holster. 'I noticed some Flying V C horses down the trail a way as I came up. We'll rope one, tie the body on it and send it home with this carrion on its back.'

'Fine!' Morgan ripped out a malevolent oath. 'Telling them their killer has come back to report.'

Bill Herriott left for Fisher Creek on his errand

to Mrs. Tetlow. The other two rounded up the bunch of Flying V C horses, roped one, and brought it back to the cabin. They found a cross-buck pack saddle in the barn and cinched it to the animal. The body was made secure to the cross-buck by a lash-rope interlaced about the load. Jeff threw the diamond hitch expertly so as to absorb any slackness that might arise. Meanwhile Morgan penciled a note, printing it in capital letters to make identification of the writing impossible.

They had to drive the packhorse many miles, to be sure it would reach its destination. To these men, who felt themselves instruments of vengeance, it was important that their enemies should know why Turley had come to his death. Both of them knew this country. They had ridden it by day and night, on business legitimate and nefarious. Roads meant nothing to them when they were in the saddle, and for obvious reasons they did not care to meet travelers.

Through a stretch of pine forest they ascended, crossed a stream, and rode down along the skirt of a grove of quaking-asps into a park green with natural grass. The horse carrying the load had been running wild for months. At first it resented this infringement on its liberty. Two or three times it bolted, but the riders easily headed it back to the course they were following. After a few attempts to escape it gave up and took guidance tamely.

A man came down a hillside to meet them, a tall, thin man wearing leather chaps shiny from much use. The shirt, wide open at the bony throat, was torn and faded. There were gaping holes in the aged boots.

' 'lo, Jeff—Dave,' he said. 'What you fellows packing?' A tarp covered the load.

' 'lo, Alec,' Brand answered. 'Just a wolf we killed.'

Alec was an oldtimer. He had a little ranch in the mountains not too far from the Diamond Reverse B to have a good yearly increase in calves. He knew no reason why anybody should be hauling a dead wolf across the country. The palm of his hand scraped a lank, unshaven chin.

'Doggone it, what for?' he asked.

'This is a particular kind of wolf,' Morgan said grimly. 'You lookin' for strays?'

'Yep. A brindle cow I'm expectin' to come fresh.'

'Whose cow?' Jeff asked innocently, with intent to divert the mind of the nester from the wolf story.

Alec glared at him. 'Dad-gum yore hide, Jeff Brand,' he sputtered, and pulled up abruptly, the flare of temper dying in him.

Jeff had turned his amiable white-toothed grin on him. Even Morgan was smiling, if a little thinly. Alec threw up his head and laughed. He was among friends. Why resent a little joke founded on a fact well known to them all?

'I bought this cow, doggone you,' Alec explained.

They left him still chuckling. A little amusement had to go a long way in his drab life.

Brand and Morgan swung around Black Butte, leaving it far to their left. On Sage Hen Flats they met a cowboy. He rested in the saddle, his weight on one foot and on the thigh of the other leg.

'Where you headin' for?' he asked.

'Just maverickin' around,' Jeff told him. 'Know anything new?'

'Not a thing. Little while ago I saw John McFaddin and Tod Collins of the Antelope Creek Ranch close to Johnson's Prong.'

'What were they doing there?'

'I dunno. Kinda loafin' around, looked like. Well, so long.'

After the cowboy was out of hearing Brand made a suggestion. 'What say we drift down in the general direction of the prong? Might as well deliver our freight there as anywhere else.'

They crossed the tableland into a hilly country where they gradually wound down toward Johnson's Prong. The two men moved cautiously now, their eyes searching the spread in front of them. When at last they came suddenly on three horsemen at the foot of a little draw, Brand noticed instantly that they were strangers. Swiftly he said to his companion, 'Don't start anything.'

The strangers were watching them, their horses motionless.

'Some freight for McFaddin and Collins,' Jeff called. 'Seen 'em?'

After a pause one of the men said, 'Yes.'

'Fine. Turn it over to them. Be seeing you later.'

Jeff wheeled and led the way round the bend, then went to a canter.

Someone shouted to them to stop, but they kept going. They heard the pounding of hoofs behind them. Just before they disappeared over another hill a rider showed at the head of the draw. He shouted again, then fired, too hurriedly for accuracy.

'This way,' Morgan called to his companion, and slid into a hollow between two rises.

The country was a huddle of hills, and inside of a few minutes their pursuers had completely lost them.

'Who were those fellows?' Morgan asked. 'They're mighty quick to burn powder. I'll say that.'

'Yes. With few questions asked.'

'Must be warriors of some of the big outfits.'

'Yes, but not cowboys.' Brand's eyes were shining with excitement. 'Part of this army the *Republican* was tellin' about.'

Morgan pulled up his mount. 'Hell! It might be that-away. We'd better find out for sure, and if it's so get word to the boys.'

'Just what I'm thinking, Dave. Let's scout around and find out how big a bunch of them there are.'

They talked it over together, then made a wide circle to strike Johnson's Prong from the pines above.

XXIV

A Texan led the packhorse back to the camp among the pines.

'Couple of fellows brought some freight in for Mr. McFaddin and then lit out like the heel flies were after them,' he said. 'The other boys are chasin' them. They acted right funny.'

McFaddin and Ellison stepped forward.

'I'm not looking for any freight,' the Flying V C man said. 'But that's my horse all right. It has been loose on the range with a bunch of others.'

'Better unpack and find what it is,' Ellison suggested.

'Sure. Hop to it, boys.'

The Texan released the diamond hitch and whipped off the tarp. A body slid to the ground. Those present stood staring at what they saw. Sunday Brown stepped closer and stooped over the dead man.

'Spang through the heart,' he said.

Ellison leaned over him. 'It's Jack Turley, one of our stock detectives,' he said.

'By God, they got the double-crossing killer,' McFaddin said bluntly.

From the coat pocket Ellison drew the note Morgan had written.

> Here is yore killer [he read]
> come back to report.

Collins looked at Ellison. 'So this fellow was the killer.'

'That's a closed chapter,' the No, By Joe manager replied.

'Closed for Turley,' McFaddin snapped. 'Whoever did this has got his nerve, bringing the body to our camp. And how did they know we were here? It's supposed to be a secret.'

They looked around at one another, startled. Before they had actually started on their clean-up their enemies had flung this melodramatic challenge at them. Were their plans known and foredoomed to defeat?

Ellison called to him the Texan who had led in the packhorse.

'What did the two men say when they turned the horse over to you?' he asked.

'Only said this freight was for Mr. McFaddin and Mr. Collins and for us to see they got it. One of 'em yelled they would be seeing us later.'

'What did they look like?'

'I wouldn't know. They weren't close. Just like any two guys on horseback.'

'That fellow you and I met, John, must have told them we were here,' Collins said.

'What else did he tell them?' Ellison asked acidly. 'That there were forty or fifty strangers with you, all heavily armed, just out having a look at the scenery?'

The rubicund face of Collins stiffened. 'How could he tell them that when he didn't see anybody but us? That's why we let him go.'

'Anyhow, we had better move fast,' Gaines said. 'After being chased off the map these two fellows must suspect something.'

'Let's go,' McFaddin said with a sardonic laugh. 'We don't have to wait any longer for Turley to guide us. He's here. A little late for his appointment with us, but I reckon he couldn't help that.'

They were off to an inauspicious start. To most of them the arrival of Turley's dead body, with the crisp, jeering note attached, was a bad omen they found it hard to shake off. Moreover, the secrecy they had depended on as an aid to swift success was gone. The men who had brought the packhorse must know there was something up. They would spread their misgivings far and wide.

The regulators, as the invaders called themselves, looked to their cinches and mounted. From the prong they wound up through the pines into a country of open range too wild for homesteaders. The spread was too rocky and too hilly to invite settlers. Presently they would cross a mountain spur from which they would drop down into a district of gulches, rock rims, and small valleys where at not too frequent intervals a few nesters and cow thieves held the fort unmolested, except when posses from the big ranches came hunting stock that was missing. On Ellison's list were the names of a dozen men who lived in this section. He and his allies meant to wipe out as many of these as they could in a few hours and sweep on up to the neighborhood of the big ranches, where they would establish a base for operations.

They straggled forward in no formation, Ellison and McFaddin in the van. From a long, rocky slope they came into a little mountain park, not far from the summit, a saucer-shaped depression fringed on the far side with jack pines. Just beyond this was the backbone of the spur they were climbing.

McFaddin lifted a shout of warning and whipped up his rifle. Two men had appeared on the rim and started to ride down, but at sight of the large company pulled up and turned. One of them flung up a hand in protest as the Flying V C man's gun cracked. The echoes of that shot rolled across the valley. A sorrel horse stumbled and flung his rider, then raced across the slope with reins flying wild. The man who had given the

Indian peace sign called to his companion. It was almost as though the dismounted man had bounced back from the ground, so quickly was he on his feet. He ran a few steps along the hillside and vaulted to the back of the uninjured horse behind his friend. Three or four Texans fired, but the horse and its double load reached the rim and vanished.

Giving the cowboy's 'Hi-yi-yippy-yi!' McFaddin brought his cowpony to a canter and pursued. The others followed him. From the summit they looked down on a tangle of huddled hills, little valleys, and dark cañons. The terrain looked like ideal cover for outlaws. A man who knew the district might hide for weeks in unsuspected pockets.

A roan horse, carrying two men, was traveling fast down the side of the spur but was already showing signs of distress.

'We've got 'em!' yelled McFaddin. Come on, boys.'

It looked as though he was right. The fugitives were losing ground rapidly. Bullets whizzed past them. Again the man back of the saddle lifted his hand to give the Indian peace sign. But there was to be no peace for him today. The invaders meant to capture him, and to hang him if his name was on the list Ellison carried.

Just ahead was a little clearing with a log cabin on the edge of a creek. A man had appeared from behind it driving a few cattle. He was at casual ease, in no hurry whatever. At the sound of the roaring guns he swung his head, took in the situation, and instantly forgot there was such a thing as leisure in the world. While the fugitives were still a good two hundred yards distant he jumped his horse to a gallop and vanished up a draw.

The hunted men flung themselves from the back of the horse and ran into the house. The door slammed behind them. The pursuers dragged their horses to a halt and many of them dismounted. Frightened by the firing, the horse of the men in the cabin splashed through the creek and bolted.

Ellison took command. He named four or five men to follow the cowman who had disappeared up the ravine. The others he distributed about the place, most of them in or back of the barn, which was over seventy-five yards from the house. Several he stationed across the brook in the brush near the edge of the clearing. A steady, intermittent sniping centered on the cabin. Already its windows were shattered. The defenders had dug spaces in the dry mud between the logs of the walls, which they used as loopholes for their guns. One had a rifle. Apparently the other was armed only with a revolver.

The door of the cabin opened a few inches and a hand came out to wave a white flag. A voice called out something that was drowned in the crash of guns. Quickly the arm and the rag were with-drawn, the door shut and bolted.

'Why not let them surrender?' Gaines asked. 'Save us some time and trouble.'

'Let 'em surrender and then hang 'em?' McFaddin asked harshly. 'No, by Jackson! I won't stand for that. If we're going to hang 'em we'll have to dig 'em out.'

'We don't even know they are on our list,' Collins said.

'We know damn well they are. They are the same scalawags who brought Turley's body back. If they hadn't been rustlers they would have held up their hands and let us take them. . . . Oughtn't to be much trouble to collect them.'

The forted man with the rifle served notice he was not to be taken too lightly. He wounded in the arm a ranch foreman who exposed himself rather carelessly. Ellison passed the word among his men not to take any unnecessary chances. A few moments later a bullet tore through the calf of one of the Texans.

The men who had pursued the cowman returned after a time. On account of his long start they had failed to catch him. This was disturbing. It meant that news of the invasion was bound to get out. The leaders held a consultation.

'We can't fool away the rest of the day here,' McFaddin said impatiently. 'To heck with this siege stuff. I move we charge the cabin and wipe 'em out.'

'Losing three or four men!' Ellison scoffed. 'That would be dumb of us.'

Collins made a suggestion. 'You're both right. What say Clint stays here with ten or twelve men and attends to this business while I take the rest and sweep the hill pockets? I can get back before dark.'

After some discussion the Antelope Creek man's plan was adopted.

'It's not foolproof, Tod,' Gaines said. 'But it looks to me as good as any.'

McFaddin said he would ride with Collins. There were some thieves in this district he had been wanting to get a crack at for a long time.

'Be sure not to let yourselves get cut off from us,' Ellison cautioned. 'And don't waste any time. We've got about four hours, I would guess. Five at the most. By that time we'll have to be on our way, or we may not get out of here at all. Whatever happens, don't be tempted to swing too wide a loop. I don't like being so deep in the enemy's country. I'll feel better when we reach Packer's Fork. Once there, it won't be so easy to cut us off from our own district.'

Collins promised to be back in time.

McFaddin nodded. 'Sure. You do your job here and we'll do ours. All I hope is that the fellow who got away hasn't warned every thief to escape. I don't see how he can have got to all of them.'

The sound of the firing on the cabin followed his party into the hills.

XXV

Ellen was making up a post-office report that had to be sent to Washington when she saw a horseman emerge from a fissure in the hills and come down the long slope to the ranch at a gallop. He was flogging his mount with a quirt. Jim Budd was at the door, leaning against the jamb, resting from the exertion of having swept the floor. It was in his horoscope that he would go through life as easily as he could.

'Seems to be a gen'elman in a hurry, Miss Ellen,' Jim drawled.

'Yes.' The girl watched the rider through the window. A faint unease stirred in her. Men did not usually ride like that except to carry bad news. She was glad to know her father was stringing barbed wire for a new pasture. It could not be about him.

The rider drew up in front of the post-office and flung himself from the horse. The man was Lee Hart. He spoke to Ellen, who had come out to the porch.

'Where's Lane?' he demanded.

'Father is down with the men fencing a new pasture,' Ellen answered. 'About three miles due west from here . . . Do you have to see him?'

Hart mopped his perspiring forehead with a bandanna handkerchief. 'Never saw it fail!' he cried bitterly. 'Need a man and he ain't there.'

'What's wrong, Lee?' the girl wanted to know.

'Wrong! Everything.' The heavy-set, bow-legged man slammed his dusty old hat on the porch floor. 'A bunch of wild Injuns is raidin' this country. They came bustin' down on my place with forty guns a-poppin'.'

'Indians?' the girl repeated incredulously.

'Well, these Texas warriors the paper was telling about. They was chasing two guys. I lit out lickety-split.'

'Who were they chasing?'

'I dunno. They're likely wiped out by now. They hadn't but one horse between them. When I took my last look they were making for my house to hole up.'

'What do you want with father?'

'Well, we got to spread the news to everybody. I'm headin' for Round Top. Someone has got to ride up the Alford road and let the settlers there know. Tell 'em to meet here. Send this nigger if you haven't got anybody else.'

'No,' Ellen said promptly. 'I'm not going to get Jim mixed up in it.'

'Mixed up in it? You tellin' me yore black

man is too good to work with us?' Hart snarled.

'I'm telling you it is none of his business.'

Hart fastened his gaze on two horsemen coming down the road at a slow trot. In his eagerness to tell the news to Jeff Brand he forgot his indignation. He bowlegged through the dust to meet the riders as they drew up at the hitching-post.

'Have you heard, Jeff? The big outfits have done brought a bunch of Texans here to run us outa the country. Paul Vallery told me this mo'ning. He got it from Lane Carey who read it in the *Denver Republican*. Well, sir, I seen them comin' down the hill hell-for-leather and lit out just in time. They was chasin' two birds.'

Brand swung from the saddle to go forward to meet Ellen. 'Chasing who?' he asked over his shoulder.

'I dunno. Couldn't wait to find out. I burned the wind getting away from there.'

'You don't know what became of the two men?'

'They got into my house and forted up, but I reckon they couldn't hold out long. Must of been a hundred in that army.'

'Fifty-eight,' Brand corrected.

'How do you know?'

'We hid on a ridge and counted them,' Morgan said.

'A bunch of warriors brought in to shoot down

innocent men!' Hart cried angrily. 'We'll see about that. I'm on my way to tell our friends at Round Top.'

'No need,' Jeff said. 'We've already sent a messenger. 'Better stay and gather a relief party to ride over to your place. We'll need every man we can get.'

'When do you aim to go?'

'We've got to get off right quick if we're going to save the boys they have trapped. Say inside of an hour.'

'We can't get together seventy or eighty men that quick,' Hart protested.

'Don't need more than ten or a dozen. We'll lie in the rocks above and shoot down at them.'

'Not me,' Hart answered promptly. 'I just got out with my skin, and I don't aim to try it again.'

Jeff looked at the man contemptuously. 'Thought your specialty was shooting from cover,' he jeered.

'My specialty ain't committing suicide,' the bandylegged man snapped, stung by the other's gibe. 'I'll take reasonable chances, but I ain't foolhardy.'

'Go hide under a bed, you louse.' The pale blue eyes of Brand burned into the man. 'But not till you've done your job. Ride up the Alford road and send down all the men you can find. After that you can go jump in a lake.'

Jeff turned away and joined Ellen on the porch.

He grinned at her. 'Well, sometimes a newspaper piece turns out to be true,' he said.

'You feel sure this crowd is the one the *Republican* told about?' she asked.

'Sure. Two-thirds of them were strangers to us. They are a tough-looking bunch, but not tough enough for the job they are tackling.'

Morgan joined those on the porch. 'I'd better ride Deep Creek and warn the folks up that way. From what Lee says looks like these fellows are headed there.'

'Yes. Better rope one of the horses in the corral.' Jeff added casual information. 'I'm going to Lee's place to see what has happened to the two trapped in his house. Maybe I can make a diversion from the rocks that will help them.'

'Must you, Jeff?' asked Ellen in a low voice.

He nodded. 'Can't desert two of our men without trying to help them.' His manner was cheerful and nonchalant. 'Dave has picked the tough job. He's liable to meet a bunch of these Texans any turn of the road. But someone has to warn our friends.'

'I suppose so. But you don't have to go and attack fifty men, do you?'

Brand's gaze followed Morgan as that young man swung on his horse to ride to the corral. 'He'll do it, too, if they don't get him first. That guy will do to ride the river with.' His attention came back to what the girl had said. She could see that excitement was quickening his blood. 'This isn't any Arnold Winkelried stuff like we read about in our Sixth Reader. I don't aim to step out and ask them to shoot holes in me.'

'I don't see what you can do alone.'

'Can't tell till I get there. Soon as a bunch of the boys roll in tell them to hop over to Lee's place fast as their broncs will bring them.'

She watched him, always spectacular, fling himself into the saddle without touching the horse. He waved his big white hat in farewell as he rode away. The girl's heart sank. He was so brave and loyal, had so many good points. But all his fine qualities were neutralized by the one fatal lack in him.

XXVI

From the Box 55 to Lee Hart's place it was eight miles across the hills. Jeff rode fast, for he knew it could be only a question of time until the defenders were overwhelmed by numbers. He had not the least idea who had taken refuge in the cabin. It might be outlaws whose activities were wholly illegal, or it might be settlers who only rustled occasionally on the side. In any case they were allies of his, men who had a claim to his support in such an emergency.

Before he had covered half the way to the hill

ranch he heard the sound of firing far to his left. The explosions came faintly, as firecrackers do when set off at a distance. First a single shot, and perhaps a minute later two more. Though he listened for more, no popping reached his ears.

To Jeff there seemed something sinister in these breaks disturbing the silence. His imagination pictured a man peacefully hoeing a potato patch or mending a fence. From the direction of the report it might have come from Wade Scott's place. If so, Wade would probably have been whistling, his mind on a girl in Cheyenne who worked in the railroad restaurant, one he was expecting to marry in a few months. Jeff could see Wade look up in surprise, to see vigilantes closing in on him. He could see him turn to run, the smoke of guns, the buckling of his knees as he went down.

Later Jeff heard more shots, but these were from the Hart place. Since this meant that the defenders were still holding off the attack, he was glad to hear them. He rode fast till he reached the top of the ravine which ran down to the Hart clearing just back of the house. Instead of taking the gulch he followed the rim, keeping to cover as he came close to the edge. Looking down, his gaze swept the clearing and picked up details. He saw two men crouched back of the barn. Evidently there were others in it, for as he stood there a puff of smoke came from the window opening in the hayloft. At least one man was stationed in the bed of the creek a hundred and fifty yards from the house. A shot from that point told him so.

There was a small alfalfa field to the left of the house. It ran to the draw leading up to the ravine. He could see the ditch crossing it in the direction of the house. Rank grass covered the edges. A wild idea jumped to his mind. Why not get into that ditch, crawl along it till he was close to the cabin, and make a dash to join the defenders? It was the sort of plan to catch Jeff's fancy. He felt the pulse of excitement beating in his throat which for him always accompanied danger. By heaven, he would try it.

Near the top of the ravine he picketed his horse, then moved down it cautiously. It was possible one or two of the sharpshooters were placed near the bottom of it in a position to command the house. As he came round a bend in the gulch, he looked down into the little basin which held the ranch. Thirty yards below him a man crouched behind a large boulder, a rifle in his hands. He was watching the log cabin, evidently hoping to get a glimpse of one of the defenders. Lower down in the draw and fifty yards to his right another marksman was also waiting behind cover for a shot.

Jeff tiptoed forward, revolver in hand. He had not been a big-game hunter for nothing. No perceptible rumor of his movements reached the lank Texan toward whom he was soft-footing. Unwittingly the sniper helped at his own undoing.

Intensely preoccupied with the job in hand, his mind was following a single track which led straight from him to the quarry in the cabin. When Brand was about ten strides from him he drew a bead and fired. As the rifle cracked Jeff flung aside caution and took the last stretch on the run.

The Texan whirled, too late. The long barrel of the .45 smashed down on his lifted forehead. His body swayed, and collapsed. Jeff pistol-whipped him again, to make sure he would not come back from unconsciousness too soon.

Nobody had noticed what had taken place. Jeff helped himself to the man's rifle and cartridge belt. He moved to the left and stepped down into the dry ditch he had seen from the bluff above. Crouching low in it, he crept forward. The alfalfa hid him pretty well. If he were seen by the attackers he would probably not be molested, since he would be taken for an ally of theirs trying to get close to the enemy.

Crossing the field was a slow business. He went on all fours, dragging the rifle beside him. The firing was intermittent. Occasionally the reverberating crash of a gun beat across the basin. He was near enough the cabin to see lead fling splinters from the logs. At this point the ditch deflected at a sharp angle. Every foot he took in it now would take him away from his destination.

He called softly, 'Hello the house,' and when no answer came back to him he called again, more loudly. It was after his fourth attempt that somebody inside answered.

'Who is it? What you want?'

'Jeff Brand. I'm gonna make a run for the door. Fling it open for me when I give the word.'

There was a perceptible silence before the man in the house replied. 'How come you there —if you're Brand?'

'Don't talk, you fool. Do as I say.'

Jeff came out of the ditch running. The distance was greater than it had looked from the bluff above; nearer fifty yards than the twenty he had guessed it. But he could not go back now.

From the edge of the valley he heard a shout. Somebody had discovered the Texan he had knocked out and was spreading the news. The guns roared. A bullet whistled past his head. Involuntarily he ducked, still racing for the cabin. Twenty yards more would do it.

He bowled over, all the power knocked out of him in an instant. That he had been hit he knew, though he felt no pain. Still clinging to the rifle, he tried to clamber to his feet. The ground tilted up at him, and he went down again. Still conscious, he crawled forward a foot or two.

A splatter of sand kicked up in front of him. Another bullet parted his curly hair.

The cabin door was flung open. Two men showed at the entrance. One ran toward Jeff, in long, reaching strides. The other covered the rescue, firing at the figures which had come into the open to get Brand. It was a matter of seconds, but they stretched interminably. The first man reached Jeff, gathered him up, and plunged back toward the house. As he crossed the threshold the man with the rifle slammed the door shut.

XXVII

Calhoun Terry and Larry Richards, on their way to Round Top to meet a cattleman who had a registered Hereford bull for sale, struck across country to hit Johnson's Prong and take the short cut down Box Cañon. They traveled at a road gait, not pushing their horses, for there was a long journey ahead of them. It was not necessary for them to make talk, since they were knit in close friendship tested by a hundred experiences shared together.

When they talked it was mostly about a new enterprise in which they were to be partners. They had made an arrangement with John Q. Powers to buy the old Terry Ranch once owned by Calhoun's father, and with it a fine stretch of river land adjoining. Larry had lately inherited some money. This was to make part of the initial payment. The rest of it was to come out of Terry's interest in the Diamond Reverse B. Six hundred cattle branded with the ⬦B⬦ were included in the deal.

There would be enough cash left for current expenses.

'You're getting the most unpopular man on Buck River for a partner,' Calhoun said. 'The little fellows and the big outfits have just one thing in common. They both agree that I'm a deserter and a traitor.'

'Inside of a year all that will be forgotten,' Larry predicted. 'The big ranches will be following your example. The bad feeling will pass away soon as the friction is removed, and the settlers will give you credit for taking the first step to straighten things out.'

They came to the lip of a small mountain park and dipped down into it. Terry pulled up his cow-pony and pointed to the opposite slope. A large body of men on horseback was moving down it.

'The Texas invaders,' Larry said instantly.

'Yes, and we'd better get away from here,' his companion decided. 'When they see us they will hold us prisoners, to make sure we don't spread the news. That wouldn't suit us. We don't want to be identified with them.'

Too late, they wheeled their horses. The sound of a rifle shot roared across the park. Larry's horse went down and flung him. His friend raised the palm of his hand to give the peace sign, but the answer was a splatter of bullets.

'Come a-running, Larry,' called Terry.

Richards vaulted to the back of the horse,

and they were on their way. From the ridge they headed down into a country of huddled hills and ravines where outlaws had their abode. The roan gelding did its best, but when Larry looked back he knew the race would be a short one.

'They're coming hell-for-leather,' he said. 'We won't reach the hills.'

He held up his hand in the peace sign, but it did not stop the crashing of the guns.

'We'll have to hole up at Lee Hart's till we get a chance to explain we're not the men they want,' Terry said.

'Yep. There's Lee down there with his stock. He isn't waiting to ask questions either.'

'Don't blame him. He's on their list.'

They reached the clearing, flung themselves from the horse, and raced for the cabin by the creek. Once inside, they slammed and bolted the door. From the window Larry saw the leader of the regulators disposing of his men.

'I could bump that fellow off with yore rifle, Cal,' he said. 'He figures we can't shoot, I reckon. It's Clint Ellison.'

Terry joined his companion at the window. 'Yes, it's Clint. He doesn't know who we are, but I don't think he would mind picking me off, sort of accidentally, even if he did.'

They could hear bullets thudding into the logs. One shattered the other window.

'We'd better move back out of sight,' Larry

suggested. 'Have to dig out holes between the logs to shoot through.'

'I'll try a white flag,' Calhoun said. 'If they'll hold back long enough to listen to us we'll be all right.'

He found an empty flour sack, opened the door a few inches, and waved the white sack. He called out his name to Ellison. The noise of the guns killed the sound of his voice. Lead tore into the door.

'Quit that foolishness, Cal,' his friend snapped. 'You'll get shot up, first thing. The darned fools are crazy with the heat.'

With their knives they dug away the mud plaster between two logs. They had to have sights for shooting and they could not use the window spaces. Already the shattered glass on the floor showed the enemy fire was concentrating there. As yet the defenders had not fired a shot and the gunmen outside were growing bolder. Some of them began to press closer.

'Have to stop that,' Calhoun said.

He did not want to kill anybody. A time would come, he hoped, when he could let the cattlemen know who they were. He had recognized Tod Collins and John McFaddin. They had been associates of his only a short time ago, and he did not want to hurt either of them or any of their party. But his warning had to be effective.

A foreman of the Circle C C ranch, a big, blustering fellow who rode his men hard, was gesticulating violently and pointing toward the cabin. Apparently he was urging them to a charge. Terry shot him in the arm, and he took cover behind the barn. During the rest of the battle he was not seen again by the besieged men. A few seconds later Calhoun's rifle scored another hit. A lumbering Texan behind a cottonwood tried to improve his position by running to another tree closer to the house. He stopped before he reached it, lurched sideways, and fell to the ground. With scarcely a moment's delay he began crawling back to his original position.

'You got him!' Larry cried.

'In the leg. I didn't want to kill him. Maybe his friends will get the idea that they haven't been invited to come any nearer.'

'Some folks can't take a hint unless a Methodist church falls on them,' Larry said lightly. 'Wish I had a rifle too. My six-gun won't carry that far with any accuracy. Looks like I'll have to be an innocent bystander until they begin to crowd us.'

Both of them knew there could be only one ending to the battle if it went to a finish. But they were cool, game men, used to danger, and they could take whatever was in store for them without weakening.

The attackers grew more wary of exposing themselves. Presently the firing died down except for an occasional shot.

'Something's up,' Calhoun said. 'Probably

getting ready to rush us.' He laughed sardonically. 'I never was in this kind of a jam before. All we have to do is let them know who we are and they would let us alone, but as soon as we poke a nose out to tell them they blast away at us.'

Larry was watching the attackers through his peephole. 'They are getting their horses.' His voice grew excited. 'By the jumping horned frog, they're riding away. They figure it would cost too much to dig us out of our hole. Seems too good luck to be true.'

It *was* too good to be true. More than forty men took a trail into the hills, but enough were left to keep up the attack on the cabin. Terry tried again, during the lull in the firing, to let Ellison know who they were, but he was fired upon the instant he opened the door. The No, By Joe manager had nothing to discuss with the two rustlers he held cooped in the house. His intention was to wipe them out.

For nearly an hour he kept up a desultory firing, most of it from the sharpshooters stationed in the barn and among the brush at the foot of the ridge. At the end of that time he stopped the waste of ammunition and tried another plan to dislodge the besieged men. Two horses were taken into the barn. A few minutes later they came out drawing a wagon with a hayrack on it.

'Will you tell me what the blazes that is for?' Larry asked.

The wagon was driven through a poor man's gate[1] into a meadow of wild hay. Near the center of the field was the remains of a stack of hay, most of it weeds tossed aside as unfit food for stock. Men began to gather this trash with pitchforks and load it on the rack.

At first Calhoun was puzzled, but the purpose of this jumped to his mind. 'You picked the right word when you said "blazes," Larry. Ellison is going to burn us out.'

Larry caught the idea. 'Sure. They aim to get behind the hay and push the wagon by the tongue up against the house. Then they will set fire to the hay.'

'Go to the head of the class, Master Richards. That's just what they intend to do.'

After a moment Larry spoke. 'You've been favoring these fellows, Cal, and that was right so far. But no longer. They mean to kill us, even if they have to burn us up. It's them or us. I won't let them rub me out without fighting back.'

Calhoun nodded agreement. 'Nor I. But maybe the time hasn't quite come for that, Larry. The thing is to delay them all we can. Help is on the way to us by now, I expect. Hart could not have recognized us. He thinks we are some of his outlaw friends. When he reaches Black Butte he

1 A poor man's gate is made by three strands of barbed wire attached to a pole at each end.

will start gathering men to save us. That will take some time, but not very much if we are lucky.'

'You mean if there's a bunch of men at the post-office. Not likely this time of day. Besides, they would have to get their rifles before they came. No use foolin' ourselves. Help won't reach us before night.'

Terry found no words to refute that. His friend had said what he too thought. When the attempted rescuers arrived it would be too late to do any good.

'If they try to rush the house I'll show myself at the window,' he said. 'When they are close they will recognize me.'

'After they have pumped lead into you.'

Terry did not answer. He was watching the wagon and the men with it. They had loaded the refuse hay and were picking up brush to pile on the top of it. The driver swung the team round to return to the gate. He was nearer the house than at any time since leaving the barn.

Calhoun took careful aim and fired. One of the horses sank to the ground.

'That will hold them for a while,' he said.

'Good shot!' Larry applauded. 'Must be four hundred yards. Watch the brave boys scurry for cover.'

There was a flurry of renewed firing at the cabin. For ten or fifteen minutes it continued to cover the activities of those with the wagon. Five or six men rode out there, making a wide circuit, and dragged the dead horse out of the way. They hitched another animal to the load. Terry fired again and missed.

A voice outside, not far away, hailed the house. It came from the side Larry was defending. Richards searched the alfalfa field and saw nobody.

'Someone has worked up right close to us,' he told his companion. 'Sounds like he's only forty or fifty yards away.'

'Ask him who he is,' Terry said. 'We can send a message by him and tell Ellison who we are.'

Larry shouted the question. The answer astonished him. He passed it on to his friend.

'Claims he's Jeff Brand and is going to make a run for the door. He must have crawled up the ditch.' Larry demanded more information from the man outside. A moment later he cried in excitement: 'Hell, it's Jeff, all right! He's coming on the run . . . They've hit him. He's down.'

Terry ran to the door and flung it open. He thrust the rifle into the hands of Richards and raced toward the man on the ground, who was crawling toward the house. The spiteful whine of the bullets whistled past him. He knew that Larry was in the doorway firing at their enemies, holding a position more dangerous than his because he was not moving.

Stooping, Calhoun picked up Brand, the rifle

still in his hand, and hurried back to the house. He reached it in safety and Larry bolted the door.

Terry put the wounded man down on the bed. 'Where did they hit you?' he asked.

Jeff Brand did not answer. He stared at his rescuer in vast astonishment.

'They got him in the ankle,' Larry said, pointing to a hole in Brand's boot.

The man on the bed sat up. He gazed at Larry, then once more at the manager of the Diamond Reverse B. This was as bad as a Chinese puzzle.

XXVIII

Jeff said bluntly, 'What in hell are you doing here?'

'The gents outside ran us in here,' Larry said, chuckling. 'Now they are fixing to run us out again.'

'But—what for? I don't get the reason.'

'They didn't wait to find out who we are. Began to make targets of us before we had a chance to explain . . . Better let me get that boot off your leg, Jeff.'

Terry was back at his loophole. He had to make sure of what the attackers were doing. Brand looked at him—and laughed. There was no mirth in his laughter.

'I take the cake for damn fools,' he said acridly.

'You surely picked a hot spot, one that's going to be hotter soon,' Larry told him. 'If I hurt you too much while I'm working the boot off, holler.'

Brand set his teeth as Richards removed the boot. Tiny beads of perspiration stood on his forehead, but he did not flinch. Gently Larry drew off the sock. While he was getting water from a bucket to wash the wound he swept the alfalfa field with his keen eyes. It was important not to let anybody else come up out of the ditch.

'Everything seems to be quiet along the Potomac,' he announced, turning away, and as he spoke a bullet crashed through a small section of glass in a window through which he had been looking.

He tied up the wound with a handkerchief he found in a drawer. Brand rose and tested his leg gingerly. Larry caught him as he started to slump down.

'Better lie there on the bed,' Terry said, without looking round. 'Let Larry have your rifle.'

'It's not mine,' Brand answered. 'I borrowed it from a guy I met at the foot of the ravine.'

'Borrowed it,' Larry repeated.

'Yep. He didn't need it right then. He was counting stars, I reckon.' Brand grinned. 'Maybe he still is. I wouldn't know . . . You can have the loan of it till I quit feelin' dizzy, Larry.'

'Better lie down,' Terry said again. 'Until you feel steadier, anyhow.'

Jeff looked at Terry's flat, strong back with

cold dislike. This was a nice pickle to be in. Without knowing it, he had come to rescue an enemy, and by another queer topsy-turvy quirk the man had saved him. He had heard of life's little ironies. This was one in which he could find no pleasure.

'I'll sit up,' he said.

'Ankle hurting much?' Larry asked.

'I can notice it,' Jeff answered dryly. 'But in a couple of minutes I'll be able to sit up in a chair and pick off some of these wolves.' He added, his hard, narrowed eyes on Terry: 'Ought to be like shooting fish in a duck pond. How many of 'em have you got?'

'They haven't ever come within range of my six-gun,' Larry explained. Cal has wounded two.'

'Fine work,' Jeff derided. 'But I reckon he hates to kill off his friends.'

'Would you call them his friends? And them bringing a hay wagon down to burn him out of here.'

Brand looked quickly at Larry. The Diamond Reverse B puncher had spoken in a voice cool and even, but the rustler did not make the mistake of deciding that he did not mean what he had said.

'You wouldn't be loadin' me?' Jeff asked.

'They are bringing the hay to the barn now. Some of them will take hold of the tongue and back the wagon against the window. Then they will set fire to the hay.'

Jeff showed his white teeth in a grim smile. 'That's what a fellow gets for coming to a barbecue when he hasn't had an invite.'

Without looking round, Terry said: 'It may not be as bad as that. When they get close I'm going to try to let them know who I am.'

Again Jeff laughed, mirthlessly. 'That will be fine—for you and Larry.'

The words of the outlaw gave Larry a shock. He had not thought of it before, but he saw now that even if he and Calhoun could save themselves by surrender, in doing so they would condemn Jeff to death. And Jeff had come here, thinking they were his allies, to fight off the invaders until help arrived.

'How soon will your friends get here?' Larry asked. 'I reckon they are gathering quick as they can.'

'I sent Lee Hart out to pass the word. My guess would be, in another hour and a half. Depends who leads them. Dave Morgan would have jumped them along, but he had to go warn the Deep Creek settlers.'

After a pause, 'We can't stand them off another hour and a half,' Terry said.

A sinister light quickened Jeff's face. He said ironically: 'You'll be able to make a nice deal for yourselves now. They won't have two to hang, but one is better than none.'

Terry did not answer. Larry flushed angrily.

'You have a fine way of making friends, Jeff,' he said.

'I'm particular about who my friends are,' Brand jeered.

'I've noticed that. A scoundrel like Lee Hart who shoots from back of a wall at a man not expecting it. A bullypuss ruffian like Jack Turley. A scalawag like—'

'Don't talk about Turley being my friend,' Jeff interrupted. 'I killed him this morning.'

Larry stared at him, waiting for information. The roar of Terry's rifle filled the room.

'Get one?' Larry snapped.

'Hit him in the foot. They are ready to start the wagon.'

Jeff hobbled to the wall, dragging a chair with him. 'Gimme that rifle, Larry,' he ordered, and got out a knife to dig a loophole.

'All right. Soon as you're ready for it. Howcome you to kill Turley?'

'We found out he was the traitor who shot Jim Tetlow and the other boys. I gave him an even-Stephen break, which was more than the skunk deserved. We found the blood money in his cabin. You and yore friends can't get it back, Mr. Terry, because we turned it over to the widow of one of the men your killer shot.'

Terry looked at him, and the eyes of the ranchman were hard as agates. 'They are starting the wagon. In ten minutes we may all

239

be dead. I told you before I had nothing to do with those murders, and I tell you so now.'

'They've stopped the wagon,' Larry interrupted. 'Someone has brought in a horse without a rider. Looks like the roan you were on. Bet a dollar they have recognized the horse and are having a pow-wow about it.'

'It looks like only one of us may be dead in ten minutes,' Jeff snarled. 'I'll take that rifle now, Larry. I aim to go out in smoke.'

Larry looked at the Diamond Reverse B manager.

'Give it to him,' Terry said, his gaze fixed on the outlaw. 'But don't make a mistake, Brand. I wouldn't have chosen it that way, but we're all in this tight together. We all come out of it alive or none of us do. Let me do the talking; that is, if any of us get a chance to do any with these fellows.'

'We're getting a chance, all right,' Larry cried. 'Someone is running out a white flag from back of the barn.'

The narrowed, glittering eyes of Brand held fast to those of Terry. The rustler trusted his friends but was suspicious of his enemies.

'How do I know you won't throw me down?' he asked harshly.

'Don't be a fool, Jeff,' Larry cut in. 'Cal and I are both square shooters. You ought to have sense enough to see that.'

Terry walked to the door, unbolted it, and waved the flour sack. Ellison and Sunday Brown came out of the barn and walked toward the house. When they were about forty yards distant the No, By Jo manager shouted a question.

'What made you run away, Terry?' he demanded irritably. 'You might have got killed.'

The Diamond Reverse B man waited until they were nearer. 'So we might,' he agreed, sarcasm riding his voice. 'Whether we ran or whether we stayed. Your hired killers are too ready with their guns. Ellison I told you it would be that way.'

'We took you for two scoundrels who had killed one of our inspectors and had the nerve to bring his body to us with an insulting note. Naturally when you ran we followed. If you had stayed and held up your hands there wouldn't have been any trouble.' Ellison smiled thinly, his eyes hard and cold. Larry guessed he was not sorry for the bad two hours he had given them.

'If you expect me to say your explanation makes everything all right, I shall have to disappoint you,' Terry answered stiffly.

'Too bad you were annoyed,' Ellison said, with smooth insolence. 'By the way, what adjustment do you expect to make to the three men you have wounded?'

'Just tell them they are lucky Cal is a good shot,' Larry retorted. 'If he hadn't been you would probably have had to dig graves for them.'

Ellison looked at him. 'I wasn't talking to you.'

'No? Well, I'm talking to you.' Into Larry's face

beneath the tan dark blood swept. 'Your hired killers have been plugging at me for a couple of hours. You're no better than that dead wolf Turley you were telling us about. The sooner you are run out of the country the better.'

Larry had made a slip, and Ellison pounced on it. 'Did I mention Turley? How do you know he was the man?'

'Never mind how I know. He has nothing to do with our complaint against you. I'm going to see that it gets into the Denver papers that you attacked us.'

Sunday Brown spoke for the first time. 'Who is the man that slipped into the cabin a little while ago?'

Terry looked at him bleakly. 'You wounded the man, whoever he is. That's enough for one day. I advise you-all to mount your horses and get out of here while you can.'

'Don't try the high and mighty with me, Terry,' the No, By Joe manager advised, restraining his temper with difficulty. 'We're letting you go. That's enough. If you want my opinion, you're no better than these rustlers you are secretly encouraging. I'm asking you two questions, and I don't intend to leave till I get answers. The first is, how do you know Turley was killed, unless you were in on the job? The second is, who did you carry into the cabin a little while ago?'

'You're out of luck in your questions, Ellison,'

drawled Terry. 'We won't answer either of them.'

'I'll satisfy myself on the last point by looking,' the leader of the regulators announced arrogantly, and stepped toward the house.

Quick as he was, Terry barred the way. 'Nothing doing. The man is our guest, and he isn't entertaining visitors today.'

Little white spots of rage dented Ellison's nose. 'By God, you're not in the clear yet, Terry. I'll tell you that. You're in with these thieves . . . or you're not. I've asked you two plain questions. If you are an honest man you won't wait a moment to clear yourself.'

Terry looked him over coldly. He too was curbing his anger not too easily. 'I'll be the judge of my honesty, Mr. Ellison. And I'm not answering your questions. That's final.'

Sunday Brown tried the soft word. The big Texan had ridden into the brush many times to drag out desperate criminals. He and his men had brought out a good many lashed to pack saddles as Turley had been, dead bodies to be identified and buried. But these two men facing him were not criminals, at least so far as he knew.

'Let's be reasonable, gentlemen,' he said. 'I don't reckon you mean to aid outlaws. You're with one of the big concerns, Mr. Terry. We'd better get together on this. Mr. Ellison's questions look fair to me.'

A man appeared in the doorway of the house.

He leaned against the jamb for support, but the rifle in his hands was quite steady.

'You've got me so plumb scared that I expect I'd better answer yore questions, Ellison,' he said, not raising his voice. 'I'm the guy in the cabin, and I'm the one who told them about Turley. I knew about it because I shot the bastard this morning. Maybe I'm one of the men you're looking for.'

The color slowly drained from Ellison's gray face. His guess was that Brand meant to kill him now.

XXIX

Sunday Brown said: 'I don't know who you are, young fellow, but yore own words convict you and I'm arresting you.'

'I'm standing in the doorway waiting for you to try it,' Brand answered. He did not move a muscle, his voice was even and gentle. Only his glittering eyes betrayed wary excitement.

'Just a moment,' Terry said. 'To avoid any mistakes, Larry and I are declaring ourselves. All three of us are in this tight together. You're not taking one without the others.'

'I'll do the talking for our side, Sunday,' Ellison told the Texan. 'No need for guns to smoke here.'

'It's been such a nice, friendly afternoon Mr.

Ellison would hate to have trouble start now,' jeered Jeff.

'The attack on these gentlemen was a mistake,' the No, By Joe manager explained. 'We didn't know who they were. I've already told them that. But about this Three Musketeers stuff. Let me get you right, Terry. Are you telling me that you are lining up with the rustlers in this fight?'

'No.' Calhoun looked at the other ranch manager, not giving an inch. 'You know damn well I'm not, but you're trying to put me where I'll have my tail in a crack. I'm not on either side. A plague on both your houses. If I catch any thief fooling with our stock I'll rub him out like that'—he made a sweeping gesture of the arm away from him, palm down. 'But that's not the point. Brand made the same error you did. He guessed we were somebody else. His friends are hotfooting it over the hills to rescue us. But he didn't wait for them. He came alone, to share our risk. We won't throw him down now.'

'Very noble,' sneered Ellison. 'I'll ask a question, since my other two have been answered. Would Brand have come if he had known who you were?'

'Not a foot of the way,' Jeff cut in tartly.

'In that case you don't owe him anything.'

'Not a thing,' the rustler agreed.

'We're of a different opinion,' Larry said. 'He and his friends are breaking a tug to help us. Jeff has been wounded. We don't have to go back of

245

the facts to find a reason. Tell your crowd to get the hell out of here before the boys come, unless you want a real war on yore hands.'

Brand offered a suggestion. 'Why drag anybody else into this, Mr. Ellison? You don't like my way of life, and not a thing about you pleases me. We can settle this right here in three seconds with six-guns. If you feel lucky, start smoking.'

'I don't fight duels with outlaws,' Ellison replied curtly.

'No, you hire killers to shoot 'em down from ambush. You go raiding their homes with sixty gunmen at yore back.' Brand's voice was heavy with scorn. 'When you open the pot you have a pat hand, and you sure play it close to the belly.'

Ellison stood stiff and straight. 'I don't explain my conduct to thieves,' he said shortly.

'Meaning me, Mr. Ellison?' Jeff asked gently, his light, blank eyes very steadily fixed on the No, By Joe manager.

Terry stepped in front of the leader of the regulators, to prevent the rustler from getting a shot at him.

'You had better go back to your men,' he said. 'And tell them we won't baby them any longer. If this battle goes on, we'll be shooting to kill.'

'Sure, run along back and hide behind the barn again,' the wounded man jeered. 'You're too soft for this game, Ellison.'

Larry was watching Sunday Brown. He guessed

the temptation filtering through the big Texan's mind to accept Brand's challenge in place of his chief and blaze away at the man in the doorway. The gunman did not move, but a preparatory ripple seemed to pass through the heavy muscles.

'Don't you!' Larry warned. 'Terry and I are sitting in on the game.'

The former United States marshal shrugged his shoulders and relaxed.

Ellison turned and started back toward the barn, his flat back straight as a yardstick. Brown followed him. Neither of them looked round to see whether Brand was going to make a target of them.

Jeff laughed sardonically. 'Where do you reckon we go from here?'

'Up to Ellison,' Larry mentioned. 'Me, I'd like to go home, and not lying on the floor of a wagon bed. All this gun stuff makes me goosy. I don't like to have a fuss dragged in and laid on my lap when I'm not a party to it. I'm a peaceable guy myself.'

'You'd ought to sue yore reputation for libel then, Larry,' Jeff droned dryly.

The three defenders moved back into the house and shut the door. Through their loopholes they watched the enemy to see what the result of the parley would be. They had not long to wait. The invaders ran out the white rag again to indicate the battle was over. Men and horses poured out of the barn and from the creek bed into the open. The outposts returned to the main body. Those ready first swung to the saddle and waited for others to mount. Presently Sunday Brown led the way into the hills along the same trail Tod Collins and his troop had taken.

'They won't go far,' Larry said. 'For fear of missing their friends. They'll roost on the top of some bluff close to the road and wait for the others to come back.'

Terry picked up a pail and threw out the tepid water in it. He walked down to the creek and filled it.

'The coast is all clear,' he announced when he returned.

Jeff lay on the bed. The fever was mounting in him. Already the numbness of the wound had passed and given place to great pain. He gave no sign of what he was enduring but kept his lips tightly locked. Avidly he drank dipperfuls of the fresh cold water.

'We'll see what we can do for your leg now,' Terry said. 'Let me have a look at it.'

Larry brought cold water and clean rags to the bedside. Terry gave Brand a wet towel with which to bathe his hot face while he unfastened the bandage around the ankle and washed the wound. He tied another handkerchief around the leg.

'It will have to do until we get you to a doctor,' the Diamond Reverse B manager said. 'If you can make it across the hills to the Box 55, we can get a wagon there to carry you to town.'

'I can stick in the saddle after the boys put me there,' Jeff said. 'I'm not the first guy who ever had his leg busted.'

The rescuers arrived about an hour later, Roan Alford and Bill Herriott at their head. A flour sack was nailed to the back door of the Hart cabin, but Roan spread his men and approached carefully. The cabin might be filled with enemies ready to turn loose a blast of gunfire at them.

Bill Herriott came forward alone, waving a white handkerchief. Terry stepped out of the house to meet him.

'What are you doing here?' Herriott asked curtly.

'I'm representing Jeff Brand just now,' the Diamond Reverse B manager answered dryly. 'He's inside the cabin wounded.'

'You shot him,' accused his former friend.

'No. It's quite a story. Maybe you had better step in and find out what Brand thinks about it.'

The blue eyes of Bill looked into his, searching for information. 'All right,' he said.

They walked into the house. Larry said, ' 'lo, Bill.' The young ranchman nodded. His gaze swept to the bed.

'How bad is it, Jeff?' he asked.

'A busted ankle.'

'Who did it?'

'I don't know who to thank. There was a whole b'ilin' of gents cracking away at me, mostly warriors from Texas, I reckon.'

'Not Terry or Richards?'

'No, Bill. They were the heroes who went out and dragged me in when I was lying on the ground with a busted leg.' There was sardonic mockery in Jeff's voice.

Herriott looked from one to another. 'Well, someone tell me about it. Where are the fellows who did it? What's the idea of this love feast?'

'It don't exactly run to that,' Jeff drawled. 'We're sorta victims of circumstances, you might say. None of us like it, but we've kind of pooled our interests for a while. It suited me fine, since if we hadn't hung together I would have had to hang by my lone. I was a liability in the partnership. All I contributed was a promise of you boys.'

'And that's what turned the trick and made Ellison's men light out,' Larry mentioned.

'I still don't know what happened,' Herriott complained.

Brand told him the story briefly.

'So that's how it was,' he concluded. 'Ellison jumped his Diamond Reverse B friends, thinking they were Dave Morgan and me, who had brought him back what was left of his killer. I butted in here, likewise under a mistake. It was what you might call a comedy of errors.'

'We had better get out of here,' Herriott said. 'I

have about eight or nine men with me, not enough to stand off this army of Clint Ellison's. Point is, can you stick it on a horse far as Black Butte?'

'Yes. Let's get going.'

Terry and Richards rode with the party as far as the Box 55. They were not very welcome. The members of the rescue posse made that clear. Wild rumors were in circulation, though none of them could be traced to a reliable source. Dave Morgan had been killed by the invading Texans. Half a dozen other men, nesters in the hill country the cattlemen were now raiding, had been trapped and shot down. Their homes had been burned.

A man galloped down a hill trail to join them. He had just come from the territory into which Tod Collins had led his troop. All he knew was that Dave Morgan had warned him, and that while he was slipping into the hills for safety he had heard heavy firing to the west and later farther to the north. He was worried about Wade Scott and Lin Harkness. It looked like they might have been taken by surprise. Then there were the two Lee families just beyond them.

Lane Carey and his daughter came out of the ranch house to get the news. From a little distance Terry watched Ellen's face as the men eased Brand from the saddle so that he would not have to put any weight on his wounded leg. He could see her breath catch and the intent fear in her eyes.

Jeff limped forward, an arm around the

shoulder of Roan Alford. He had lost his hat, and his close-cropped curly hair was shining in the sun. His face was flushed with fever, but a gay, devil-may-care light was in his eyes.

'Back from the war,' he told Ellen. 'With a sure-enough hero story for you. Only trouble is two other guys were the heroes.'

'Are you badly hurt?' she asked in a low voice.

'No. I ought to be a sieve, but these Texans are false alarms. They can't hit a barn door.'

'We had better have him carried upstairs,' Ellen said to her father. 'He can have the spare room.'

Jeff shook his head. 'Sorry, but I have to say "No, thanks," lady. If I stay here these Texas wolves would be liable to collect the only scalp I have. The boys are going to take me to Round Top in your wagon.'

Ellen had Jim bring down a mattress and put it on the porch. The wounded man lay down on it, protesting that there was no sense in babying him. The girl made him a pitcher of cool lemonade and he drank several glasses of it.

Meanwhile the men hitched up the wagon and piled hay in the bed. The mattress was put on top of the hay and Jeff assisted to the place on it. Ellen arranged a pillow for his head. Her father put a canteen beside Brand. She waved a good-bye at him as the guarded wagon rolled down the road.

Apparently noticing them for the first time,

Ellen walked over to the Diamond Reverse B men. Since their arrival they had taken no part in the preparations. The friends of Brand had pointedly ignored them.

Watching her, Terry thought there was a kind of light, flying grace in the girl's movements. He liked the mobility of her lovely face, with its fine-drawn planes and the eager look that was almost luminous.

'Will you tell me all about it—just what happened?' she asked.

'Larry saw him in the ditch working toward the house where we were prisoners, so we opened the door for him,' Terry said.

'No, no. Begin at the first. What were you doing there? I don't understand it. Jeff said you two saved his life.'

Calhoun Terry gave her a dry skeleton sketch in five sentences.

Ellen turned to Larry impatiently. 'Can't you tell a story better than that?' she asked.

The eyes of the cowboy were quick with interest. This was a select audience of two, for Lane had joined his daughter. It was one he would like to make a favorable impression upon, as would any other young man on the range.

He described their adventure in detail, from the time that they had first sighted the invaders until they reached Black Butte, and he told the tale vividly. The girl did not lift her entranced eyes from him, but she was very much aware of the quiet gray-eyed man with the lean, sun-tanned face who listened without comment. When his companion used adjectives she knew a satirical smile was twitching at his lips. None the less she thrilled to the danger of their hazards. She could hear the booming of the guns and see the spatter of the bullets against the logs. She raced breathlessly with Cal Terry to pick up the wounded rustler, and her heart lifted when he was telling Ellison that all three of them in the cabin meant to stand or fall together.

'I expect they hated to let Jeff go,' Larry concluded. 'The blamed idiot stood in the doorway and told Ellison he was the man who had killed his spy Turley.'

Ellen gave a little groan. 'Did you say that Jeff . . . killed Turley?' she asked. What Larry had said she had heard quite dearly, but she did not want to believe it.

'Yes. He found out somehow that Turley was the fellow who killed Buck Hart and the other boys. Jeff says he gave Turley an even-Stephen chance. I'll bet he did, too. They don't come gamer than Jeff. You'd ought to have seen him standing in the doorway of the Hart cabin. He had to lean against the jamb to keep from falling, but he was that cool and easy as he defied Ellison to come and get him.'

The color had washed out of Ellen's face. 'I'm

responsible for Turley's death,' she said in a low monotone. 'I . . . told Jeff the man might be Turley, and I said the writing on the note left by the killer looked like his.'

'Then you did a service to this district,' Terry told her bluntly. 'Don't worry about that. The fellow had to be killed.'

'Yes, but—why did I do it? I might have known what Jeff would do. And I wasn't sure. Maybe—maybe Turley wasn't the right man.'

'They found the money in his cabin. He was the right man.' Larry nodded reassurance. 'He's better dead. Don't waste any pity on him.'

'You're so sure about that, aren't you?' the girl cried in passionate protest. 'Only God can make a life, but it's all right to cut one off if you take a fancy to play at being His agent.'

Terry explained gently: 'When a mad dog is loose it has to be shot to protect people. That is what Turley was. You can't go back to thinking of what he used to be as a little boy or as a lad before he sold his soul to evil. A hired killer is a menace to a community just as a man-eating tiger is in India. He has to be wiped out. Think of Jim Tetlow's wife and three little children up on Fisher Creek. Jim was a rustler, no doubt, but he was a good husband and a good father too. When a man chooses to be a killer for profit there is no stopping him. He has lost all sense of moral values and he will kill whenever he thinks it will pay.'

'Calhoun is right, Ellen,' Carey agreed. 'You are not in the least to blame, but you surely would have been if you had concealed any information you had about the identity of the killer. Nor is Jeff to blame, according to his own sense of right. Any of us would have joined a posse to hang Turley, after he had been proved guilty. Jeff did better than that by him. He gave him a chance to fight for his life. I know that, because I talked with a man who was present. As a matter of fact, Turley started to draw first. In many ways I don't approve of Jeff, but I can see no blame attaching to him in this case.' Lane brushed the doubts of his daughter aside as of no weight. 'What has happened to Turley doesn't matter. What may happen to any number of better men is of importance. I am thinking about the outcome of this raid. I don't see how a pitched battle can be avoided, and if so a great many will be killed. Isn't that your view, Calhoun?'

'Yes, and Ellison's men will be defeated in the end. This invasion has been botched from the beginning. The Texans won't escape without heavy loss unless they get out at once.'

'Why did Mr. Ellison start so crazy a thing?' Ellen cried. 'Ever since I came home this dreadful bitterness has gone on, getting worse and worse. Now nobody seems to be safe. Must it go on forever, one crime leading to another? Isn't there any way to stop it? Can't you do something, Mr. Terry?'

Calhoun shook his head. 'How can I, since both sides distrust me and I have influence with neither? I have thought of one thing—to ask the government to send troops from Fort Garfield to stop the war. I have no influence at Washington. Mr. Powers probably has, if I could get word to him.'

'I could send a messenger.' The ranchman snatched at the proposal of an appeal to Washington. We could get signatures to it, if we had time.'

'That's the trouble. There will be a clash between the two forces within a few hours. Larry and I are going to town. I'll see Horace Garvey and try to get him to join me in a wire.'

'Good. I'll come to town as soon as I can get off. That will be after the down stage passes.'

Larry went with Carey to saddle fresh horses from the Box 55 corral. Terry started with them but was detained by Ellen's voice, smaller in volume than usual.

'Just a minute, please, Mr. Terry.'

He waited, his gaze on her. She seemed to have difficulty in beginning. Beneath the tan of her soft cheeks pink was glowing. Calhoun found her glamorous loveliness exciting. He was a man not easily moved, but he felt the blood in him drumming faster.

'I want to 'fess up,' she said at last, trying for a light note.

'You must think I'm a dreadful little prig, the way I have treated you.'

His voice sounded cold, because he was keeping a tight rein on his emotions. 'I haven't any complaint, Miss Carey,' he began, and pulled up short. That wasn't what he wanted to say, or the way to say it. 'I knew you didn't like me, but I didn't blame you for that. I'm not used to being liked these days.' He smiled, to let her know he was standing up under the general dislike pretty well.

'I didn't like you,' she admitted. 'I thought you were horrid. And I was wrong. In all this dreadful business nobody has been as right as you.' The color in her eyes deepened as she looked at him. Her heart was fluttering against her ribs, and she told herself not to be a fool. 'It was splendid, the way you ran out of the cabin to get Jeff. I know you don't like him. But you went just the same.'

'I like him as well as he does me,' Calhoun said wryly. 'As to picking him up, there was nothing to that. I handed the dangerous job to Larry—to stand them off while they plugged away at him.'

'Yes,' she said with sweet derision. 'I know you would give the dangerous place to somebody else. Jeff did not tell it that way, but he probably didn't know.'

The girl was in love with Brand, of course. He had no doubt of that. To think of it sent a chill wave over him. The man had his good points, many of them, but he was the last one a fine, brave girl like Ellen Carey ought to love. It was natural that her heart should go out to him. He was gay and young and good-looking, and there was that dash of the devil in him that women always find fascinating in men. He supposed it was the mother instinct in her, the feeling that she alone had influence enough with the likable scamp to snatch him from ways of evil. Of course she was wrong. A man blazed his own trail, and the woman who loved him had to take him as he was. But she would not learn that until too late.

Calhoun understood that she was thanking him for saving her lover. In doing that he had wiped out any prejudice she might have had against him. Any merit he had acquired was through his service to Brand.

He nodded good-bye to her stiffly and walked away to join her father and Larry at the corral.

XXX

Terry and Richards came into Round Top after dark. As they rode along the railroad tracks they became aware of unusual activity in the town. More men than usual were on the lighted business street ahead of them, and the breeze brought to them the sound of excited voices. In the shadow of a loading chute they drew up. A man with a

259

rifle in his hands cantered past. He shouted at them, 'We aim to get a second troop of the boys off inside of an hour.' He did not wait for an answer.

'This town has gone wild,' Larry said. 'I reckon maybe we'd better scout around here a little before we show ourselves. We're not exactly popular.'

His friend agreed. They detoured through a pasture that lay back of the main street and tied their horses to a willow growing on the creek. Cautiously they advanced toward the town square. A light gleamed from the back window of the *Gazette* office. When they came closer they could see the dried-up little editor sitting at a desk near the front of the building. He was writing an editorial on a torn sheet of paper with the stub of a pencil.

Calhoun Terry tapped on the window and Horace Garvey slewed round his parchment-like face.

'Who is it? What you want?' he snapped.

The Diamond Reverse B manager tapped again. He did not want to shout his name aloud. Garvey grunted impatiently and turned back to his work. At the third tap he flung his pencil down with annoyance and moved to the rear of the building. He peered out of the window.

'Don't you know I keep this back door locked with piles of paper in front of it?' he called out.

'Who is it anyhow? Go round to the front door.'

Calhoun's face came out of the darkness close to the window.

'Goddlemighty!' Garvey exploded. 'Haven't you got any sense at all?'

He began to haul bundles of paper from in front of the door. Presently he opened to let them in and led the way to a dark corner back of a press.

'What's the idea of coming to Round Top after your friends have pulled such a crazy outrage as this invasion?' he demanded. 'Don't you know that this town is about ready to tear you in two? Some of the boys brought in Jeff Brand wounded. All kinds of rumors are going around. They say these Texans have killed eight or ten settlers in the hills back of Lee Hart's place.'

'I doubt it,' Calhoun replied. 'Maybe one or two. No more. Dave Morgan rode in there and warned all he could.'

'How do you know so much about it?'

'We were among those present when Jeff was wounded,' Larry told the editor.

'You mean you were with this bunch of Texas killers?'

'Not exactly with them,' Larry explained. 'They were trying to collect our hides. Cal saved Brand's life—dragged him into the cabin after he was wounded.'

Over his spectacles Garvey's eyes searched the face of the cowpuncher. 'Is this some kind of a story you're making up?' he inquired, his thin voice sharp. 'Brand was brought in only ten minutes ago, and I haven't heard the facts yet.'

'Honest Injun!' Larry laughed. 'Sounds like I'm loadin' you, doesn't it? Well, I'm not. Listen, and you can get a piece for yore paper.'

He told the story of their adventures for the day. Garvey's eyes gleamed. 'Good for you,' he said. 'Since you have broken with Ellison and his crowd it ought to fix you up with your old friends, as soon as I can get the *Gazette* out with the story. They will be glad to shake hands and make up.'

'We'll be hobnobbing with cow thieves in a couple of weeks, Cal, don't you reckon?' Larry said with a sardonic grin.

Garvey paid no attention to the cowpuncher's jeer. 'I think you boys had better get out of town as soon as you can,' he warned. 'Folks don't yet know your new position.'

'We haven't taken any new position,' Terry answered. 'We stand just where we always have. If we catch any rustlers fooling with Diamond Reverse B stock it will be good night for them. Neither Larry nor I are repentant sinners at the mourners' bench.'

'That's all right, but I wouldn't talk that way round here yet a while. The thing for you to do is to hit the trail soon as you can. Next time you come to town everything will be fine as silk.'

'He's telling us "Here's yore hat, boys," and us

all set to see the elephant,' mourned Larry. 'I figured on a little write-up about how we came to town and reported the cow business good on the Buck River range.'

'This isn't the first time he has hurried me out of town, Larry,' Calhoun said, fixing the editor with an accusing eye. 'It doesn't go this time. We came in to see a cattleman about buying a bull for the new firm of Richards & Terry. Probably he has been waiting for us all day at the Holden House. We wouldn't think of going without a confab with him.'

'Well, I'll bring him down here. I'll not have you crossing the courthouse square. Some fool would probably take a crack at you.'

'We wouldn't like that,' Larry admitted. 'Several fools have been doing it most of the day and we're fed up with being targets.'

Terry discussed the matter of sending telegrams to Washington to induce the President to order troops from Fort Garfield. Grudgingly Garvey admitted that he thought it would be a good idea. Before morning, he told them, four or five hundred armed men would have left town to engage the invaders, and as many more would pour in from the ranch country to join them.

'Not that Ellison and his gunmen have any right to complain, after what they have done, but if we can save a lot of lives that will otherwise be lost we shall have to do it,' he growled.

'What you going to say in your telegrams?' Larry asked Calhoun.

'I'm going to tell the truth, that this means war with a heavy loss of life, probably including the destruction of the whole invading force.'

'That's right,' Garvey approved. 'Don't underplay the situation. I'll sign with you.'

Inside of thirty minutes the appeals for troops were on the way to Washington, and the story was spreading through the town that Calhoun Terry had wired the President to send government troops to fight with the big outfits and their hired Texans against the settlers.

Garvey brought the cattleman to the office from the hotel, and inside of five minutes of his arrival Terry and his new partner were the owners of an imported pedigreed Hereford bull. The editor hovered over them while the bargain was being struck, like an anxious hen with one chick.

'All right,' he sputtered. 'Now you've made your deal it's time to get out of town, Calhoun. It was foolish of you to have come, with the boys so worked up they are liable to explode any minute.'

'That listens like good medicine,' Larry agreed. 'We're going right damn now.'

But they had waited too long. An irruption of angry citizens poured into the office through the front door to ask Garvey what he meant by signing a telegram requesting that troops be sent to help the invaders.

'It had Lane Carey's name on it too, and that scoundrel Terry's,' Lee Hart yelped. 'What's eating you and Lane? Are you and he laying in the same bed with Terry and his friends?'

'Who told you to sign Lane and Cal's names?' a redheaded rustler demanded. 'I know Lane ain't here, and Cal Terry wouldn't be fool enough to stick his nose into a hornet's nest after he had stirred them up to sting.'

Horace Garvey felt goose pimples run down his back. The Diamond Reverse B men were in the shadowed semi-darkness back of a press. They had slipped out of sight as the first of the group showed in the doorway. But at any moment they might be discovered. The editor pushed through the crowd toward the desk in the front of the room.

'Well, now, Red, I'll explain that,' he said nervously. 'First off, Cal Terry isn't in with the big outfits any longer. He has broken with them. I'm writing an editorial now for the next issue of the *Gazette* dealing with that. Let me read it to you.'

'Read nothing,' Hart snarled. 'We've done asked you questions. Answer them. And tell us how much Ellison paid you to throw us down?'

'You're getting this all wrong, Lee,' the harassed editor insisted, his voice shrill with excitement. 'Maybe you don't know that Cal saved Jeff Brand's life today when these Texans had him lying wounded on the ground.'

'Who told you that fairy tale?' demanded a rough, unkempt nester who had a Winchester in his hands.

'Why—ask any of the boys who came down from Black Butte with Jeff.'

'Who? Which one? Put a name to him.'

Garvey felt the sweat drops standing on his forehead. He did not know who had brought Brand to town.

'I didn't get it direct,' he admitted weakly. 'But I've heard talk, same as some of you must have done.'

'Sure we've heard talk,' Red answered, with a short, unpleasant laugh. 'We've heard these hired killers have rubbed out eight or ten of our friends and that you are trying to get the troops in to side with Ellison's men now they are getting in a jam.'

'Not to side with them,' Garvey explained desperately. 'To stop a war where dozens of you boys will be killed. I'm not throwing you down but trying to stop a terrible slaughter. Can't you see where you are heading for if you don't keep cool? We don't want—'

'Cut it,' interrupted Hart harshly. 'We don't want any more guff from you. Howcome you to sign Terry's name on that telegram? Talk, fellow.'

The nester with the Winchester in his hands craned a long scrawny neck forward. 'Someone hiding in the back of the room,' he announced.

The rifle leaped to his shoulder. 'Come outa there with yore hands up, whoever you are.'

Terry and Richards came out, not with their hands up.

The Diamond Reverse B manager answered the question Hart had put.

'My name was on that telegram because I'm the man who sent it,' he said quietly.

The men who had come to question Garvey stared at Terry in surprise out of angry, hostile eyes.

XXXI

There was a shift in the half-circle of men who fixed their attention on Terry and Richards. Lee Hart had been in the foreground, crowding the editor with snarling questions. Now he was back of the big nester with the Winchester. Over the shoulder of his shield he flung a triumphant shout at his enemy.

'Got you at last, you damn fool!'

Looking round on the grim faces of these men, all armed, most of them ready to start out on a long ride to exterminate their foes, Terry guessed that never in his turbulent life had he been in more deadly peril. In the war against the invaders he was the first victim to fall into their power. How many they had lost they did not know, but they were not likely to lose this chance to help even the score.

'Larry and Horace are not in this,' he said quietly. 'Garvey has not thrown you down. He's on your side still. Larry is a hired rider. He is not responsible for what the Diamond Reverse B has done. I'm the manager.'

Calhoun Terry was a tried man, tested in many an emergency. Some of those present had seen him in self-defense kill the two bad men from Cheyenne a few years earlier. Watching him now, cool and strong and lean, his blue eyes points of frosted steel, they knew he would go down with his soul unconquered. Marked for destruction though he was, he was master of the situation.

'If Larry Richards claims he's not on yore side he keeps mighty bad company,' Red jeered.

'I'm not claiming it, Red,' Larry cut in coolly. 'My chips are on the table alongside those of Cal.'

Shrilly Garvey begged a chance to talk. 'For God's sake, don't make a mistake, boys!' he cried. 'Listen to me. Calhoun Terry is our friend. Take time to find out—'

'He's your friend, but not ours,' Hart interrupted savagely. 'We don't need any more time. I say, right now.'

A man had walked in the front door and joined the group. He was Sheriff Hart. One sweeping glance was enough for him to size up the situation. He crowded through and took his place beside the Diamond Reverse B men.

'Don't push on the reins, Lee,' he said evenly. 'These two men are my prisoners.'

'How do you mean yore prisoners?' his brother blustered. 'Ellison's warriors aren't taking any prisoners. That goes with us too.'

The hard, unwinking eyes in the long-jawed, bony face of the sheriff looked almost contemptuously at his older brother. 'Come out from back of Houck if you have anything to say, though it won't be important anyhow. I'm the law, and I'm arresting these men. Don't any of you get the wrong idea about that.'

Terry knew that the sheriff had no friendliness for him, but he had no doubt that Nate Hart had interfered to prevent him and Larry from being killed.

'What are you arresting us for doing?' he asked. It did not matter what pretext was offered by the officer, but as a matter of form Calhoun made a protest. 'We're peaceable citizens going about our lawful business.'

'For conspiring to bring about an armed insurrection in the territory,' the officer answered.

'Hmp! We came here to buy a registered bull from Mr. Murdoch here,' Larry said. 'We have done bought it. Now we're ready to leave and go back to the ranch. Looks to me like these gents who were working themselves up to bump us off when you sashayed in are doing the insurging.'

'No use littering up the jail with them,' Lee Hart urged. 'I say hang them to a telegraph pole.'

The sheriff drew a revolver. 'I know all of you boys,' he said quietly. 'I'd hate to have to kill any of you, and I don't want to be killed myself. But I'm going to take these men to jail. If anybody interferes there will be trouble.'

In the West 'trouble' meant only one thing, a gun battle. These men knew that the sheriff would do exactly what he had said. He might pass out in smoke, but if he was still able to walk he would keep his prisoners. Moreover, both Terry and Richards were armed. They were men notable for gameness in a country where courage was taken for granted.

The cowboy Red threw in the hand for his group. 'All right, Nate. If you want these fellows, take 'em. But be sure you don't let 'em go. We'll be hearing from the hills soon as to whether any of our friends have been murdered. And if they have, hell and high water can't keep us from busting into yore calaboose and hanging these birds high as Haman.'

Red and his allies followed the arrested men to the jail, to make sure the sheriff did not release them. They posted a guard at both the rear and front doors. The leaders adjourned to the Crystal Palace and the Red Triangle to drum up sentiment in favor of a lynching. It was all very well for Nate Hart to put up a good bluff, but they knew that excitement in Round Top was so high that enough men could be gathered to storm the prison. Already a large party of armed riders were almost ready to leave for the battlefield in the hills. If word came that the invaders had killed any of their party, Lee Hart knew that these men could be induced easily to turn on Terry for revenge.

He did not know it any more surely than Terry and Richards did. Calhoun put the matter bluntly to the sheriff.

'Getting down to cases, Hart, what is your idea in locking us up?' he asked. 'Are you holding us here till your friends are ready to lynch us?'

'I'm holding you here for your own safety. If I turned you loose you would never get out of town alive. You wouldn't get fifty yards from the jail door.' Impatiently he added, 'Why in hell did you come to town now?'

'Why shouldn't we come?' Terry wanted to know. 'We have nothing to do with this crazy invasion. Ellison's men attacked us today and almost killed us. We rescued your friend Jeff Brand. The Diamond Reverse B is being cut up into small ranches, of which Larry and I are buying one. What have you against us except that we won't stand for having our stock rustled? The trouble with this town just now is that it is seeing red and can't think straight.'

'If I could get Red and some of the other hot-heads to go up to the house where Jeff is and talk with him they might get some sense thumped into their heads. But no chance of that now. They figure you are one of those who paid that two thousand dollars to Turley to ambush their friends. You may have been, at that. Even if you have quarreled with Ellison since then, that doesn't prove a thing, and far as that goes they only have your own say-so that you're not hock deep in this invasion.' The sheriff slanted a suspicious look at Terry. 'Looks like you are, when you get off a telegram to the President asking him to send troops to support the big ranches in this business of killing settlers.'

'That's not what I asked him to do,' the Diamond Reverse B manager said. 'Since the operator was in such a hurry to give out a private message he might at least have done so correctly.'

Larry tossed a question at Hart. 'Let's know where we're at, sheriff. Is it yore intention to ask us to give up our guns and wait in a cell for these galoots outside to break in and send us west? Because we have other views.'

Nate Hart was a harassed man. 'I didn't get you in this jam, Larry,' he said. 'You didn't have to come here and drop a match in a barrel of powder. I'm trying to save you, but I'll tell you straight that if any bad news comes to town the boys will attack the jail. It's only a flimsy shack.

You know that. I aim to protect you if I can, and if it comes to a showdown I'll give you back your guns to help me stand them off. More than that I can't promise.'

'Fair enough,' Terry said. 'Do we stay here in your office or go to a cell?'

'You don't have to be locked up, but I'd like you upstairs out of sight so as to give the boys a chance to forget you if they can.' He added after a moment, 'If I could get a chance to let you slip away I would.'

'Since we're not prisoners you'd better let us keep our guns,' Larry suggested. 'You might be where you couldn't get them back to us when we have to have them.'

The sheriff did not like that, but he recognized the force of the argument. 'All right,' he said. 'Keep them. I don't need to tell you if you begin shooting you are sunk.'

He led them to a room on the second floor.

XXXII

After supper Ellen walked out into the soft, moonlit night to see where her father was. She found him in the stable putting harness on Sam and Buck.

'You have decided, then, to go to town,' she said.

'Yes. I can't help here. I might be able to do something there.'

'I'm going with you,' the girl told him.

She was prepared to argue it, but to her surprise he made no objection.

'I think you had better,' he agreed. 'There's a chance these invaders might come this way. Pack a valise with things to last you two–three days. Until things settle down you'll be safer at Round Top than here.'

Ellen hurried back to the house and packed a telescope grip for her father and a valise for herself. By the time her father had brought the buckboard to the front door she was ready. The solitude of the night swallowed them. Countless stars studded the sky. When the road ran between pines they could hear the rustle of the wind in the foliage.

Lane Carey reached over to tuck the buffalo robe over his daughter's knees. 'You warm enough, honey?' he said. 'It's right cool.'

He had felt her shivering, but it was not because of the temperature. There had flowed through her a swift and unexpected sense of imminent danger. Not peril which involved herself but someone else dear to her. Was it her father? She did not know. The premonition was not clear as to details, but it was so vivid as to fill her with fear.

'I love this country,' she said to her father, 'but I wish we did not live here.'

He patted the robe covering her thighs. 'I know. Right now it is no place for a woman. Maybe it will clear up instead of getting worse.'

'It's no place for a man either. It gives me a scunner, as mother used to say.'

Lane pulled up to listen. 'Someone is riding a trail parallel to this road,' he said.

A queer dread flooded the girl, as if it had been no mortal man riding that trail but a black shape out of the spirit world.

Lane clucked to the horses and they started again. Presently the trail ran into the road. A man came out of it at a canter.

Ellen drew a deep breath of relief. He was a man of flesh and blood, and one she knew. His name was Wade Scott. He had a place up in the hills. She recalled having heard that he was soon to marry a girl now living in Cheyenne.

'Ellison's men got Dave Morgan and Sib Lee,' he blurted out.

'Got them?' Ellen murmured.

She knew of course what he meant, but her imagination could not at once vision Dave Morgan as dead. She had danced with him at the Sleepy Cat Ranch, and she remembered a certain dark fierceness in his brittle manner. Only a few hours ago she had seen him start for Deep Creek to warn the settlers.

'Yep. Dave killed one of 'em before they finished him.' Scott stopped to steady his voice.

'They got him about an hour after he warned me. He kept on up the creek. A dozen folks got out soon as he gave 'em the word, but they jumped him and Sib near the foot of Blue Mountain.'

Ellen said in a low voice, 'Poor Dave.' She thought of what Jeff Brand had said, that Morgan would do to ride the river with. They had left together, without a moment's hesitation, to face great risk in order to save others. Now one was dead and the other wounded.

'Was anybody there?' Lane asked. 'Do you know how it happened?'

'No. Sib's brother found them dead with their guns in their hands.' Scott brushed a hand across his eyes, as if to wipe away the memory of what he had seen. 'I helped take their bodies back to Sib's house . . . Never was anybody gamer than Dave. He was wild and reckless, but he went through for us fellows on Deep Creek. Maybe if I'd gone with him—But he wouldn't let me. One of us had to ride across to the Bromleys' and warn them, he said. I feel kinda responsible for what happened to him. He would have been alive now if I'd gone up to the Lees' instead of him.'

'You couldn't tell that,' Lane comforted.

'No. I offered to go. For all we knew, these Texans might be cutting across to the Bromleys'. It was fifty-fifty. At least it looked that way to us.' He flung out a low, bitter protest. 'What right have these big ranches to raid this country like

276

Cheyennes or Sioux? I hope to God we wipe out every last man of them.'

Carey shook his head. 'No, Wade. That's not the answer. We're all off on the wrong track. I wish I knew the right one, but I don't.'

Scott rode down beside or behind them to Round Top. He dropped off at the Crystal Palace to tell his news. The place was boiling with life, as was the street outside. He caught sight of Lee Hart and Red. Both of them showed signs of having had a good deal to drink.

The man from Deep Creek banged a tumbler on the top of the bar for silence. When the voices died down he told his story to a stilled and shocked audience. They waited till he had finished, then poured questions at him.

Lee Hart slammed his fist on the walnut. That settles it. We'll take those fellows out of the calaboose and string 'em up, no matter what Nate says.'

A little wrinkled man with a wide, gray, weather-beaten hat walked into the place. He had just ridden down from his ranch to find out how large a force Round Top expected to send as allies of the settlers against the invaders. Roan had arrived just in time to hear Hart's snarling threat.

'Who is Lee aimin' to string up now?' he asked the nearest man.

'Cal Terry and Larry Richards. These warriors

of Ellison's have rubbed out Dave Morgan and Sib Lee, and we aim to start evening the score.'

'But Terry can't be here in town—or Larry either.'

'That's where they are. In Nate's jail. He arrested them this evening. We're gonna bust in and get them.'

Roan scraped his wrinkled, unshaven face. 'Why, I don't reckon the boys had better do that. Larry is only a cowboy. As for Cal, he ain't so bad, and anyway he has cut loose from Ellison's crowd.'

'Like Ned he has! He sent a telegram about an hour ago to the President asking him to send troops to wipe out our boys.'

'That doesn't sound like Cal. Unless he has changed a heap since I knew him.' Alford walked to the bar and stood at Lee Hart's elbow. 'You don't want to get on the prod too sudden, Lee,' he said mildly. 'I heard up at Black Butte as I came through that Cal Terry saved Jeff Brand's life today. It takes only a li'l while to hang a man, but only God Almighty can bring him back to life again.'

Hart turned on him angrily, a glass of whiskey halfway to his mouth. 'Not a thing to that story. Horace Garvey started it. He has done been bought and gone over to the big fellows. Cal Terry has come to the end of his last crooked mile.'

'What does Nate say about this?'

The bowlegged man brushed that aside with a violent gesture. 'Never mind what Nate says. He's sheriff, and he has to put up a bluff. It's our say-so tonight and not his.'

Red indorsed this instantly. 'Y' betcha! We're the top dogs.'

The others at the bar voiced savage assent.

Alford was worried, but he said no more in protest. He knew it was of no use and might involve him in trouble.

'How is Jeff?' he asked. 'Where is he?'

'Doing all right, I reckon. He's at the Round Top hotel.'

Roan left his horse tied at the hitch-rack and started for the Round Top, which was really only a boarding-house. On the way somebody stopped him for a moment to discuss the chances of trapping the invaders. He mentioned casually that he had just seen Lane Carey at the Holden House. Lane and his daughter had reached town. Alford decided to consult with the Box 55 man about the best thing to do. He knew that Terry and Richards were in very great danger. Only a determined effort could save them from mob vengeance. The streets were crowded with men, nearly all of them excited beyond reason. They talked of nothing but the invaders, the fate of Morgan and Lee, and the prospective lynching of the Diamond Reverse B men.

Carey and his daughter were still in the lobby

of the Holden House. They were waiting there for a maid to finish changing the bed of a room recently vacated. Alford walked across to them.

'Hell has broke loose in Georgia,' he said to Carey. 'I've just left the Crystal Palace, where they are all talking about lynching Cal Terry and Larry Richards. That's all they are discussing on the streets too, except the trouble on Deep Creek. They'll be heading for the jail mighty soon, looks to me.'

All the color washed from the face of Ellen. She stared at the little man, lips parted, fear dilating her eyes. 'But—but—how can that be, when they fought with the Texans today and saved Jeff Brand's life?' she asked.

'I told 'em that. They won't believe it. They have gone crazy. We have got to get it across to them that Cal isn't tied up with this bunch of Ellison's. I figured maybe they would listen to Jeff, if we could get him to the jail. He's at the Round Top Hotel.'

'I'll go to Jeff,' the girl cried. 'I'll bring him.'

Lane Carey ignored what she had said. 'You go see Jeff and talk with him,' he said to Alford. 'I'll run down to the corral and bring the wagon to move him if he is able to go. See you soon.'

'I'm going with Roan, father,' Ellen cried.

The Box 55 man hesitated. 'All right,' he said after a moment. It had occurred to him that she might have some influence with Brand if any was necessary. 'But you'll stay at the Round Top till this is all over. The streets are no place for a girl tonight.'

Roan got Ellen off the main streets as soon as he could, but not before she sensed the intense feeling of the men they saw. It beat on her like the heat from the open door of a furnace. Instinctively she hurried her steps, as the chill of fear filled her breast.

The old woman who was nursing Jeff thought that he ought not to be disturbed, but they brushed her aside and went into the bedroom.

'It's life or death for two men,' Roan explained. 'We've got to see him, doctor's orders or not.'

As soon as Jeff saw Ellen his face lit. 'I been thinking about you,' he said.

She could see by the light of the lamp that he was flushed with fever, but she had to tell him for what they had come.

'Oh, Jeff!' she cried. 'The town has gone mad. Nate Hart has arrested Calhoun Terry and Larry Richards, and Lee Hart is gathering a mob to lynch them.'

Jeff sat up on an elbow and stared at her in surprise. 'What for are they doing it?'

'Because Ellison's band of killers shot Dave Morgan and Sib Lee today.'

The wounded man's gaze did not shift from her, but Ellen knew he was seeing something else. His face had gone rigid.

'How do you know?' he asked, after a long silence.

'Wade Scott rode down with us. He helped carry the bodies to Sib's home.' Ellen pushed past that to the terror crowding in on her. 'They think Terry is in with the invaders. He sent a telegram asking the President to send troops to stop the trouble. Father thinks he did right. Nobody can talk these crazy men out of what they are going to do—unless you can do it, Jeff.'

'How can he talk to them when he is sick abed?' the nurse wanted to know. 'Even if you were to bring them here? The doctor said he was to be kept quiet.'

Jeff hardly heard what they were saying. He was thinking about Dave Morgan. They had frolicked a lot together and they had ridden lawless trails side by side. Between them had been a close comradeship. Each of them had trusted the other completely, had known his friend would not fail him at a pinch. Now Dave was gone.

Out of the fog of his thoughts Ellen's voice came to him. '. . . so father is coming with the wagon to carry you to the jail if you can go.'

'He can't go,' the nurse snapped. 'I wouldn't think of letting him.'

Roan Alford said: 'We hate to ask it of you, Jeff, seeing how sick you are. It's up to you. Lane and I can carry you to the wagon. I dunno as it will do any good, but we figured maybe if you would tell the boys about how Richards and Terry stood by you they wouldn't be so bull-headed.'

The nurse said, 'No, he's going to stay right there on that bed.'

'You know Cal Terry didn't have anything to do with this invasion, Jeff,' the girl urged. 'He had a quarrel with Ellison and broke with him. Mr. Powers himself told father and me that Terry had persuaded him to break up the ranch and sell it to settlers. These gunmen attacked him and Larry just as they did you and your friends.'

'Bring me my clothes,' Jeff told his nurse.

'I ain't a-going to do it. The doctor said—'

'Doc didn't know I had important business on hand,' the wounded man said. 'Roan, you bring me my shirt and pants.'

'I knew you would, Jeff,' Ellen said, and walked into the corridor.

Jeff's eyes followed her, in them the knowledge of defeat.

XXXIII

Calhoun Terry and Larry Richards played seven-up with an old deck of cards the sheriff had given them. Occasionally one or the other of them strolled to the window and looked out through the bars at the crowds milling on the street. Both of them felt uneasy. Their disquiet took the form of sardonic jesting.

'The Crystal Palace and the Red Triangle must be doing a land-office business tonight,' Larry said. 'I reckon a war must be good for trade. A lot of redeye must have gone down the hatch since supper time.'

Calhoun came and looked over his shoulder. The noise of excited voices beat up to them. A group below caught sight of them. Someone shook his fist at the prisoners and cupped his mouth to fling a jeer at them.

'We'll have you out of there presently,' he threatened.

The others sent up a roar of approval.

'A mob is sure a crazy thing, with no more sense than cattle in a stampede,' Larry said. 'Those birds down there are all het up till they haven't a lick of judgment.'

'Bad as a bunch of lobo wolves,' agreed Calhoun. 'If they get tired milling around it would be all right with me for them to go home.'

'Me too. I haven't lost any mob.'

Sheriff Hart came upstairs with bad news. 'I wish to heaven there was a way to smuggle you two out of here,' he said. 'Wade Scott got to town half an hour ago with word that Ellison's gunmen got Sib Lee and Dave Morgan. Afraid that means trouble.'

The prisoners knew what the officer meant.

The minds of these excited men lumped them with the invaders as common enemies, and their first thought would be that an easy revenge was waiting for them.

'There are ideas afoot,' suggested Terry evenly, the inflection of a question in the words.

'Yes.'

'So where do we go from here?' Larry asked ironically.

'I have two–three men downstairs. You have your own guns. They can't have you without a fight.'

'We knew that already,' Terry said dryly. 'When do the fireworks begin?'

Though no friend of the Diamond Reverse B, the sheriff found it difficult to tell these men that the hour of doom was at hand. He hesitated.

Larry laughed hardily, without mirth. Like Terry, he was a tough and hardy realist, not afraid to face a situation which had to be met.

'Spit it out, Nate. When do the guns go boom?'

'Soon. I'd say in ten or fifteen minutes.'

'Who are the trusty men you have downstairs?' Terry asked, a note of irony in his voice.

He knew that the sheriff was a game man. Nate would do his best within reason to save his prisoners, but it would not be possible for him to prevent a determined mob from breaking into such a ramshackle building.

Hart said that the men were his two deputies and a volunteer, Horace Garvey.

At mention of the editor's name Larry said: 'I'll be doggoned! The little rooster must have sand in his craw.'

'Let's have him up here,' Calhoun said. 'I want to talk with him.'

'What do you reckon ever got it into Garvey's head that he is a fighting man?' Larry asked his partner after the sheriff had gone to fetch the editor.

'I did him a service once, and he is trying to square the account. Probably he is scared stiff. We don't want him here, Larry. He'll only get killed, and it won't do us any good. I'm going to send him away.'

'Sure. I give the little cuss good at that for coming through. But like you say, no sense in his making one more victim.'

Garvey was white to the lips. He carried a Colt .45, at a right angle to his body, as if he was afraid of it. But it was quite clear that he had nerved himself to stand by his friend.

Cheerfully Terry greeted him. 'Hello, oldtimer. I hear you've enlisted for the duration of the war.'

The editor did not try a smile This was serious business with him. He could stand up and take whatever was in store for him, but he could not make light of it.

'I felt I ought to come,' he said.

'Bully for you, Horace. I'll remember this. But we don't need you here and we sure do need you outside. What I want you to do is find the fellows who brought Jeff Brand to town. They know what happened in the fight at Lee Hart's place. Take them to the leaders of these crazy men and make them tell what they know.' He gave the names of the men who had guarded the wagon that brought the wounded man to town.

Garvey looked at him suspiciously. 'You're trying to get rid of me because you think I won't be of any use,' he ventured.

'I'm sending you out to make a stab for our lives, and you've got to hurry to do any good. Listen.'

On the light night breeze was lifted the yell of those ready for the kill.

The editor made up his mind instantly. 'I'll do what I can, Calhoun. I hope to God I can help you.'

'Sure you can,' Larry encouraged. 'Hop to it, old man. And you might tell these birds out there to order eight or ten coffins. We'll be behind cover, and we won't be fooling the way we were this afternoon against the Ellison crowd. We aim to take a few of these anxious lads with us.'

Garvey hurried away and was let out of the front door of the jail. He was at once seized by those outside and questioned. Through the window the prisoners watched him as he was hustled along.

'He might do some good, at that,' Larry said.

'But I would hate to bet a plugged dime on it.'

Terry had no hope, but he did not say so. It was up to him to keep his chin up. He meant to go out as a man should, without flinching. After all, there was only the quick agony of the bullet, and then painless sleep.

XXXIV

Roan Alford helped Brand put on his coat. Jeff sat on the bed gripping the covers to steady himself.

'Gimme my gun belt,' he said.

'You don't need no gun tonight, Jeff,' Roan told him. 'You couldn't use one good if you needed it—and you won't.'

'I'll take the belt, Roan. I wouldn't feel dressed without it.'

Alford buckled the belt around him. Lane Carey walked into the room.

'How you feeling, Jeff?' he asked.

'Fine and dandy. Let's be going.'

They supported him to the wagon and helped him to get into the hay-filled bed. Ellen arranged a pillow which she had brought from the hotel.

She said in a low voice to her father, 'I want to go with you.'

'No,' Brand said. 'We won't have a girl in this. It's a man's game.'

'Jeff is right,' Carey agreed. 'You stay here,

honey, and don't worry. We'll work this out some-how.'

Ellen knew she could not talk them into with-drawing the veto. She moved to one side, her heart filled with a leaden despair, and watched the wagon roll down the street. But she could not go back into the Round Top Hotel and sit there quietly while the man she loved was being lynched. At least she could return to the Holden House, which was much nearer the jail. She came out of the quiet residence section where the Round Top was situated to the main business street leading to the square. Even this was now deserted except for a couple of running men. She knew they were hurrying to be in at the death.

A queer suffocation choked her throat. Even now men were making ready to batter down the door of the jail, if they had not already done so. They might be dragging out the victims of their mad blood-lust. She could hear the dull roar of many voices, and she shuddered at the sound. There was no more mercy in that call for the kill than there would have been in the hungry howl of a wolf pack.

Ellen had come to a street corner from which she could see a segment of the milling crowd. Every step she took now toward her hotel would carry her farther from the jail. She found she could not do it. She could not walk away and leave Calhoun Terry to his fate. Perhaps she could not help him. Her father would be angry, knowing that she was making herself a subject of critical gossip. None the less, she had to do her best. She turned to the left and ran down the street to get to the mob.

As she drew nearer, the roar of the voices died down. Ellen knew that some critical moment had arisen to still the clamor. But it was not until she reached a street corner where she could see the prison that she knew the reason for it.

Lane Carey drove the team through the square and down the road leading to the jail. He did not wait at the outskirts of the crowd but continued to urge the horses toward the door.

'Make way there!' he shouted. 'We've got to get through. Open up. Open up.'

Men turned on him angry and excited faces. One of them caught the bridle rein of the nearest horse.

'Here. What's eating you?' the man cried. 'You can't get through here . . . Why, holy smoke, it's Lane Carey!'

'Help get us through, Bill,' Carey urged. 'I've got Jeff Brand here. He's wounded and can't get to the front afoot, but he has something to say. It's important.'

'Nothing is important right now but getting those scoundrels out of jail and hanging them,' Bill answered. 'But I'll help you if that's what you want. Open a way, boys. Jeff Brand in the wagon, wounded, and he has come to see the show.'

The pack around the jail door was more dense. Somebody had been sent for an axe, and those nearest were already throwing their weight against the door.

The sheriff shouted down a warning. 'A lot of you are going to get killed, boys. Terry and Richards are armed. We mean to fight.'

He was standing on a little railed balcony which faced the street. Terry and Richards came out and joined him. At sight of them a roar of rage beat up from the lifted faces of the packed mob. It struck the two prisoners like a blast of heat.

Larry said, 'We're not popular today, Cal,' in a voice carefully even.

His friend flung out the palm of his hand as a signal that he wanted to speak. The thunder of the mob redoubled, started to die down, swelled out again in crescendo. Terry waited, his lean, strong face showing no sign of fear. He knew they were no longer individual thinking men, but part of the pack straining to get in for the kill. The sight and sound of them were appalling. Yet he clamped down any fear that rose in him. A man had to face the music without any sign of dismay.

The voices stilled at last. There would be entertainment in listening to whatever plea this man made for his life. But Terry surprised them. He did not ask for mercy.

His scornful gaze swept the crowd. In it he recognized half a dozen who had once been his friendly neighbors, many more with whom he had had a pleasant acquaintance. All that seemed to be forgotten now. He represented, for this hour at least, the enemy against whom their hatred was boiling.

'No use to tell you I'm against this invasion of the Texans,' he began. 'No use to tell you that I'm responsible for the breaking up of the first of the big ranches in this district, and that on my advice the owners of the Diamond Reverse B are dividing it to sell to small settlers. You haven't brains enough to take in a simple little thing like that.'

He was interrupted by yells, but his strong, clear voice made itself heard above them. 'I'll tell you something you can understand. The stairway is barricaded. Before you storm it we can shoot down eight or ten of you. Think that over, and then listen to my proposition.'

'To hell with yore proposition,' someone shouted. 'We're gonna string you up to a telegraph pole.'

From the wagon seat Carey shouted another opinion. 'Sure we'll listen. Go ahead, Cal.'

Alford and two or three others backed Carey. The crowd fell in with their view. In due time they would hang these fellows, but while they were waiting to break down the door Terry might as well talk. A good many were curious to hear what he had to say.

'I'm the man you lunkheads want,' Terry went on, taking his time. 'Larry hasn't a thing to do with this. He's only a hired hand, and today he saved Jeff Brand's life from these Texans. You haven't a thing against him. All he did was take a job at cowpunching when he needed one. And Sheriff Hart is a good man. He means to do his duty and defend us. Very likely he will be killed. That would be a pity. Here's my proposition. I'll surrender without a fight if you'll let Larry go.'

Larry's voice rang out instantly. 'No, I won't have it that way. If you muttonheads don't know any better than to kill Cal Terry you will have to kill me too.'

'All right. Have it yore own way. Let's go, boys. Here's the axe.'

The sheriff called down an answer to that. He knew the voice. 'Come out into the open, Lee. If you're so anxious to have good men killed don't stand away back there but step out and lead the attack.'

Somebody laughed at that and momentarily eased the tension.

Assisted by Roan Alford, the wounded man in the wagon got to his feet. It took him a moment to clear his head from the unsteadiness that went over him like a wave.

'Good old Jeff!' a black-headed youth shouted. 'They didn't get you this time, if they did cripple you.'

The light-headedness had passed and Jeff had found his voice. 'Why didn't they?' he asked. 'Ellison's gunmen were plugging at me plenty, and I hadn't a chance to get away. This fellow you're going to hang—this bird Terry—ran out from the cabin where the Texans were shooting at him and Larry, and he carried me back to cover while these hired warriors shot at him. If you-all had the sense of a rabbit you would know neither one of these two men up there are friends of Ellison's crowd. The Texans shot a horse under Larry today while he was trying to escape—and now you feeble minded jackasses want to hang him because he's a tillicum of these invaders. Can you beat that? You fool away a couple of hours trying to bump off some guys who are more on our side than against us when you ought to be riding hell-for-leather to get to the war.'

What Jeff had said came to most of those present as a complete surprise. The men who had brought Jeff to town had departed almost at once to join those in the field, and they had not had time to tell the story to many.

'How do we know these Texans shot a horse under Larry Richards?' somebody shouted.

'Lee Hart saw Terry and Richards ride in on

one horse, with these birds chasing them like a bunch of Cheyennes. Isn't that right, Lee?'

'I saw someone come riding in thataway—two guys on one horse—but I don't know who they were, Jeff.' The admission came reluctantly.

'That's right. You didn't stay to find out, did you? Well, I don't say I blame you.' Jeff's hit got a laugh, but he pushed on to make his point. 'But I found out who they were when the two of them came out of that cabin, one to drag me in and the other to hold Ellison's warriors back while he was doing it.'

'You wouldn't be loadin' us, Jeff,' Red said, making of the statement a question.

'Why would I?' Brand flung at him. 'I don't like a hair of this bird Terry's head. Twice I came near bumping him off. But I'm not like you dumb geezers. I don't need a mule to kick me before I can take a hint. Terry and Ellison are at outs, probably because the Diamond Reverse B is going to be offered for sale to small cowmen. The Texans jumped these two men up there and drove them into Lee Hart's place. They were emptying a ton of lead at them when I drifted into the doings. These boys not only yanked me into the cabin. They told Ellison later, when he came with his flag of truce offering to let them go and hang me, that there was nothing doing since we three were all in the jam together.'

A shrill voice in the background made a contribution. 'He wired the President for him to send troops from Fort Garfield to help these hired killers wipe out us boys.'

Lane Carey said his piece. 'I signed that wire, Brad. And you have it wrong. We asked the President to stop the fighting. I didn't want a lot of your children made orphans. Jeff is right about the Diamond Reverse B going on sale to any of you who have a little money to buy some land. Mr. Powers himself told me Cal Terry had persuaded him to sell. You've made a mistake. Better admit it and call this off.'

'Or come a-smokin',' Jeff told them recklessly. 'Count me in with these men upstairs.' He poured out a dozen blistering epithets at the mob, and finished up by telling them they didn't know enough to pound sand in a rat hole.

Some of the men in the crowd began to laugh. They knew the lynching was off, and deep down they were glad of it.

'All right, Jeff,' one of them called. 'You have sure given us a good cussin' out.'

Larry sat on the rail of the balcony and grinned down at Brand. 'Heap fine oration, Jeff. I'm for sending you to Congress. I'll bet you'd twist the lion's tail proper.' He had grazed death by a very close margin, and the swift revulsion from despair to joy was flooding him.

'I learned how from you fellows today,' Brand said.

He clutched at Roan Alford for support and slid down to the hay in a faint.

Already the crowd was thinning. The rest would be anti-climax. A girl on the outskirts of it drew the curious glances of several as they passed. She was standing against a wall, her white face limned in the darkness by a lantern hanging above the door of a near-by brothel. They wondered what she was doing here. She could not be a house girl, not with a face like that. Yet no decent young woman would be in such a place, at such a time.

Ellen came out of her terror to awareness of herself. She turned and hurried back to the Holden House.

XXXV

Ellen was too excited to sit in her room at the Holden House and wait for her father to come and tell her the news. She went down and took a seat in an inconspicuous corner of the lobby, from which she could hear scraps of talk as men surged into the hotel, either to gather in knots there or to pass through to the bar.

'You got to give it to those Diamond Reverse B birds. I never did see anything gamer than the way they came out on the balcony and faced us . . . Jeff Brand saved 'em in the nick o' time. We'd of had 'em out of there in another ten minutes.

Lucky for them. Maybe lucky for some of us . . . Another troop of the boys has just started to the front. Ellison's killers won't have a look-in.'

There was no more danger for Calhoun Terry. Ellen knew that. He could walk the streets of the town unmolested. The hatred that for an hour had threatened to obliterate him had been born of a misunderstanding, and that was now cleared away. But she did not want to sit there neglected while everybody else was living over again in conversation the thrills of the evening. Why did not her father come and bring the rescued men with him? That was what she wanted—to see and talk with Cal Terry, to look into the deep blue eyes set in the strong, lean head.

A thought flashed to mind. Her father would be at the Round Top Hotel, where of course he must have driven Jeff after the storming of the jail had been abandoned. He had told her to stay there, so she had better return to it. Slipping through a side door, she walked swiftly down the dark street.

Several men were standing round the doorway of the Round Top when Ellen drew near. A buggy pulled up at the door and somebody got out. It was Doctor Harris, a fat, fussy little man of irritable disposition who had endeared himself to the district by his unwearied service and his careless-ness in the collection of fees.

'Goddlemighty!' he ripped out. 'What's the sense in patching up you dunderheads when you start rampaging over the country soon as my back is turned? Get out of my way and let me through to Brand. Serve him right if he never walks on that leg again.'

A drawling voice answered, and at the sound of it a wild and primitive emotion fluttered in Ellen's heart. 'You fix that leg up right, Doc,' it said, 'for if Jeff had stayed in bed Larry and I surely would never have walked on ours again.'

A moment later Ellen was face to face with Calhoun Terry. None of the tumult that filled her found expression. She said in a small murmur, 'Is my father here?'

Terry looked at her, surprised. She ought not to be out alone on a night like this. 'Yes. He's with Jeff. I'll tell him you are here. Better wait in the parlor.'

He led the way, closing the door behind them. 'Jeff saved our lives, with your father's help,' he said.

'Yes, I was there. He saved yours, as you did his this afternoon.'

'You were there?' he repeated.

'Yes. Jeff and father wouldn't let me go with them, but I couldn't keep away.' A vibrant wire strummed in her voice. She wondered if he could look at her and not know the truth.

'You heard Jeff talk to them?'

'Jeff—and you.'

He thought he knew why she had been unable

to stay away, and he said gently: 'I think Jeff will be all right in a few days, though his fever is high now. He was fine, wasn't he?'

Calhoun had a sudden sense of the tragic futility of life. She was so young, so eternally young, and she demanded all good things of life. The girl was dancing on the quicksands of the future, the warm hope in her heart of a happiness ever after. But life would maul her. For all his good intentions Jeff would fail her, because of the fatal lack of stability in his character. And some day her fine, tempered beauty would fade. She would grow old, and no longer would she walk as if life, the mere living, sang a song in her veins.

'Yes—and so were you,' she said, the memory with her of a strong man facing the end with a courage that did not know defeat and would not admit fear.

He said nothing for a moment, but his look gave a significance to his silence that kindled in her bosom a hot excitement. Yet when he spoke his words ignored this.

'Would you like to see Jeff from the door? I don't suppose the doctor will let you go nearer now, because he doesn't want him excited.'

'Not tonight,' she said. 'I'll wait here for father.'

'I'll tell him you are here.'

He returned in a minute. 'Your father has to take the wagon back to the corral. I have offered to see you to your hotel.'

His restrained manner chilled her. She said in a mincing voice, 'If it isn't too much trouble.'

'No trouble,' he answered. 'I am going there anyway to get a room for myself.'

As she walked beside him, Ellen caught herself thinking how strange was a woman's fancy. Out of a thousand men it flew to one. When his voice was kind, it played on chords in her heart. If he walked beside her in friendliness, she trod the hilltops in a world reborn. But when his eyes had no gifts for her, she was drenched with woe.

Her arm rested lightly on his. She felt a pulse beating in it that she hoped did not betray her.

Terry spoke of Jeff. 'I haven't been fair to him,' he said. 'I don't know another man in the world who would have crawled through a line of forty enemies to join two men in such a tough spot as we were. There's a fine generous streak in him too. Sick and wounded as he was, he didn't need to come out tonight on the chance of saving two men he doesn't like.'

Without enthusiasm, Ellen agreed. Many a time in the future she would warm to what Jeff had done. But she did not see why her companion had to harp on it just now. She wanted him to talk of something so much more personal. And he would not, for the simple reason that he did not feel any of the emotion that welled up in her.

'He is very loyal to his friends and will go to any lengths for them. I suppose you know he sent the money found in Turley's cabin to Jim Tetlow's wife to support the little children.' Calhoun did not know exactly why he was marshaling talking-points in favor of Brand, unless it was because he had been a little less than fair to him and felt he ought to acknowledge it to the girl who loved the reckless scamp.

'Yes,' Ellen agreed listlessly, and turned the conversation to the first subject that came into her head. 'What do you think is going to happen when the settlers meet these invaders? Will there be a battle and a great many men killed?'

He shook his head. 'I don't know. Your father and I are riding up the Buck River valley. We are leaving as soon as we hear from Washington. I don't think we shall get any favorable response from the government. Ellison arranged for it to keep hands off. Our idea is to try to be mediators between the two parties and fix up a settlement of some sort.'

'I don't see how you can do that, with both sides acting outside the law trying to destroy their enemy. You and father had better not get mixed up in it. You will only get into trouble.'

'I'm glad Jeff Brand didn't feel that way tonight,' he said, smiling at her. 'He took a lot more risk than we are going to run. He might have done himself great harm. Perhaps he has, though I don't think so. But he did his job just the same.'

Ellen lifted her shoulders in a weary shrug,

'You'll both do as you want to do, of course.'

They had reached the Holden House.

He said to her in the lobby before they separated. 'You had better try to go to sleep now.'

'Yes,' she assented. 'Will you please tell father, if word comes from Washington during the night, to be sure to wake me up to say good-bye?'

He promised. They said good night, neither of them happy in their parting.

XXXVI

The raiders under Ellison reached Packer's Fork safely and found the wagons waiting for them. After a hot meal they bedded down for the night. Guards were set round the encampment, to be relieved every few hours. Morning found them unmolested, and after an early breakfast the little army broke camp and headed north. They rode in a fairly compact body, moving as fast as they could and still keep touch with the supply train.

A No, By Joe rider came across the hills with the news that a large body of men was following them about three miles in the rear. He could not tell how many, since he had seen them through the dust their horses had stirred up, but his guess was that there were at least a hundred. The invaders threw out a rear guard under the command of Collins to protect the wagons against a sudden attack.

A few minutes later one of Sunday Brown's men who had been scouting in advance of the others came back at a gallop to report that he had been fired on by men hiding behind large piles of baled hay on a hilltop which commanded the road. After a short consultation McFaddin took a dozen men with him to feel out the strength of the party.

They exchanged shots for a few minutes without damage to either party, after which McFaddin brought his men back to the main army. There were, he guessed, forty or fifty men behind the rampart of bales. The leaders quickly decided to avoid a fight with this body if possible. They gave orders to leave the road and took to the foothills in a wide detour. The country was rough, and the loaded wagons made slow progress. After an hour's travel they came to a wire boundary fence of the Diamond Reverse B. This they cut, crossed a corner, and came out again in open country close to a ranch known as the Wagonwheel Gap.

The enemy had picked up their trail and was already pressing on their heels when they came in sight of the ranch. It lay below them in a swale surrounded by rolling hills commonly known as hogbacks.

The invaders dropped down into the swale to the ranch and took possession of it. For the time at least it was plain that they must fort up here and be prepared to stand a siege.

Collins swung from his horse and stepped to the porch. Bluntly he stated the situation. 'Hell has broke loose in Georgia, boys. The whole damn country is headed this way for the war. That means we're in for a fight. We don't want to be caught in the open, and this spot is made to order for us. McFaddin and Ellison agree with me. What do you think, Sunday?'

The big Texan marshal nodded his head. 'I would say we are in luck to find such a place. We have all the food we need and the creek runs right past the house. It would take an army to dig us out.'

The rubicund little ranchman wasted no more time in talk. 'Then get busy, boys. We'll occupy the ranch house, the stable, and the bunkhouse. Get out your picks and shovels from the wagon. We'll run a triangle of trenches connecting the buildings so that we can't get cut off from each other.'

A sleepy-eyed little man came out from the house. 'Say, what's going on here?' he wanted to know. He was the ranch cook. The boss and his family had gone to Larkspur for the day and left him to take care of the place.

Collins grinned at him. 'You haven't lost your job, Doc. Here are sixty or seventy hungry men. You can flunky for our cook. You'll like that.'

The Wagonwheel Gap cook did not like it, but there was nothing to do about it. He was in the army by draft and accepted his position philosophically. Inside of ten minutes he was busy making a great batch of bread.

Built in the Indian days, the Wagonwheel Gap had been designed to resist attack. A seven-foot log fence surrounded all the buildings, the poles set so close together as to make it impossible for a man to crawl through. All three of the main buildings were constructed of heavy logs. Near the stable was a pile of thick timbers. These were used to barricade windows and doors.

The ranch was excellently situated for defense. On all sides of it were low, rolling hills with little large brush except in a few gullies. Plenty of water for the horses could be got from Bear Creek, which ran close to both the stable and the house. An adjoining corral had a large haystack near the barn, in case the supply in the loft gave out.

The arrival of a large body of settlers interrupted these preparations. Bill Herriott was in command. He stationed his men along a ridge to the north of the house, and they began to pour down a scattering fire that drove the ditch-diggers and the timber workers to cover. As word spread that the cattle barons and their Texans had been trapped, reinforcements poured in to join the attackers. Another detachment arrived from Round Top, and out of the hills came rustlers, nesters, and honest homesteaders to punish the invaders. They dared not venture too close, and the heavy discharge of rifles was ineffectual.

Clouds scudded across the sky and obscured the moon so that nightfall brought darkness. The ditch-diggers went to work again, protected by ramparts of logs built between them and their enemies along the bluff. The firing did not die down entirely, but it became intermittent and sporadic. Food was carried to those in the bunkhouse and in the stable from the ranch house. Most of the men were in good spirits. The Texans were not cowboys but officers, and of late years they had not done much riding. They were very saddle-sore, and they were glad to be at rest with a roof over their heads. The prospect of the battle ahead did not greatly disturb them. Their way of life had inured them to gunfire.

The leaders of the party held a conference in the living-room of the ranch house. They did not deceive themselves about the ultimate outcome of the battle. In time the settlers would overpower them by sheer numbers, unless help came to them from outside. That help could come only from government troops.

Collins lit a cigar as he lounged in an easychair. He laughed sardonically. 'We fixed it all up so nice to have the soldiers looking another way when we pulled off our raid that I don't reckon it will be easy to attract their attention now. Like as not the Great White Father can't hear us when we holler.'

Ellison paced the floor anxiously. He more

than anybody else had got them into this trap, and he was worried about the outcome. To the others he read a telegram he had written. It was directed to the Governor, and it asked him to urge the President to order troops from Fort Garfield to the Wagonwheel Gap Ranch at once. Any delay might result in the extermination of the beleaguered force, which was at the mercy of thousands of armed men. Ellison suggested that all the cattle-men present sign it.

After reading the message as it was written McFaddin pushed the paper across the table to Gaines.

'Don't like the way it's worded,' the Flying V man said curtly. 'We're in a jam, sure enough, but we don't have to yell quite so loud for help.'

Irritably the No, By Joe manager looked at him. 'If we don't make it emphatic we won't get the troops.'

'Yeah, and maybe we won't get them anyhow,' McFaddin retorted. 'Like as not our messenger will be caught. If he is, I don't want those birds on that bluff out there to think we've turned yellow. I'll not sign unless the wording is changed.'

Collins agreed with McFaddin. 'We have a lot of men here, well armed, with plenty of provisions and ammunition. We're forted up in comfortable quarters. They can get us, but they will have to pay a damned high price first. My idea would be to state facts and let the Governor draw his own inferences.'

The telegram was rewritten and a volunteer called for to get it to Cheyenne. It was decided that the safest place from which to send the wire was Jim Creek. The station agent there was friendly to the big cattle interests and would not hold up the message.

A dozen men volunteered to try to run the enemy lines and get the telegram through. A young Texan named Hal Yancey was chosen. He was not married, and he had once worked on the Two Star Ranch and knew the country fairly well. Moreover, he was a seasoned man, game and determined.

'I'll get the message through if I can,' he promised.

'You'll have to hoof it unless you can pick up a horse somewhere,' McFaddin said. 'Take care of yourself, boy. Until you are through their lines you'll have to lie low when the moon comes out from behind the clouds.'

'Don't get panicky,' warned Ellison. 'The lives of a lot of men depend on whether you get through.'

Yancey looked at the No, By Joe manager. 'I'll remember that,' he said dryly.

As soon as the clouds obscured the moon again the Texan and Collins slipped out of the house and down the bank of the creek. The ranchman went with the messenger for thirty or forty yards, then shook hands with him and murmured 'Good luck' in his ear.

Yancey followed the stream, moving through the water carefully in order not to make a misstep on a slippery rock that would cause him to stumble and make a splash. The creek was lined with willows after he had passed out of the cottonwood grove in which the ranch buildings were situated. The Texan left the creek and crept toward the log fence which separated him from the enemy.

He waited until a dark cloud swept in front of the moon, then clambered over the fence and moved forward through the brush. A gulley wound up the hill, and he stuck to this until it ran out near the top of the incline.

A voice hailed him. 'Hello, fellow! Where you been?'

The messenger knew he had been mistaken by one of the other party for a friend.

'I slipped down to that log fence to have a look at it,' Yancey answered. 'Nothing doing there. The logs are too close to crawl through.'

'Hmp! I could of told you that. Got the makings?'

The Texan handed the man a sack of tobacco and his little book of paper wrappings. He had to wait while the homesteader shook out the tobacco and rolled the cigarette. The hillman had not taken a second look at the donor, but Yancey felt very nervous. He heard somebody else moving toward them through the brush.

'Say, I gotta be beatin' it,' he mentioned. 'I'm supposed to be with the remuda.'

'Hell! This ain't no regular army. We don't have to take orders.'

The advancing man loomed out of the darkness. Yancey recognized him. He had known Lee Hart when he had worked on the Two Star Ranch three or four years earlier. Hart spent a good deal of time loafing at Round Top and everybody in the county knew the man.

'Just had word there's a big bunch of boys coming down from Larkspur to join us,' he said. His gaze rested on the Texan. It was a moment before his memory placed the young fellow. 'Why, it's Hal Yancey! What you doing here? Thought you went back to Texas.'

'I did. Got into Larkspur only three days ago. I'm on the bread line. How's everything, Lee?'

'Fine. We've got these sons-of-guns where we want them at last.' Hart pulled his talk up abruptly. He stared at Yancey blankly. A sudden suspicion had disturbed him. 'Say, we'll go talk with Bill Herriott. A lot of Texans have come in mighty recently. Maybe—'

The barrel of Yancey's revolver pointed at Hart. 'Let's not talk with anyone, Lee. Let's all three move deeper into the brush. I'm on an errand, and I don't want to talk with Bill. Drift along to the right, boys. I'm not allowing to harm either of you if you behave.'

They drifted, but unfortunately directly toward another group of three or four men. Yancey bolted into the brush as Hart yelled out a warning. Bullets whistled in the darkness. The Texan knew he had been hit, but kept going. He dodged into a draw and ran limping down it. When he reached a clump of aspens he buried himself in them and sank to the ground. He believed he had evaded the pursuit.

A low voice, not six feet from him, asked, 'What seems to be the trouble?'

XXXVII

When Terry and Carey offered their services as mediators to the little group who seemed to be leading the attackers the proposal was rejected at once. The Diamond Reverse B superintendent was not in favor with the people's party, even though he had escaped lynching by a narrow squeak. Lane Carey had always been liked by the settlers, but he too had signed the telegram asking for the soldiers and was temporarily under suspicion.

'We don't aim to do any mediating,' Lee Hart sneered. 'We're figuring on wiping out this bunch of killers the cattle barons have brought in, and with them some of the high moguls themselves.'

Bill Herriott was less ferocious but just as uncompromising. 'They can hang out a white flag if they want to surrender,' he said. 'Until then we haven't any terms to offer.'

'What terms will you give if they do decide to surrender?' Carey asked.

Herriott's bleak gaze rested on the face of the Box 55 owner. 'I wouldn't know. We'll cross that bridge when we come to it. The fellows who hired Turley to kill our friends will have to pay the price. So will those who murdered Dave Morgan and Sib Lee. There won't be any compromise about that.'

Argument was of no use. The bitterness of the feeling was too great.

'We might as well sit back until Nate Hart gets here,' Carey told his companion. 'The sheriff has a lot of influence with these fellows, and he keeps his head.'

'He has influence,' Calhoun agreed. 'But not enough to save Ellison and McFaddin and Collins. Do you think we could do any good by riding over to Fort Garfield and seeing the commandant?'

'We might get him to wire the War Department.'

When they went to get their horses they were met by the announcement that they were to stay here for the present. They had not been asked to come, but since they had done so they were not to leave.

'Who says so?' asked Terry.

313

'Doesn't matter about that. You stick around.'

Terry strolled down toward the firing-line, from which occasional flashes came. He was not apparently under surveillance, but the horses were being watched. A draw brought him to an aspen grove. Calhoun hesitated, uncertain whether to go round it or go back to the summit of the hill from which he had just come. He passed into the aspens.

Guns sounded, close to him. What surprised him was that they were revolver shots. The distance was too great to reach the ranch house except with rifles. He heard excited voices, and presently the sound of a runner coming into the aspens. The escaping man collapsed and sank to the ground.

Almost in a murmur, Terry said, 'What seems to be the trouble?'

The man on the ground turned a startled face toward him and reached for a gun.

'Not necessary,' the Diamond Reverse B man said. 'I won't hurt you or call anybody.'

Yancey recognized him. 'What are you doing here with these fellows, Mr. Terry?' he asked, surprised.

'I came to try to fix up a truce, but the settlers wouldn't have it.' Calhoun asked a question. 'Was it you they were shooting at?'

'They hit me in the leg. I'm one of Sunday Brown's Texans. They sent me from the ranch to get a telegram through to Washington asking for troops.'

'Hit bad?'

'Not so bad. I can't travel, that's sure. Not on that game leg.'

'You have a written message?'

'Yes.' He added, worried, 'They're depending on me at the ranch.'

'I might get it through for you. But I can't leave you here. Not with these men as filled with revenge as they are. . . . There's a horse tied to a sapling in a draw near here. If we had two . . .'

'I could ride all right,' Yancey said hopefully.

Terry gave instructions. 'Stay here. I'll have a try for the horse. When you hear me coming move to the edge of the aspens.'

Terry walked up the incline toward the draw and met Lane Carey.

'I heard some revolver shots,' Lane said. 'Hope they weren't firing at you.'

'No. At a fellow named Yancey who was trying to get through a telegram from the beleaguered men to send to the Governor. They hit him, but he got away and is hiding in the aspens. I'm trying to get a horse for him—that one in the draw there.'

'How badly is he hurt? Can he ride?'

'He says so. If I could get two horses I'd try to go with him.'

'You'd be shot down before you got twenty yards.'

'I'm not so sure. It's dark when the moon is under a cloud. More men keep riding in to join the attackers. Nobody is paying any attention to us.'

'Not as long as we don't try to get away. But they have sentries out. I ran into one and he warned me back.'

They were moving in the direction of the saddled horse. It was a rather heavily built sorrel gelding.

'I'm going to try it,' Terry said. 'They will find Yancey soon if I don't get him away, and if they do he's a goner.'

He untied the horse, and the two men walked back with it toward the aspens. They met a man whom they recognized as the owner of a wagon yard at Round Top. He said, 'Hello!' and passed without question.

Yancey was waiting at the edge of the aspens.

'How is your leg?' Terry asked.

'Fine,' the man answered in a thin voice.

'Let me look at it,' Carey said.

While he examined and dressed it as best he could, Terry took the horse deeper into the aspens where it would not be seen. Carey called him when he was ready.

The Box 55 man said in a low voice, 'This man can't make it alone to the railroad.'

Terry frowned. 'I've been thinking that. I'll go with him. Later on we'll pick up another horse somewhere.'

'You mean, both go on this horse?'

'Yes. He isn't going to make it without help.'

Yancey spoke up stoutly, but in a weak voice. 'I am too. Boost me into the saddle and I'll burn the wind out of here.'

They helped him to his feet. He leaned heavily against Terry. The eyes of the ranchmen met. Each was telling the other that the Texan would not get far alone.

Out of the darkness a man walked. He asked peremptorily, 'What you fellows doing here?'

The voice was that of Lee Hart. He bowlegged forward, and pulled up abruptly as he recognized the two ranchmen. His gaze slid to Yancey. They could see understanding of the situation filter into his eyes. He opened his mouth to shout, and was a fraction of a second too late.

Terry had plunged forward, his right lashing at the man's jaw. Hart went down, and Terry was on him instantly, his fingers closing on the hairy throat to prevent an alarm. Calhoun dragged the heavy body into the aspens.

'Give me your bandanna,' he said to Yancey, and with it gagged the prisoner. The rope from the saddle he used to tie the man securely.

The moon came out for a moment, then went behind a cloud. Yancey was boosted to the saddle and Terry swung up behind him.

'If you can slip through the lines you'd better do it,' Calhoun told the Box 55 man. 'When they

317

find Hart and he tells what he knows they will be some annoyed at you.'

'I'll make out,' Carey said. 'Good luck, Cal.'

Terry moved into the darkness. Carey waited and listened to the sound of the retreating hoofs. There was a long minute of silence, then the crash of guns and the lift of excited voices.

'Who was it?' somebody asked.

'Don't know. He wouldn't stop when we gave orders. We missed him, looks like.'

Carey very much hoped so.

XXXVIII

Ellen found it impossible to sleep. After tossing in bed for two or three hours she got up, dressed, and went down into the hotel lobby. Roan Alford passed through it, on his way from the bar to the street. The gray-haired little man's beady eyes fastened on the girl.

'What you doing up this time of night, Miss Ellen?' he asked. 'You don't want to be losing yore beauty sleep, though gosh, I don' reckon *you* got any need to worry about that.'

'I can't rest, Mr. Alford. I'm worried about father. I want to go back to the ranch, where I'll be nearer him if anything happens.'

'There ain't a thing going to happen to Lane,' he promised. 'Neither side is unfriendly to him.'

'Anyhow, I want to go back. Do you know anybody leaving for there tonight?'

'I am. Right away. But you don't want to go traipsing off in the middle of the night. Wait till morning and go up then, if you got to go.'

'I want to go now. If you'll let me ride with you, I can get a horse.' Ellen gave him her most wheedling smile.

'Sure you can ride with me. Only I wouldn't want you to go if yore father would have objections.'

They rode through the night, sometimes in darkness and again under the shine of a moon that had escaped from behind the scudding clouds. It was a long ride, and they reached Black Butte in the small hours just before the faint light of early morning had begun to sift into the sky.

As they rode up through the darkness to the ranch house Roan caught at the rein of Ellen's horse and pulled it to a halt.

'Wait a minute. There's someone there—on the porch.'

Already Ellen's gaze had picked up two horses at the side of the building, vague and shadowy in the gloom. The object on the porch stirred. It was a man. Or was it two men?

'Who is it?' Alford called.

'Calhoun Terry,' the answer came.

A pulse began to beat in the girl's throat.

'Is that father with you?' she asked.

Terry rose from where he had been kneeling. 'No. Your father is all right, Miss Carey. This is a wounded man. He slipped out of the Wagonwheel Gap Ranch with a message, and they wounded him as he was trying to get through the lines.'

'The Wagonwheel Gap,' she repeated.

'Yes. Ellison's men are surrounded there. They want a telegram sent to the Governor.'

'Has there been a battle?'

'Not yet. The settlers are besieging the invaders, who are pretty well forted up. I'm afraid there will be a heavy loss of life if the troops don't stop it.'

'Where is father?'

'He is with Bill Herriott's men. We offered to mediate, but they wouldn't let us.'

Ellen looked down at the man on the floor. 'Is he badly hurt?' she asked.

'Shot in the leg. Could you take him in here, until I can arrange to have him moved?'

'Of course. Mr. Alford will help you carry him upstairs. I will get a light.'

'I hate to trouble you, ma'am,' Yancey said.

'Don't worry about that,' she told him.

The men carried him upstairs and put him to bed. They dressed the wound as best they could, after which Ellen joined Calhoun on the porch.

'I'll rope one of your horses, if you don't mind,' he said to her. 'I have to get this message off to the Governor.'

320

She took instant alarm. 'You're not going back to Round Top?'

'No. I'll send the telegram from Jim Creek. It would probably be held up if I tried to get it off from Round Top.'

'Will you send a wire to Doctor Harris and ask him to come up and look after our patient here?'

'Yes. He'll probably be needed at the Wagon-wheel Gap Ranch too. On the way there he can stop here.'

Ellen walked down with him to the corral. Roan Alford was taking care of the wounded man, and for the time she could be spared. She moved with a fine animal vigor, shoulders and hips in a straight line vertically. Calhoun noted the rhythmic grace of the slender figure. He had never met another woman like her, so fine and gallant and animated with life. There strummed in his blood a strong desire for her—for the dark beauty tempered as a Toledo blade, for the sweetness and the courage that she carried like a banner. There would be gifts in her eyes for some lucky man, but they would not be for him.

'Larry Richards and I are buying a slice of the Diamond Reverse B,' he told her. 'I've been thinking we might have a place for Jeff Brand when he gets able to work.'

She flashed a quick look at him, surprised. 'Do you think that would suit Jeff?' she asked.

'He's so restless. I wonder if he would be content.'

'He'll have to settle down sometime, won't he?' Calhoun said.

'I don't know. He's so wild.' She went on, almost as if she were talking to herself: 'It would be terrible for a girl to be married to him. With a husband as reckless and unstable as he is, no woman would be able to keep step. He would bring her great and lasting unhappiness, though very likely she would keep loving him till the end.'

Calhoun pulled up in his stride. 'I thought you were going to marry him.'

'Did you think I would marry a rustler?' she reproved gently.

'Do you mean—that you're not in love with him?' he asked, looking directly at her.

She laughed, a little tremulously. 'Where did you get that ridiculous notion?'

He stared at her, a heat beating through his body. 'Then you're not in love with him . . . or with any other man?'

She said in a low voice, 'We aren't talking about any other man, are we?'

Some hint of her deep emotion reached him. A swift hope blazed up in him. He had thought never to tell her what was in his heart, but now he flung away restraint.

He said, 'I couldn't be the man.' But his voice asked for a denial.

When she did not reply, he pressed home his question.

Ellen looked up, her face a soft and shining answer.

Riding through the night to send the message to the Governor, Calhoun was filled with a sense of the nearness of the girl whose warm body he had held in his arms. The lift of the hour was still on him. With the extravagance of a lover, he was sure that no man since Adam had ever had a sweetheart comparable to his. He loved everything about her—the parted lips and shining eyes, the flowing grace of movement, the turn of the lovely head.

His ecstasy amazed him. He had counted himself a hard man, cynical, not given to sentiment. Yet a girl with a windblown skirt had crossed his path and changed the world for him. He thought, with a smile, of the verse of the hymn he had once quoted to her:

> Though every prospect pleases,
> And only man is vile.

He was ready to revise his opinion about that too. Jeff Brand—Dave Morgan—Sheriff Hart. Tough, hard men all of them, but with a light shining in their hearts that separated them a million miles from vileness.

XXXIX

That the soldiers reached Wagonwheel Gap Ranch just in time to save the invaders is written in the history of Cattleland. Ellison and his men surrendered to the commanding officer of the troops stationed at Fort Garfield. To Sheriff Hart and to the best of the attacking settlers the sound of the bugle sent out by the approaching troops had been almost as welcome as to the beleaguered party.

Collins strutted out of the ranch house undaunted by the yells and curses flung at him and his associates. He stood on the porch and waited for a chance to speak, and when the angry shouts died down flung back defiance at the enemy.

'To call me a murderer doesn't make me one,' he said, no more disturbed than if he had been sitting with cronies at the Cheyenne Club. 'We're honest men fighting for our rights. Some of us have been here since the Indian days. Every cattleman among us has helped build up this territory and has been a good citizen. I can call out the names of a dozen thieves I see among you, scoundrels who came here without a cent and have obtained herds at our expense, every hoof of them stolen from some of us.'

He waited till the roar of rage had spent itself,

then went on hardily. 'I'd do just what I have done again. The time has come when either honest men or the thieves have to get out, and by God! I stand for hanging every rustler I can find until the law will punish them by putting them behind bars. We are not fighting small settlers but thieves. If I have to go to prison for what I have done, I'll still say I did right in trying to rid this country of outlaws.'

Neither Collins nor any of the other invaders went to the penitentiary. Their trials were postponed for many months. Witnesses vanished. The intensity of the feeling against the cattlemen declined. Moreover, the cost of the trials was so great that there was likelihood of county bankruptcy. In the end the indictments were dismissed.

But it was plain that the big ranches were doomed. One after another they followed the example of the Diamond Reverse B and went out of business. With the increase in the number of small cattlemen the chances for undetected rustling grew fewer. Most of the thieves were known, and one by one they flitted to Montana or Idaho or Mexico.

Jeff Brand joined a cattle outfit in the Argentine. At long intervals his friends heard of him. He came back to the States to enlist for the Spanish-American War. A bullet took him in the throat as he was going up San Juan Hill.

In the reorganization of the cattle country after

the breakup of the big ranches Calhoun Terry took an important part. He was recognized as a strong man, and as the years passed his influence became more than local. There came a time when he had to go to Washington to represent his people. He was never quite happy there, for he was no politician, and he was glad when his term of office expired. So was Ellen. It seemed to her that a city was no place to bring up a large family of boys and girls, and she gave a deep sigh of relief when they were all home again in the West she loved. Her father was an old man by that time, and she knew it made him happier to be near them.

In private, sometimes, her husband tells Ellen that she is still lovelier than the slim, dark-eyed daughters who trouble the hearts of the young men of the neighborhood. She smiles wisely, and is content. For she knows that both Calhoun and she have had a happy life in spite of the occasional storms that have beat up to trouble them.

Center Point Large Print
600 Brooks Road / PO Box 1
Thorndike ME 04986-0001 USA

(207) 568-3717

US & Canada:
1 800 929-9108
www.centerpointlargeprint.com

C1/1

hf 10.13.14   HA 4.2.16   ba 3.17 (11)
+c 2.27.15   HU 9.14.16
bk 6.16.15   SU 12.4.16

NNS   NC